Pra

"The Lucky Diamo... is a gem, fast-paced and convincing, with an unusual quest and characters you'll want to know. A great read." Livi Michael, author of *The Whispering Road*, winner of Nestle Children's Book Bronze Award.

"A hit for any middle grade readers who like magical quests and fantasy." *LoveReading4Kids*, UK premier book recommendation site.

"A fast-moving action adventure in an amazing world full of magical creatures – and evil – that is sure to have young readers on the edge of their seats." Lindsay J. Sedgwick, author of the *Wulfie* series.

Books by Valinora Troy

THE LUCKY DIAMOND

VALINORA TROY

The Lucky Diamond
Copyright 2021 Valinora Troy

Cover art by Elizabeth Eckstein
Map illustration by Dewi Hargreaves
Internal illustrations by I. Murphy
Formatting by Polgarus Studio

First Print Edition
Disresponsible Nodpots Publications
ISBN 978-1-7399903-0-5

To Iseult, the good twin

Contents

MAP OF NIVRAM

Prologue

The trial was held in Hanging Square, not far from Lowdar's town gate. A large crowd had gathered for the judgement to be delivered, as per the custom, after sunset. That way, if the verdict was guilty, the sentence could be carried out immediately.

"Excuse me, please." A young girl pushed her way through the crowd, squeezing between rough-hewn jackets and coarse shawls. It was her uncle on trial. Tears stung her eyes as she attempted to make her way to the front. "Please let me pass."

"He'll get the rope for sure." A broad-backed man blocked her way. "If not something worse."

The woman standing beside him pulled her shawl more tightly about her shoulders. "Don't even suggest such a thing. To throw that poor young man to the monsters of the Great Forest, to leave him to be torn apart by the fiends at our very gate – why, it makes hanging seem merciful."

"It's what they did to Farley Fieldson last week, and to Farley's brother the month before. There's no mercy with Judge Death," the man said.

Overhearing, Yvonne shuddered as she ducked under the man's elbow. In Lowdar, criminals locked outside the gates at nightfall were never seen again, but surely that couldn't happen to Uncle Matt? He was such a kind uncle, and had been looking after her and her siblings since the fire. Yvonne couldn't imagine him doing anything wrong.

She wriggled her way to the front of the crowd as the judge arrived. Yvonne glared at the judge as he lowered himself into an enormous raised throne. The crimson torchlight cast great wells of shadow across the judge's face, making him appear as cruel and relentless as the carved birds of prey adorning his chair.

Uncle Matt faced the judge, so his back was to Yvonne. She hated to see his wrists manacled, and the soldiers, hands on sword hilts, guarding him, but at least his head was up and his shoulders back, and that gave her hope that he would be freed.

"You are charged with the dreadful crime of treason against our country." The judge spoke contemptuously, not raising his eyes from the sheaf of papers in his hand. "I hold here the sworn statements of your accusers, loyal servants of Nivram and beyond reproach. Have you anything to say before I pronounce judgement?"

Uncle Matt tried to step forward but his ankles were shackled and he stumbled. Yvonne sucked her lip and blinked hard.

The prisoner regained his balance, shook away the soldier's hand, and cleared his throat. "Sir, I wish to plead for clemency."

Even by lamplight, the heavy frown that marred the judge's brows was obvious. "On what grounds?"

"Not on the basis of my innocence," Uncle Matt said. "Although I am innocent. But my brother's children – five orphans, the eldest only ten years – who is to look after them? They have no one but me."

It was true. Yvonne couldn't imagine what would happen to her family without him. Where would they live? How would they eat?

"You need not concern yourself," the judge said callously. "This town shall look after them. But to return to the matter in hand: the tradition of Lowdar has always been to offer criminals the choice between death by hanging, or banishment beyond the safety of our walls. I need not remind you that none survive being left to the mercy of the Great Forest – we have all heard the screams of those foolish enough to choose that fate over the hangman's rope." He paused significantly. Yvonne felt sick, as if she were being torn to pieces on the inside. "However, because your crime was treason, and to serve as an example to all citizens of Nivram, especially to young men like yourself who may be tempted to do likewise, only one sentence is just: total banishment from Lowdar, and all townships of Nivram, for the duration of your life."

It took a moment for Yvonne to grasp what the judge meant – that Uncle Matt was to be devoured by the monsters of the forest. Her uncle shouted something, and tried to break free of his bonds, but a soldier knocked him to the ground. Three others drew their swords and pressed their blades against him. Yvonne wanted to run over to him but she was too terrified to move.

"Go home, the rest of you, or you will all follow," the judge roared, as a low hum of anger ran through the crowd. "And you, Captain of the guard, find those five orphans and reunite them with their uncle – outside the gates!"

Yvonne found herself caught up in the press of people hurriedly leaving the square. She saw the guards drag her uncle away towards the town gate as she was borne in the opposite direction. She heard the clang of the great bar – once to open the gate, a second time to close it – and knew her uncle had been tossed outside the walls. She could do nothing to help him now.

"Goodbye, Uncle Matt," Yvonne whispered, tears rolling down her cheeks. She wiped them away. It wasn't time for crying. The judge's last words echoed in her head and she knew none of her family were safe. She broke away from the crowd and fled down a side alley, the thought of the town guard chasing her spurring her on. *If they find us, we'll be thrown to the monsters.*

She crossed half a dozen empty streets before reaching a laneway, where she slowed, her eyes searching for the others. A low whistle caught her attention and drew her towards a darkened porch. The faint light was enough for her to see her sister Susan, sitting on the step, two smaller children leaning against her on either side, sleeping. Susan held a protective arm around each twin, and gazed up anxiously at her.

Vicky's disembodied voice from the shadow-filled porch spoke softly. "Well?"

Yvonne heard the fear in the seven-year-old's voice, and saw it in eight-year-old Susan's eyes. She wanted to say *I don't know what to do, I'm only ten*, but she was the eldest and there was no one else to help them. Swallowing back her fears, she shook her head.

"We're in trouble; we must go into hiding, at once. Uncle Matt is - gone, but don't worry, I'll look after you." She bent down to shake awake the sleeping youngsters. "The town guard is after us," she added in an urgent whisper. "We must hurry."

FIVE YEARS LATER

Chapter One
THE DIAMOND

Cathy perched on a step by the water pump and watched the lamplighter at work. She couldn't help fidgeting anxiously with the chain around her neck. Her eldest sister, Yvonne, had told her to wait with Alan in Front Square for Vicky, but Vicky was late and dusk was falling, which meant it was almost curfew. While Alan, her twin, was happy to be with a group of boys kicking a bundle of rags across the cobblestones, Cathy knew what being caught out after dark by the town guard meant – banishment from Lowdar.

Front Square was also far too close to the forest for her liking. An archway and a short lane were all that separated Cathy from the town's gate. She tensed, hearing shouting from the direction of the gate, expecting, as she did every day, a monster from the Great Forest to enter the town. Then she heard the heavy clang of the gate shutting, the gatekeeper ringing the bell for sundown, and she relaxed.

Not for long, as there was still no sign of her sister and curfew was minutes away.

The clip-clop of horse hooves drew her attention to the nearby lane leading from the town gate. Whoever had entered Lowdar barely made it in time – they must have been the cause of the rumpus. She watched curiously to see who the late arrival was.

A huge coal-black horse, shining with sweat, stepped gracefully through the archway. Its rider was dressed in the uniform of a colonel from the Nivram National Army, and he was deep in conversation with the captain of the town guard.

Cathy looked at the horse admiringly but didn't pay the men any attention until they stopped beside the boys playing nearby. The captain grabbed hold of Alan by the shoulder and shook him.

Cathy jumped to her feet in alarm and ran over to them.

"This is Colonel Thrand," the captain said. Cathy could see Alan squirm but he was unable to get free. "You're to take him to the governor's house at once. I know you, so no tricks, unless you wish to find yourself thrown to the Great Forest tomorrow."

Alan scowled at the ground. In response to a shove from the captain, he grudgingly led the way across the cobbles. Colonel Thrand followed. Cathy ran after them and fell into step beside Alan. Maybe the colonel would reward Alan with a coin, or perhaps beat him, but either way she was going to be with him.

Alan led the way through narrow, badly lit streets, strewn

with refuse. The sightless eyes of the tenement buildings loomed over them, but the street remained silent other than the sound of the horse's hooves and the creak of its saddle.

"Why are you taking me this way?" the colonel demanded. Cathy was furious to see him grasp Alan's shoulder. As he did so, the colonel's sleeve shot back, revealing a small dark mark etched on his wrist. He hastily pulled his cuff down over it.

"It's the only way I know," Alan said simply.

As if satisfied with this answer, the colonel released his hold on Alan.

As they entered a once fashionable square, now badly dilapidated and only partially lit, Cathy felt a stab of pain in her foot and stumbled. Something was caught in her shoe. She sat upon a pile of rubble and removed it, emptying the large pebble into her hand.

Except, it was a precious stone, a gem, crystal-clear and filled with light. A word popped into her head: *Diamond.* She cupped it in her hand, unable to believe her find. Its brightness spilled through her fingers, illuminating the dark alleyway. Instinctively she shoved it into her pocket. Looking up, she found both Alan and the colonel staring at her.

"Come here," the colonel ordered.

Instead, Cathy dashed off into the shadows. She expected Alan to follow, and when he didn't, she peeped around the side of a building. Colonel Thrand had Alan held by his ear and was shouting at him.

Alan's face contorted in pain. Cathy didn't know what to do but a bright light from her coat shot through the gloom, causing the stallion to buck. Thrand strove to control the horse, and Alan tore himself free and ran.

"Come back at once," the colonel shouted angrily, jerking on the bridle. "Show me what you found. You can't hide from me. I'll see you're fed to the beasts in the forest, I promise you."

Cathy heard every word he said. She didn't want to be thrown to the beasts of the forest, like her uncle. Crouching behind a water barrel, she watched the colonel calm the horse, and retrieve something from the saddlebags. It was the strangest box Cathy had ever seen, pyramid-shaped and seemingly formed from shiny black metal. The colonel placed it on the ground, removed a cloak from his saddle, and held it above the box.

The colonel's face glazed over and he started to chant.

"Fire and Night,
Darkness Delight,
Destroy the light…"

A tiny flame flickered at the apex of the box and the cloak began to billow in a non-existent breeze. As it inflated, a voice Cathy didn't recognise came from her pocket, speaking one word:

"Run!"

The cloak now towered over the colonel. Cathy didn't know what was beneath it, but she didn't want to find out. She dived down a side street, and into a narrow alleyway. The windows of the houses were boarded up but Cathy knew where one board was loose, pushed it aside, and scrambled inside. As the board swung back into place, she pulled the Diamond from her pocket.

This thing had told her to run.

It blazed with light, dispelling shadows and blinding Cathy. She had to turn away until the light dimmed and she was able to look at it.

The Diamond was about three inches in height, with sparkling facets, and fuelled by a pulsating interior flame. Cathy could make out facial features, indentations which were clearly eyes, and a mouth curved into a smile. The Diamond felt soft and warm on her palm, and she had never seen anything so alive. Liquid fire held captive in glass, she thought.

"Who are you?" Cathy whispered. She had no doubt the Diamond was a living creature of some kind.

"Permit me to introduce myself." The Diamond gave a strange little bow, its voice a musical tinkling. "I am Princess of the Ancient Order of Diamonds, the most noble species of all. You may call me Lucky."

Scrabbling at the window made her jump. The loose board swung back and Alan fell into the room. Cathy had expected him to find her there, it was their favourite hiding place, even Vicky didn't know about it.

"Did you see that cloak-y thing, Cathy?" Alan said, panting hard. "The colonel sent it after us."

"I was afraid of that," Lucky said.

Alan stared open-mouthed at the Diamond. "You're *alive*?"

Lucky glowed a little brighter before answering. "What else would I be?"

"This is Lucky, Alan," Cathy said. "Do you know what that cloak is, Lucky?"

"It's a half-grolsch," Lucky said. The name sent a shiver rippling through Cathy. "What's a half-grolsch?"

The Diamond cast a little trail of light as she hopped from Cathy's hand to her shoulder. "Not something you want to meet. It appears as shadow, but is able to hunt and destroy Diamonds – and will kill anything in its way. Cathy, let's see if it has followed us here."

Cathy didn't like the sound of that, but she obediently pressed her face to the gap between the boards covering the window. Twilight filled the street with shadows, colouring everything grey. Cathy bit her finger as she stared at the darkening street. Then she saw it, a cloaked figure gliding among the shadows. On the far side of the street, directly opposite where they hid, it stopped.

She held her breath. If that was a half-grolsch, she'd hate to meet a full one.

Alan joined her at the window. "Can you see it?"

"Yes." Cathy gulped. As she spoke, it turned towards them. Two burning white orbs stared directly at her, full of venom and hate. She had never seen a monster before, even though she had grown up beside the Great Forest. She hadn't realised it would be so terrifying.

"Don't worry," Lucky said. "It's after me. Can you take me somewhere safe to hide?"

The only place Cathy could think of was the tiny garret where she and her siblings lived. They had stayed hidden there from the town guard for five years, so it must be safe.

"Home." Cathy met Alan's eyes and he nodded.

"Better go," Lucky said.

Cathy needed no second urging.

The building lay in darkness but the Diamond's glow shed plenty of light. Cathy longed to know more about the Diamond, so although she meant to keep quiet, the questions kept spilling out.

"Where do you come from? What are you doing in Lowdar? Why does the half-grolsch hunt you?"

"Time for that later," Lucky said.

Alan dragged open the back door, and Cathy followed him into a small back yard.

"Better hide in my pocket," Cathy said, concerned the Diamond's light would alert the half-grolsch. "So it won't see you."

"Very well," Lucky said. "But if you meet the half-grolsch, leave me behind and run – for it will surely kill you if you get in its way."

Cathy swallowed and slipped the Diamond away.

"I'll draw it off, Cathy," Alan said. He scrambled onto the back wall. "You go by Hollow Square and I'll pass through Fisher Lane. I'll lose it easily there, and meet you on the roof."

Cathy wasn't happy with this plan. "What if it catches you?"

"It won't – it's after the Diamond. But I'll get you more time." He jumped off the wall and out of sight. Cathy counted to ten - *one for every year of her life* - and followed.

Night had descended upon the streets of Lowdar, but there was no sign of either the half-grolsch or the angry colonel, nor any of the town guard. All the same, Cathy broke into a run, her heart thumping in her chest, terrified that every corner or laneway would reveal one of their enemies.

A derelict building, one of many in Lowdar, served as the secret entrance to their hideaway. Cathy clambered onto a barrel, reached up and caught the top of the porch and swung herself up. She squeezed through a window, climbed the three flights to the attic, and emerged onto the roof. Pinpoints of light lit up houses around the town, in stark contrast to the large area of darkness signaling the abandoned streets where Cathy hid.

Where was Alan? She wished she had Vicky's telescope so she could use it to find him.

"Alan should be here by now," she said miserably. Lucky didn't reply. Cathy was afraid to take the Diamond out of her pocket in case she shone brightly enough for the half-grolsch to see. She twisted her fingers anxiously until Alan eventually climbed through the window to join her on the roof.

He didn't look as calm and unconcerned as earlier. His jacket sleeve was torn, he had a scrape on his cheek, and his hair was full of cobwebs.

"Took longer than I thought to give it the slip," he said. "It followed me all the way to Moonlit Square. Did you find out any more about it? Or the Diamond?"

Cathy jumped to her feet.

"Let's get home first," she said.

A short scramble across the roofs brought her to a skylight. Cathy prised it open and dropped through into a small room. It was furnished with a collection of boxes and heaps of tattered blankets that served as seats and tables. Candles burned in glass jars, bathing the room in a soft yellow glow that hid the rotting walls and the damp patches on the ceiling.

Two girls sat on a makeshift couch. Yvonne's dark head bent over a cardigan she was darning, while Susan polished a metal flute. Vicky, her plait over one shoulder, sat cross-legged on the floor, looking annoyed, though her frown vanished when Cathy and Alan arrived.

"I knew you were all right," she said triumphantly. "I *told* Yvonne there was nothing to worry about."

Yvonne paused in her darning. "You shouldn't have come home without them, Vicky, you *know* that. Where were you, Cathy?"

Cathy had forgotten Vicky was meant to collect them from the square. It wasn't her fault that Colonel Thrand needed an escort, but none of that mattered anymore.

"Look," she said and flung down the Diamond.

Instantly the room was filled by a dazzling light. For a split second, she was blinded. Then the light subsided, the room became dim again, and her eyes were once more riveted by the Diamond pulsating gently on the table.

Behind her, Vicky gasped loudly. Yvonne dropped her darning. Susan stared, entranced. Nobody spoke.

"This is the Lucky Diamond," Cathy announced proudly. "She needs our help."

Cathy was pleased to see the looks of amazement on her sisters' faces, but the Diamond's next words startled her.

"I came to ask for your help in leaving this town," the Diamond said, "but I'm afraid you no longer have a choice. If you wish to live, you too must leave Lowdar. Tonight."

Chapter Two
FLIGHT

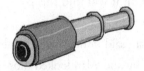

Vicky stared at the Diamond. Despite spending all of her twelve years in the shadow of the Great Forest, she had never seen anything as strange or as wonderful as the Diamond. It *couldn't* be real.

"Where did you find it, Cathy?" Vicky said, trying to work out what it was. "How did you get it to speak?"

The Diamond blazed briefly and Vicky had to cover her eyes. When Vicky was able to look at the Diamond once more, several people spoke at the same time.

"Who are you and why do we have to leave?" Yvonne said

"I thought you said the half-grolsch only went after Diamonds?" Cathy said.

"How beautiful! Is your name really Lucky?" Susan's sapphire-blue eyes shone with happiness.

It seemed the Diamond was truly alive. Vicky felt chilled and excited at the same time.

"Are you from the Great Forest?" she said.

A shudder ran through the Diamond at Vicky's question.

"No, only evil things dwell there. My home is many miles from here, in North-East Nivram. Thanks to the evil machinations of – well, it doesn't matter who – but I find myself stranded here, unable to make it back to The Rock on my own. Unfortunately, there is also a half-grolsch hunting me. Soon it will find this place. Even now it draws close. Will you help me?"

"I will," Susan said immediately, brushing her fair hair out of her eyes. Cathy and Alan looked more twin-like than ever, with their untidy brown hair and green eyes, nodding in unison. Vicky hesitated. She wanted to help as well, of course, but she liked to know more about what she was getting into.

Yvonne put her head in her hands. "I don't understand any of this."

"What do you need us to do, Lucky?" Vicky said.

"Take me back to the Rock of Diamonds, my home. The home of all Diamonds. Diamonds draw their energy from the Rock, but I have been away so long, I am too weak to get there by myself."

"What about that half-grolschy thing?" Vicky said. "And why must we leave tonight?"

"The half-grolsch will kill me," Lucky said. "And anyone who gets in its way, including Cathy and Alan, and everyone here."

Vicky didn't know whether it was fear or excitement that shivered through her but the Diamond had convinced her they had to leave Lowdar. "When do we go?"

Yvonne raised her head from her hands and tucked her

chestnut hair behind her ears. "This is crazy. We're not going, this is where we live. I'm the eldest…"

Vicky groaned. Yvonne thought she was in charge, and constantly told Vicky what to do: *wear a dress and cut your hair, girls your age don't wear leggings, do something useful like work in the fields, look after the twins…* She wasn't going to listen to Yvonne this time, either.

"I don't want to be here when the half-grolsch comes, so I'm going with Lucky," Vicky said firmly.

Yvonne looked shocked.

"But our home is here…" Her voice trailed off.

Vicky didn't consider Lowdar her home. Since her parents died and her uncle was killed, she'd hated the town. They'd spent five years living in hiding, never seen together in case the town was still after them, sleeping in a mouldy attic and struggling to get enough to eat. *Anywhere* would be better than this town. She could see Susan and the twins felt the same.

"I can promise you a most generous reward," the Diamond said, in an off-hand manner.

Yvonne frowned at Lucky, and she took a moment to answer.

"North-east Nivram means going through the Great Forest," she said. "Are you going to protect us from the monsters there?"

"I would," the Diamond replied, "but we won't be travelling through the Great Forest at all. We'll travel by sea."

Vicky was so happy to hear they wouldn't be going

through the forest that she didn't worry about a sea voyage.

"And that monster you mentioned," Yvonne continued, frowning at Vicky. "If there is danger to any of my family, I will fling you to it."

A moment's silence followed her words. Vicky waited for the Diamond to flare up but she didn't.

"I will not allow it harm your family, even if it costs me my life," Lucky said solemnly.

"All right," Yvonne said with forced cheerfulness. "We'll be ready to leave early tomorrow."

"Too late," Lucky said. "We need to go in the next few minutes. It won't take the half-grolsch long to find us here. Travel light. Only bring what you need."

"Not a problem," Vicky said, who barely had a change of clothes. The only thing she wanted to bring was her telescope.

"But…" Yvonne began but broke off, accepting they had no choice.

"Hurry," Lucky said. She glowed a little brighter and, despite the danger, somehow Vicky felt brave enough to face the monster.

Yvonne put food and some clothes into a basket and slipped it over her arm. "Are we ready? Susan, you have your flute?"

Susan nodded.

"Vicky, your –"

Vicky slapped the front of her jacket. "Of course."

"We must leave as unobtrusively as possible," Lucky said. "Move quickly and silently."

"We can do that. Even our shadows won't notice us,"

Vicky said, hauling herself through the attic window.

It was a chilly evening. Stars shimmered overhead, and a full moon sailed across the sky. Vicky pulled out her only valuable possession – her telescope. When she held it to her eye, the dark, quiet streets sprang to life. Despite the curfew, carriages were on the move in the wealthy streets. It looked like the governor was having a party, with colourful lanterns strung along his railings, while inside his ballroom, musicians were tuning instruments. Vicky checked the town gate. She could see all the streets clearly, even Front Square and the town wall, and the guard on patrol.

No sign of any monster.

If she wanted to, Vicky could look beyond the walls and into the forest, but she hastily looked the opposite direction. Beyond Lowdar, the mountains rose like jagged teeth towards the sky, and stretched beyond the harbour to fall into the sea in a steep precipice.

Something moved in the dim streets below. Slowly, but purposefully. A tall, cloaked figure turned towards Vicky. Beneath the hood, flames burned amidst a swirling darkness. It felt so close she cried out, fearful of being sucked into that void.

"Come on," Yvonne said urgently.

Yvonne's tug on her sleeve pulled Vicky back to her surroundings. She lowered the telescope and pointed. "It's there."

"How far to the harbour?" Lucky stood on Susan's shoulder.

"Five minutes that way." Vicky jerked her head in the opposite direction.

"Hurry." As she spoke, Lucky disappeared into Susan's pocket.

Everyone immediately scrambled across the roof. Vicky was fastest, but she let the others go ahead while she checked the streets again. The telescope showed nothing but derelict buildings and empty alleys, but she felt the half-grolsch's nearness, a prickling on her spine.

By the time she reached the street, her family were well ahead. Vicky sprinted after them, and was in sight of the harbour entrance when she tripped and fell, dropping her telescope, which rolled away.

Ignoring her grazed elbows and knees, she stretched out a hand to grab it – too late. A shadow fell across her. She raised her head and forgot to run or even cry out. All she saw were white eyes floating in a sea of darkness and fire.

She was going to be burned to cinders by its dark flame.

Then a bright light shot in front of Vicky and the spell was broken.

"Run, Vicky." It was Lucky's voice, faint but insistent. "I can't hold it for long."

Vicky scrambled to her feet, snatched up her telescope, and ran, terrified the monster would grab her long fair plait as it swung behind her.

A single street lamp cast soft yellow light, and the harbour itself was dappled in moonlight. The others were farther along the quay. Vicky cast a quick glance over her shoulder as the half-grolsch turned into the harbour and glided after her.

The sea slapped against the wharf and boats creaked as

Vicky reached the end of the jetty. A small fishing boat was moored there, the words *Sea Flower* scrawled in cracked white paint on its prow.

"Come on, Vicky!" Susan called from the deck.

Steps were cut into the quay, but they were greasy with fish oil and muck from the tide. The gap between jetty and boat looked enormous. Vicky couldn't face the leap to the deck. She would surely drown in the sea or break her neck on the *Sea Flower*'s rail.

The half-grolsch was moving swiftly towards her.

"Jump!" Lucky urged.

Drowning looked a better option than half-grolsch fire, Vicky thought, as she shoved her telescope into its pouch and launched herself forward. She felt the boat rock wildly as she landed, lost her balance, and fell on the deck.

"Loosen the rope," Lucky said urgently.

Vicky pushed herself up on bruised knees. The half-grolsch was halfway along the quay. Alan tugged at the thick rope tethering the boat. He was taking too long to undo the knot; the half-grolsch was almost upon them.

"I can't untie it!' Alan shouted.

Four boats away...three...

A spark flew from the Diamond and sliced the rope in two. The little fishing vessel ploughed forward through the water.

Vicky shook with relief as she watched the half-grolsch, a moment too late, stand on the receding pier and stare after the boat.

The moon rippled across inky sea swells as the boat

gained the entrance of the harbour. The bay lay ahead, sheltered on one side by the mountains.

Vicky stood on the deck, still breathing quickly. Around her were creaking planks, coils of thick rope, fishing nets, and above all, the strong smell of fish. The boat surged through the waves, Lucky at its helm. Already the lights of Lowdar twinkled far behind them. Vicky took out her telescope and raised it to her eye.

Between them and the harbour, a small boat moved rapidly across the waves, faster than the *Sea Flower*. A tall, thin, shadow stood at its prow.

"Lucky! It's after us. I can see its horrible eyes shooting flames."

Lucky didn't reply.

"Lucky!" Vicky swung around to see why the Diamond ignored her. Her words died in her throat.

Ahead, the mountain ended abruptly, its precipice plunging into the sea. Beyond, huge dark rocks were visible. Lined up like warriors, they towered forty feet above the water. Waves crashed against them, churning the sea into white froth.

The Living Rocks.

The *Sea Flower* was headed directly for them.

Panicked, Vicky ran over to Lucky, a beacon of light in the darkness.

"No one can sail past the Living Rocks," she said frantically. The fishermen of Lowdar were terrified, she knew, and refused to sail near them. "It's certain death – we won't survive."

Above the wind, the roar of the sea and a strange humming from the rocks, Lucky's silvery voice was clear.

"It's the only way of escaping the half-grolsch," Lucky said.

The *Sea Flower* passed the precipice and headed closer to the Living Rocks. Vicky looked desperately behind them. The vessel chasing them was gaining. The half-grolsch stood at its helm. She didn't need to use her telescope to see the fires burning beneath its hood.

The others were silent, staring at the approaching rocks. Yvonne put a protective arm around each of the twins and held them tight.

Vicky swallowed. The Living Rocks were sure to kill them if the half-grolsch didn't get them first.

The *Sea Flower* neared the first of the rocks. A cold shadow fell across the deck and Vicky felt a strange weakness come over her.

Lucky's words reached her ears. "I need to concentrate. All of you, lie on the deck. Do not look up."

Vicky pressed herself against the damp deck, inhaling the strong smells of resin and fish and salt, and waited for the end. The boat strained, but didn't move forward. A numbing chill crept along her legs. It grew very dark, as if the moon and the stars had been blotted out. Vicky slowly raised her head.

The *Sea Flower* was midway between two of the rocks, in a channel which suddenly narrowed. Lucky shone brightly at the prow. Close behind, almost near enough to step into their boat, came the half-grolsch.

In a rush, they passed between the rocks, the half-grolsch in the raft at their heels. With a groan, the two living rocks came together. The half-grolsch leaped forward towards the *Sea Flower*. It was clear of the rocks, about to land on their boat, but at that same moment, a gigantic stony hand reached out and snatched the half-grolsch as it touched the deck. The last Vicky saw of the creature was it caught between the two rocks as they slammed together.

Chapter Three
WHIRLCLOUDS

The living rocks came together with a great bang. At the same moment, a sudden swell raced across the sea, rocking the boat. The numbing shadow passed and the *Sea Flower* was bathed in moonlight.

Alan sat up. The half-grolsch was gone. The living rocks had drawn apart and resumed their sentinel position. Their boat had passed through the rocks unscathed.

Which, Alan was pleased to remember, was more than any of the Lowdar fishermen could say.

"Are we safe?" Cathy asked, her face still pressed against the deck.

"I think it's dead." Alan got to his feet, rapidly losing interest in the half-grolsch but eager to discover more of the world beyond the rocks.

"The living rocks destroyed it." Lucky sounded tired, and glowed a little less brightly. "As I hoped."

Although glad the half-grolsch was dead, sailing

interested Alan intensely. A strong breeze blew in his face, leaving salt on his lips. The sky was a midnight-blue blanket pierced with millions of tiny stars. Ahead there was nothing but water, deep swells running across the dark sea. Land, if it existed, was impossible to distinguish from the water. The *Sea Flower* had taken them where no one else could sail.

Alan inhaled the sea-scent, listened to waves slap against the *Sea Flower*, touched a thick coil of rope, and felt the deck roll beneath his feet. He decided he would become a sailor. This voyage was only the start of his adventures.

"Talking Diamond, monsters, a boat theft, and now passing through rocks no one else can," Yvonne said slowly, getting to her feet. "What else will we face, Lucky?"

"Let us go below," Lucky said. "It will be easier to talk."

Inside the tiny cabin, sheltered from the wind, the creaking planks sounded louder, and the swaying of the boat felt stronger. A spark from the Diamond lit the lantern hanging from the ceiling, and its yellow light illuminated two wooden benches, a small table, and some lockers in the corner.

Alan sat on a bench beside Vicky. "Those living rocks were incredible, weren't they? They must be fifty feet tall. Did you see the faces carved into the stone, grinning evilly at us?"

"Yes. I also saw the claw that snatched the half-grolsch," Vicky said sombrely, which made Alan quite envious.

"How did we get through the living rocks?" Cathy said. "They rip every boat to shreds. *No-one* survives."

"Diamond magic," Lucky said. She stood on the centre of the table, and rotated slowly. Alan felt she was studying them all. He stared at her, admiring the way she shone with pure light. He longed to know more about her.

"Are we sailing to your home, Lucky?" he asked hopefully.

"No," Lucky said, to Alan's disappointment. "We will sail around the mountains tonight but most of our journey will be by land."

"Where to?" Yvonne said. "Lowdar is the most eastern point of Nivram, there's nothing beyond the mountains."

"You are only familiar with west Nivram, and its coast, where humans live. The country is actually divided in two by the Blackhand Mountains. Permit me to show you." A spark flew from the Diamond and hovered inches above the table, where it started to stretch and shape itself. "That's the coastline of western Nivram."

It looked like clear and fluid glass to Alan, until a dark speck materialised at one end, followed by another, and he realised it was some kind of map.

"That's Lowdar – there's Senten, and Marron, and the other towns in the country, stretching all the way along the coast to Denstar."

A number of specks sprang up at intervals along one edge of the Diamond map, which continued to grow while Lucky spoke. The speck she had called Lowdar became large enough so that miniature blocks, arranged like buildings in streets and squares, were visible.

"Look, there's the forest that covers most of west Nivram." Tiny black crystals sprang up behind the towns, stretching into the distance. "As you can see, you humans only inhabit the narrow coastal strip between the sea and the Great Forest."

"Amazing," Alan said. He recognised Lowdar now, and was convinced he could distinguish Front Square, the governor's house, and even the derelict building they lived in.

Beside him, Cathy shivered. "Scary."

Alan knew what she meant. The Great Forest was much larger than he'd guessed. He almost felt swamped by the black crystals, clustered so thickly together against the clear glass of the coast and dominating the specks of the towns. Evil, just like the real Great Forest.

To the right of Lowdar, a series of tooth-like mountains protruded, smothered on one side by the black crystals. The mountains swept down past Lowdar and into the sea. The small town of Lowdar was totally dwarfed by them.

"Now look east of the mountains."

Alan focused his eyes on the other side of the magical map, where the clear glass expanded once more to almost the same size as west Nivram. Eastern Nivram was free of black crystals. The terrain undulated gently, sapphire glimmers hinted at rivers and lakes, and at the far end was a mountain, taller than the rest, the top of which was bent at an angle.

"That's Mount Slant, our destination," Lucky said. "As you can see, this half of the country is a much pleasanter place than the other."

Without the shadow of the Great Forest, the eastern

country was bright and appealing. Alan was disappointed. Much as he had taken to sailing, he had also hoped the Diamond princess would take them into the Great Forest and destroy all the monsters living there.

"I thought your home was somewhere called the Rock?" he said. "Where's that on the map?"

"The Rock of Diamonds is within Mount Slant," Lucky said.

"So why did you leave it?" Vicky said. "I mean, I'm glad you did, but what were you doing in Lowdar?"

"Making my way home, as I told you," Lucky said. "I did not leave Mount Slant by choice."

Silence followed as everyone waited to hear more. Eventually Susan spoke.

"Is it to do with the half-grolsch?"

"Yes." Lucky sparkled a little brighter. "An old enemy of mine stole me from the Rock and cast me far from home, hoping I'd die. I believe the same person is responsible for sending the half-grolsch. But now it's dead, so we don't have to worry about her anymore."

"She could send another one after you," Vicky said darkly.

"The living rocks will not allow a half-grolsch through," Lucky said.

"Good," Yvonne said, too cheerfully. "I had no idea Nivram was so large. How do we get to Mountain Slant? It looks a long way from Lowdar."

"Once we are clear of the mountains, we will put to shore," Lucky said. "And head due north."

"Couldn't we stay on the boat, Lucky?" Alan said. He pictured himself sailing around the world, exploring new countries and meeting magical creatures like Lucky.

"My route is the fastest and safest," Lucky said. "Now, it's getting late. You should rest while you can." As she spoke, the crystal map dissipated with a musical tinkle, and the cabin seemed a little gloomier.

Lucky asked Alan to carry her on deck.

"I want to set a course for the *Sea Flower*, so we can land at a place with the shortest journey to Mount Slant," she said.

The wind had increased and the sea swell had strengthened. Alan made his way to the tiller, pleased with how well he could keep his balance on the tilting deck.

For a few moments, the Diamond shone brightly, and Alan had to avert his eyes.

"That's done," Lucky said, reverting to a dim glow. "The *Sea Flower* will take us safely to shore. Now, I must sleep for a few hours. Could you take me somewhere suitable to rest?"

Alan couldn't think of anywhere but his pocket, which didn't seem right for a Diamond princess, but Lucky graciously accepted his offer and he carefully stowed her away.

Back in the cabin, his sisters had found some blankets in one of the lockers and were curled up on the floor. Alan took the extra coverlet which lay beside Cathy.

"Where's Lucky?" she whispered.

"Sleeping in my pocket. This is really exciting, isn't it?"

"Frightening – and fantastic," Cathy said. "Are we imagining it all?"

"No, and it's brilliant." Alan had never experienced anything so exhilarating in his life. "Can't wait to see what happens tomorrow."

"As long as it doesn't bring another half-grolsch," Cathy said doubtfully.

Alan was first to wake, and immediately ran outside. The wind had dropped and the sun shone on glassy blue waters that matched the translucent colour of the sky. To the south and west, nothing was visible but the sea. To the north, a thin dark line on the horizon indicated land. The *Sea Flower* sailed on a parallel course.

He heard the cabin door open followed by Vicky's voice. "This is my type of sea, calm and flat."

"I've thought of what we should ask for our reward," Alan said. "A boat like this, so we can keep sailing."

"I don't want a boat," Vicky said, to his disappointment. "It's uncomfortable and stinks and the waves make me feel sick. We can get something much better than that."

Before Alan could respond, Yvonne poked her head around the cabin door. "Anyone for breakfast?"

They sat on the sun-warmed deck and ate bread and cheese while the *Sea Flower* sailed serenely onwards. The narrow alleys and dirty lanes of Lowdar seemed far away. Alan had almost forgotten them.

Vicky finished her breakfast, took a drink and said: "Where is the *Sea Flower* taking us? Lucky's map showed that once we passed the Blackhand Mountains, we would be in East Nivram. Why aren't we closer to the shore? Where's Lucky?"

"Still asleep," Alan said.

It was strange the boat wasn't heading towards land. As time passed and Lucky didn't appear, Alan became uneasy. He slipped a hand into his pocket and withdrew the Diamond.

He held a dull grey stone, absent of any of the light which previously animated her.

"She's dead." Cathy started to cry.

Alan stared in disbelief at the Diamond. "Lucky? Can you hear me?"

The Diamond did not respond.

Vicky peered at Alan's hand. "She *can't* be dead."

"She must have used up all her energy," Alan said numbly.

"Great." Yvonne folded her arms. "She set the boat on a course east and died on us. Now we'll never reach land."

Alan put Lucky back in his pocket, sorry and upset that the Diamond was lifeless. It looked like he was getting his wish of sailing forever after all, but he wondered what they would do when the food ran out.

"If we were closer, perhaps we could swim for shore," Susan said.

"If any of us knew how to swim," Vicky said.

Yvonne sighed. "Could we turn the boat and point it to the coast?"

"It's powered by magic – how can we control it?" Vicky said.

"Maybe you could suggest something, Vicky?" Yvonne said.

Vicky frowned and thought for a few minutes. "Make a raft, using the sail and some of these planks and rope, which we can control ourselves. It wouldn't be hard, and land isn't that far."

"That's the stupidest idea I've ever heard," Yvonne said.

While his sisters argued, Alan nudged Cathy and led her to the tiller.

"This controls the direction of the boat," he told her. "I'm going to change it." He placed both hands on the tiller and pulled.

The tiller didn't budge.

He tried again, feet pressed against the deck as he strained to move it. Cathy, her tears ceasing, did the same.

The *Sea Flower* turned in the water, its nose pointing towards the shore.

"Hey, we've changed direction," Vicky said.

"Thanks to us," Alan said, as Vicky didn't seem to have noticed Cathy and him at the tiller.

"Do you need a hand?" Vicky said.

Alan shook his head, unwilling to admit that it took all his strength to hang on. The tiller was like a coiled spring, ready to bounce back to its former position if given a chance. The boat seemed determined to go in the direction Lucky had set. His face grew warm from his efforts. It was worth it, though. The *Sea Flower* ploughed towards the shore, and soon they drew close to looming mountains, bare of trees, and bays and inlets, and a rocky shore.

"What's that?" Vicky said, pointing to something out at sea.

"What?" Alan glanced back.

At first he thought it was a low lying cloud, but it rose from the sea towards the sky. Then it started to spin across the surface of the water, travelling towards them.

Susan jumped to her feet in alarm. "What is it?"

Alan anxiously watched the cloud of water increase in size until it was a massive forty or fifty feet high. Although still some way off, it made a terrifying sight. Fear kept Alan's eyes fixed on it as it exploded in a shower of water and sent a series of waves towards the boat.

The *Sea Flower* rocked a little in the aftermath. Alan's arms ached as he hauled on the tiller, but he managed to hold its position.

Another one appeared, and a third, expanding as they travelled across the water before crashing back to join the sea. New ones, towering masses of water, rose to replace them, faster than the old ones disappeared. The surrounding sea seethed with movement.

"Whirlclouds," Cathy cried, her face tense. "Whirlies."

"They're everywhere," Alan gasped.

The tiller pulled and tugged to escape from Alan's grasp. His arms and shoulders throbbed in pain but he clung on. He was soaked by sea spray but held the direction towards land. The water between the boat and the shore began to seethe, and a new column of water formed. Faster and faster it rose, gathering more and more water as it headed directly for the *Sea Flower*. Alan pushed hard on the tiller as the whirlcloud reached the size of a house and still it came towards them. When he thought that it was too late, that the whirlcloud would hit them full on and it was impossible to escape death, the boat moved a little in the water and the whirlcloud passed, leaving the *Sea Flower* rocking madly in its wake. As the whirlcloud headed towards the open sea, it burst into a cascade of water. A few seconds later, the white crest of a wave raced towards them, smacking against the boat, and knocking everyone off their feet. Alan lost his grip on the tiller and the boat spun madly in the water.

His sisters' shrieks echoed in his ear as he pulled himself up.

Now the whirlclouds erupted on all sides, buffeting the boat first one way and then the next, sending Alan sprawling from one side of the deck to the other. He couldn't stay on his feet long enough to reach the tiller. Yvonne and Susan clung to the mast. He couldn't see Vicky or Cathy as waves washed over the side, drenching him.

The *Sea Flower* couldn't take much more of this battering. Alan grasped the end of a rope secured to the rail and clung on as the sea began to froth once more. He watched in terror as yet another column of water rose up and sped towards them.

The boat turned, but not quickly enough. The whirlcloud crashed into the *Sea Flower*. At the same moment a bright light flashed, the boat was caught up by the whirlie, tossed twenty feet in the air and dashed downwards. Alan was flung away from the *Sea Flower* and plunged into the sea. As he sank, he cried out in fear, but his words were drowned by the cold water.

Chapter Four
EAST OF THE MOUNTAINS

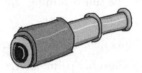

Vicky opened her eyes. She was lying with her face pressed against thousands of smooth round pebbles. Her first thought was for Cathy, who had been swept overboard with her. Where was she? Had the others survived? She pushed herself up and looked around.

She was on a gently sloping pebble beach. Straggly grass struggled to grow on low sand banks, and the Blackhand Mountains were unexpectedly close. Below her, Yvonne waded through the shallows. The twins appeared over a dune and Susan sat nearby. Pieces of wood, the remains of the *Sea Flower*, floated on the water, although some of the debris had washed up on the shore. The sea was frothy, the only sign that the whirlies had existed.

Vicky tried to blot out the memory, but her fear as she was submerged by waves, certain that she was about to die, could not be banished. She shivered. Her clothes stuck to her and she felt bruised all over, but she got to her feet and slid down the slope to the shore.

Yvonne splashed on to the beach. "Is everyone all right?"

"Great," Vicky said. She squeezed the end of her shirt and water dripped to the ground. "We're cold and wet, our ship has sunk, and we don't know where we are." She noticed Cathy staring at her in dismay, and added brightly: "But we're alive, the sun is shining, and this is the greatest adventure I've ever had."

"I've better news than that," Susan said. She held up her hand. Lucky stood on her palm, alive.

Vicky skipped in delight. "I thought you were dead."

"I was in a deep sleep, as I told your brother. I needed to rest." The Diamond twirled on Susan's palm, glinting a little in the sun. "I'm sorry about the boat. I didn't expect it to be destroyed. I set it on a course to avoid the whirlclouds."

Alan studied the sand. "Er - I moved the tiller and changed its direction, Lucky. Sorry."

"That explains why we are so close to the mountains. I wanted to land farther along the coast, but never mind, here will do almost as well."

"What do we do now?" Vicky jumped up and down and swung her arms, but despite her efforts, she couldn't get warm.

A spark flew from Lucky and landed on Vicky's shoulder. Instantly a warm glow spread through her, steam rose from her clothes, and the trauma of the shipwreck vanished.

Once her clothes were dry, the spark leaped to Cathy. Vicky noticed Cathy's hair curl as it dried and counted up all the times Lucky had used magic. Six, or maybe seven.

"Why don't you magic yourself home, Lucky?" she said.

"Diamond magic doesn't work like that," Lucky said. "Sending a little spark your way is easy. Floating home is also easy, but it would take me weeks. I don't have energy for that."

Vicky checked for her telescope – still in its pouch about her neck. The only other possession she still had was the water bottle on her belt. Unscrewing the cap, she took a long drink.

"Go easy on that, Vicky," Yvonne said sharply. "We don't know how long we'll need it. We've no food either. Unless Lucky can magic some up."

"No, but I don't have to." Lucky sounded a little tired, Vicky thought. Maybe the sinking of the *Sea Flower* had woken her prematurely. "Over there."

Lucky nodded towards a heap of debris nearby. Among the broken planks and pieces of timber was the water casket from the *Sea Flower*, the blankets, several coils of rope, and the basket of food. All intact, and the bread wasn't even soggy.

"That's what I call magic," Vicky said, grabbing her knapsack and checking inside.

Yvonne picked up the basket. "What now, Lucky? How far to your home?"

"We have several days travelling, perhaps as much as a week," the Diamond replied. "I suggest we make a start now and see how we get on."

"A *week*?" Yvonne said. "We have food for two days. We won't survive a week."

"Don't worry," Lucky said. "We shall find another source of food in a day or two. Shall we go?"

Before they left the beach, they filled their water bottles from the casket, packed up the blankets, and, on Lucky's advice, collected up some of the smaller pieces of driftwood.

"Which way, Lucky?" Vicky asked.

"Follow the line of mountains northwards," Lucky said. "As far as we can go."

"I can do that," Cathy said. She pulled at a silver chain around her neck, revealing a small bronze disk that had been hidden under her top. Opening the battered case, she stared at the cracked glass. "This way."

Vicky followed her up the sloping beach. She could have pointed out to Cathy that her compass wasn't needed, that the mountains would serve as their guide, but Cathy loved her compass, damaged and rusted as it was, in the same way Vicky treasured her telescope.

When Vicky reached the grass, she stopped to look back at the sea, stretching serenely to the horizon. Ahead were the mountains, next to them was a plain that seemed endless. The land was devoid of life. Nothing stirred, not even a bird.

Only the roar of the sea broke the absolute silence. Vicky, used to the noises of a large town and the unending buzz of people, found it weird.

"Do you see anything?" Susan said, stopping beside her, the Diamond on her shoulder.

Vicky shook her head.

Yvonne muttered something but Vicky didn't catch it. She put away the telescope, glad to be walking on solid earth. Boats were not for her, she decided. Too unstable and uncomfortable.

A few clouds scurried across the sky, but otherwise warm spring sunshine brightened the landscape, turning the farthest mountains a misty blue, and the plains a hazy green. Their path lay across the lower slopes, over a series of uneven ridges. As she scrambled in and out of the gullies, Vicky's brow grew warm, and it became harder to ration her water.

"Isn't there an easier way?" she said, stopping to gaze at the level ground that spread below them to the east. "Why can't we travel down there? It would be faster."

"Dangerous mudflats lie below us," Lucky said. "Which would take far longer to cross."

Vicky said nothing more and marched on. She was sure they were making no progress until she glanced back mid-afternoon and saw that the sea was far in the distance.

Eventually, Yvonne called a halt. "We've been walking all day. We can't go on any further."

Vicky was happy to stop. The sun was low in the sky, preparing to dip behind the mountains, and the evening had grown chilly. Her shoes, already full of holes, felt as if they were made of paper, and her feet hurt. The rocky slopes of the mountains were different from the streets of Lowdar but equally hard.

Yvonne selected a sheltered gully to stop in for the

evening, and Vicky was grateful that Lucky had insisted they carried some of the debris from the boat. They stacked the pieces of wood and a spark from Lucky set the pile ablaze.

Vicky warmed herself by the fire and happily munched her supper. She could never have imagined the events of the last day. Despite her close encounter with the half-grolsch and being shipwrecked, she discovered she was enjoying the journey.

"Play something on your flute, Susan," she said. She loved to hear Susan play.

Susan obligingly took out her flute from a velvet pouch, which, like Vicky's telescope, hung about her neck. The flute was a dull grey metal, roughly cut and damaged, yet Susan played the most beautiful music on it.

"I don't really play it," Susan said. "It seems to play itself."

"Don't be modest," Yvonne said. "None of us can do it."

Night had fallen, and the only light came from the white blaze of the Diamond and the yellow flame of the fire. Susan raised the flute to her lips and a sweet melody filled the air. Vicky felt warm and comforted.

"Where did you get the flute?" Lucky said once the music had ended.

Susan slipped the flute back into its holder. "My mother left it to me. I know it's old and battered, but it is very special to me."

"And it works really well," Vicky said. "Like my telescope."

"Did you see my compass?" Cathy held it up for Lucky. "It always points me in the right direction."

"All gifts from your mother?" Lucky said.

Vicky nodded.

"Our mother left each one of us a special gift when she died." Yvonne lifted a chain around her neck on which dangled a small rusty key. "I love my present but it's not a bit useful. What good is a key without a lock? Our house was burned down. Whatever it locked must have been there."

"Perhaps one day you will find that lock," Lucky said. "What special gift were you given, Alan?"

"I don't have one," Alan said. "Lucky, why are there whirlies and living rocks between east and west Nivram?"

"So that no one may cross from one side to the other. Would you like to hear the history behind this?"

"Yes, please," Vicky said, trying to get comfortable on the hard ground.

"Very well." The Diamond was silent for a moment and when she spoke again her voice sounded different, more solemn and mysterious.

"Since the beginning of time, this land, as well as many others, was given over to the guardianship of the Diamonds. For countless years, we took an active stewardship, closely watching over all species that dwelled in our lands, ensuring their well-being. Yet, over time, as our own concerns grew in importance, the need for an attentive guardian appeared to lessen. So much that now we choose *not* to interfere with other peoples and their squabbles. I fear that this is perhaps a mistake, that we should take a stronger interest, but the king, my father, is adamant that we remain isolated. In particular, my father is prejudiced against members of the human race."

As she spoke, a spark flew from her and lingered in the air. The surrounding darkness pressed closer as Vicky listened, enthralled.

"Because of our guardianship of these lands, Diamonds were given the gift of changing their form, at any time, to anything, large or small, that appealed to them. This gift was rarely used – being perfectly formed already, why would we wish to adopt the appearance of another? The birds and animals were all our friends, but we had no wish to emulate them. No human being, at that time, had entered Nivram."

The spark hovering in the air began to expand, displaying a picture of a mountain with a drooping summit. Streams and rivers snaked across a green landscape, and an immense blue lake spread at the foot of the mountain. Absorbed in the story, Vicky watched the picture form in awe.

"I should say, *until* that time, no human had set foot on Nivram soil. Princess Varya, eldest and most beloved daughter of the king, was fond of strolling alone across the hills and boundaries of Mount Slant. One day, she came home with a strange light in her eyes. She spoke of a handsome two-legged creature that had trespassed into Nivram. Despite all her family's entreaties and her father's exhortations, she insisted on assuming a human form and returned to the place where she had seen the man."

A beautiful young woman walked among a blanket of flowers that covered the shores near the lake. She moved away from the mountain and disappeared over the hills. A light sparkled from the upper slopes of Mount Slant.

"The king watched her go in great sorrow. A shadow darkened his heart, for he knew he would never see his daughter again. Immediately, he banned all form-changing and aimless wandering. Diamonds were – and still are - strictly forbidden to venture beyond the confines of Mount Slant.

"All but one of his daughters obeyed this decree. Fearing for Varya's life, she continued to search the hills and mountains for a trace of her eldest sister. One day, she found her, lying in the shelter of a tree, her long fair tresses swathed around twin human babies. The light was dying in her eyes, but despite her human form, she was still recognisable as Varya. A gash pierced her side, and a jewelled dagger lay near, but Varya was unable to speak, and died shortly afterwards."

As the Diamond spoke, the picture changed to depict the dying girl, with trembling lips and eyes full of pain, clasping two babies. A jagged knife lay close by. Blood gushed from her heart. A single tear ran down her cheek, and her eyelids fluttered closed.

"No sign of the father of the children was discovered, nor could the sorry truth of Princess Varya's demise ever be established. The only evidence was the knife, a crooked instrument with a lizard for its emblem, but this clue led nowhere. The truth of what happened to Varya was lost in oblivion. The king cursed all members of the human race and forbade any involvement with them.

"However, he did not neglect his grandchildren. Human in physical appearance and mortality, they had retained all the strong passions of their mother's race. As time passed, the little girl's resemblance to her mother grew stronger. She loved birds and animals, walking and singing, in fact everything in the world around her. The little boy was different. Perhaps he took after his father? He loved trees and plants, and had an immense curiosity about new and exotic things, but, as the years went by, his interest turned to darker pastimes.

"Despite the sister's peace-loving nature, squabbles continually erupted between the two. The king bequeathed Nivram to them as their inheritance, but later was forced to raise up these mountains to divide the land, to maintain peace by keeping them apart."

The division of the country was displayed by an upheaval in the land, as vast cragged mountains thrust their way up from the ground. Valleys and rifts were created, rivers and streams changed their courses, and the flowers, which had covered the foot of Mount Slant, faded away.

"The king made one path through the mountains, much farther north than here, almost as far as Mount Slant itself. It is known as Peacemaker's Pass, and the king allowed this so that someday the brother and sister could meet, shake hands, and so reunite the divided country. To prevent passage by sea, obstacles were also created there – the living rocks destroy all who attempt to pass them in west Nivram. Whirlclouds spin along the coast of east Nivram to sink approaching ships. But for my intervention, the rocks would have crushed you. Again, you would not have survived the whirlclouds without my aid. No one may pass from one half of the country to the other until the country is unified.

"Despite the efforts of the Diamonds, the Nilkens, and many others, the brother and sister never reconciled, but the mountains which divided the land in two did prevent their squabbles and so at least brought peace – hence we call them the Mountains of Contentment, not Blackhand. Each twin busied themselves with their own half. Scatherina, the sister, cared for animals of all kinds, and was sorely missed when she died. She left the Nilkens to cultivate the land, as they do to this day.

"Caralan, the brother, planted trees to cover every inch of his territory, and so the Great Forest was born. In the deepest, darkest part of the woods he built himself a black castle. Many strange creatures were invited into his land, and from his home he conducted various experiments, his mind always delving into the dark arts. No one mourned for him when he died, and evil creatures still inhabit the forest, such is his legacy."

Vicky watched a shadow creep over one half of the country in the picture, and the whole image started to fade. It finally vanished with a tinkle of glass, leaving them in darkness broken only by the soft glow of the Diamond and the flickering flames of the fire.

"I'm not skilled at showing stories. It is a rare but wonderful Diamond talent," Lucky said.

"That's the most awful story I ever heard in my life," Susan said. "I thought at first it was going to be romantic, Princess Varya falling in love with an ordinary human, but why did it have to end so horribly?"

"Who are Nilkens?" Cathy said.

"Have you seen the black castle in the heart of the forest?" Alan said.

"Who do you think killed Princess Varya?" Vicky said. The mystery of Princess Varya's death intrigued her the most.

"Nilkens are natives of Nivram. We'll probably meet some on our journey. I told you the story to explain why the barriers dividing this land exist. It is also the cause of Diamonds' traditional mistrust of humans. It is thought that Varya's husband caused her death and fled, and it is believed it was her children's human blood that prevented them from living harmoniously together, a fact which your own history of wars bears out. But I myself believe that there was something else, a malignant force at work, something that killed Varya and caused her husband's disappearance, and continued to exert its evil influence on their son, but we shall never know the truth. As far as the king is concerned, it was Varya's association with the human race that led to her doom."

The fire burned low but still provided plenty of heat. Vicky stared at its glowing centre and thought about the story. It was a tragic tale, especially that Caralan left such a terrible legacy as the Great Forest. The threat of the Great Forest beasts had cast a shadow over her childhood. Not only hers, the whole town of Lowdar, and for all she knew Senten and Denstar and the other towns along the coast.

"Lucky, when did people first arrive in Nivram? West Nivram, I mean," she asked.

"About two hundred years ago. A long time after Prince Caralan and Princess Scatherina died. The narrow strip along the coast remains free from the forest, and humans settled there."

Vicky made a face. "Maybe I should have asked *why*? Who would want to live beside the Great Forest?"

"Money," Yvonne said. "Lowdar used to be really wealthy."

"It's getting late," Lucky said. "You should get some rest. The fire will last the night."

"But…" Vicky had other questions she wanted to ask, such as if it was Lucky who found Varya, and what was the significance of the knife with the lizard, but the Diamond seemed reluctant to answer any more.

"Not now. Go to sleep. We'll have plenty of opportunity to speak tomorrow." Lucky glowed a little brighter as she spoke, before dimming once more.

With so much to ponder, Vicky didn't think she would get to sleep. She lay back on her blanket and gazed at a magnificent display of stars. It was strange to feel a light breeze caress her cheek instead of the stuffy attic space where they used to live. Lowdar seemed so far away. As she was drifting off to sleep, she thought about the promised reward and whether they would get one each. Deciding that this would be the case, and torn between being free of bossy older sisters or never needing to eat again, she drifted off to sleep.

Chapter Five
THE MARSH

Alan woke with a start, and for a moment did not recognise his surroundings. In the pale light of dawn, he could make out the sleeping forms of his sisters. A small, bright object watched over them. He realised it was Lucky and remembered where he was.

He got up immediately, his body stiff from sleeping on the hard rock, and climbed out of the gully to sit beside her.

"Morning, Lucky."

"Good morning, Alan. I trust you slept well?"

"Like a..." Alan struggled to think of a suitable analogy. "Like the governor after a twelve course dinner and several flagons of wine."

Lucky glowed a little. "Your governor probably *wouldn't* sleep well after such a meal."

In the east, the sun appeared over the horizon, sending tentative fingers of light across the land. The lower slopes of the mountain still lay in shadow. Northwards, the line of mountains continued into the misty distance. Nothing stirred.

"I wish I could use Vicky's telescope," he said. "I can't see anyone following us, but there might be."

"Would Vicky not lend her telescope to you? Your sisters are waking – why not ask her now?"

"It's not that," Alan said. "I can't see through it. It won't work for me."

"Like Susan's flute?" Lucky said slowly.

Alan nodded.

Vicky scrambled up to join them. She took out her telescope and surveyed the landscape.

"Nothing," she said.

Alan grinned. "Don't be disappointed. Another half-grolsch could pick up our scent yet."

"Don't jest about such matters," Lucky said sombrely.

"I don't want anything like that to happen," Vicky said with a shudder. "But we've spent three days scrambling over these rocky mountains and we don't seem any closer to anywhere."

Yvonne was doling out breakfast so Alan jumped into the little hollow where they had spent their third night in East Nivram. Fortunately, there had been no shortage of tiny streams trickling among the rocks, so they had refilled their canisters regularly. Other than that, their supply of food dwindled and Alan spent most of the day hungry.

Vicky dropped down beside him.

"The coast is clear," she announced. "Another day beckons, full of healthy mountain climbing, followed by a night's slumber beneath the stars."

"I like going to bed under the stars," Cathy said. "They lull me to sleep."

"Me too," Vicky said. "But I now appreciate the lumpy old mattress I had in Lowdar. How soft and comfortable it was."

"Stop complaining," Yvonne said, as she handed out breakfast, the last of the bread and cheese. "That's the end of our supplies so enjoy it."

"I won't complain again," Vicky said immediately. "Except about food. The lack of food, I mean."

"Don't worry," Lucky said. "This morning we will join the plains, and you will have plenty to eat."

Alan was glad to hear this. He finished his breakfast and rolled up his blanket, and was pleased when Lucky chose to sit on his shoulder.

"How far is it, Lucky?" Vicky said. "My boots won't last much longer. I have two holes in one already." She made a face. "My feet won't last either."

"Not far," Lucky said. "We are almost at the plains. By travelling across the lower slopes, we have avoided those dangerous mudflats. The terrain will be pleasant to walk on now."

A short steep climb down the rocky mountain slope was all that lay between them and the edge of the plain. As they clambered down, Lucky told Alan the names of each mountain. "Mount Dearth – the first of the mountain range, the inhospitable one. Next is Mount Grimstone and Mount Helmstad. That double-humped one is Mount Mellion…"

Alan gazed at the mountains, picturing the Great Forest smothering the western slopes.

"… Mount Sentine is split for Peacemaker's Pass," Lucky said.

"Can you enter the Great Forest there?" Alan said eagerly. His desire to enter the Great Forest (with Lucky, of course) had grown stronger as they crossed the mountains.

"If we can go in, what's to stop something coming out?" Vicky said.

Cathy gave a little cry and clutched Alan's arm. "I didn't think of that."

"That won't happen," Lucky said soothingly. "The pass has its guardians too."

"What kind of guardians?" Alan imagined the sides of the mountain slamming together like the living rocks, and violent gusts of winds spinning along the pass, like the whirlies.

"Catchills," Lucky said. "Gigantic birds of prey, with talons like knives and beaks sharper than scythes."

Susan shivered. "I hope we won't meet them."

"Don't worry. The catchills never leave the pass, and we won't be entering it. You're quite safe," Lucky said.

They reached the grasslands which stretched for miles in every direction, broken only by a streak of silver and the dark blur of a wood some way off. Lucky told Alan to keep to the fringes of the plains and walk in the direction of the wood.

It was pleasant walking over the soft turf under bright spring sunshine, a welcome change from the previous three days' journey. Occasionally, Vicky clapped her telescope to her eye to survey the landscape.

"Lucky," she said, after they had been walking for a while. "Through my telescope I can see giant dust clouds rolling across the grass. What are they?"

"Nothing to worry about," Lucky said. "As long as we keep close to the mountains."

Alan stared across the plains. At first he could see nothing, but after a few moments he spied dust clouds on the horizon and felt the ground shudder beneath his feet.

"What's happening, Lucky?" he said.

"Merely the Demerai," the Diamond said. "Quite far away, so we are safe."

"Who are the Demerai?" Alan said. "Another monster?"

"No, no," Lucky said and smiled. "Quite the opposite. They are shy creatures and as anxious to avoid us as we them. The plains belong to them, and we don't want to encroach."

"Are they causing the dust clouds?" Vicky asked.

"And the ground shaking?" Alan said.

"They are beautiful, intelligent creatures who love the ecstasy of running," Lucky said. "Which is all they do all day long. We are skirting the plains so that we do not get accidentally trampled by them."

The earth trembled again, but the tremor only lasted for a second before the Demerai moved out of sight.

Behind Alan, Yvonne muttered something but he couldn't make out the words. He guessed she wasn't happy about this new danger.

After they had walked for a couple of hours, Yvonne called for a break.

"Walk a little further," Lucky said. "Look – is that not a good place to rest?"

A couple of hundred yards ahead, a small group of trees sprang out of the ground. As he drew near, Alan saw clusters of fruit hanging from the branches.

"You were concerned about food, Yvonne," Lucky said. "No need to worry any longer."

"Fruit won't fill us," Yvonne said. "We need something more substantial."

Alan reached for the nearest bunch. Each bunch was a mixture of different coloured fruit. Some were translucent plum or ripe red, others fresh green or warm peach. The size and shape of the fruit varied too, and when Alan touched the fruit, he found one had a silken skin, another a rough peel, while the third had a furry rind.

"What are they?" He didn't believe they were edible.

Yvonne dropped her basket on the ground beside him. "I've never seen fruit like these. And the trees – they should be in blossom. We're in spring."

"Nilkens once roamed across this land and grew these trees so there always would be food, not only for themselves but for any traveller, no matter the season. See – four trees, and merely a single tree in fruit."

The Diamond was right: only one of the trees in the little copse was laden with produce. A second one was in blossom, a third stood stark and bare, while the leaves on the fourth had turned copper and gold.

"Are they safe to eat?" Vicky said.

An enticing aroma tickled Alan's nostrils, making his

stomach rumble, so he plucked one of the red fruits. The texture was stringy but the flavour strangely good.

"Like cheese," he said, "but tastier."

Vicky seized a green one, bit into it and made a face. "Urgh. Tastes like cabbage." Flinging it away, she tried another. This time she smiled. "Lovely."

Alan had some more, testing the different flavours. Some fruit were bitter, others sweet, and most somewhere in-between.

"The Nilkens had foresight," Lucky said. "This fruit should keep you going until we reach Mount Slant."

"What do you call them, Lucky?" Susan said. "They're sweet – like peaches and apples."

"Papples," Cathy said. She liked to name things.

"As good a name as any," Lucky said. "Papples."

Vicky plucked a lustrous black one. As she took a bite, it burst open and sprayed her with a thin clear liquid.

"For drinking as well as eating," Lucky said.

Alan found the same fruit and pulled one off the stem. Nibbling the top of it, he pierced the skin, and lifting it up to his mouth, he drained it. It was like refreshing sweet water. He decided to carry as many papples as he could fit into his pockets.

They sat for a while under the trees, enjoying a rest.

"What are Nilkens?" Vicky said. "Are they human? It's a bit late to ask, but their food won't poison us, will it?"

Lucky looked a little displeased. "No. Nilkens have similar tastes to humans."

"What happened to them?" Alan said.

"Nilkens gave up wandering once they found the place

they wished to live. Princess Scatherina allowed them make their home close to Mount Slant. If you are rested, I suggest we move on. We don't want to delay."

Their route continued along the outskirts of the plain. The ground was springy beneath Alan's feet, and apart from the occasional set of papple trees, he saw no other sign of life. Every so often, Vicky used her telescope to check the sky and then she'd shrug her shoulders. It seemed that they were still alone.

By late morning, the wood had drawn close. To the east, the plains still stretched interminably, and ahead mountains continued in a series of rocky ridges and sheer cliff faces.

Alan curiously eyed the wood and the dark mist engulfing it.

"Are we going to the wood, Lucky?" he said.

"No, we wish to avoid it." Lucky answered from Susan's shoulder. "Keep close to the mountains."

Immediately ahead, the soft turf that had been so pleasant to walk upon gave way to marshier ground. Millions of reeds and rushes grew waist high, and he heard the hum of thousands of insects.

"Wait," Lucky said. "I didn't expect long grass here." Alan was surprised to hear the consternation in her voice.

"Can't we walk through it?" he said.

"It would be better not to," Lucky said

The reeds stretched from the wood to the mountains.

"Should we walk on the other side of the wood?" Susan said.

"Crossing Demerai lands is too dangerous," Lucky said.

"What about the mountain slopes?" Vicky held her telescope to her eye. "No, forget that. The marsh meets sheer cliff."

"So we're stuck?" Yvonne said.

"What's wrong with going through the wood?" Alan said. Its murkiness intrigued him.

"Too dangerous," Lucky said. "We don't have time to retrace our steps to find a way over the mountains, so we will risk the marsh. A path should wind through it, but it is difficult to find. Susan and I will lead the way. Make sure you follow exactly, and do not let yourselves be distracted by anything. Avoid gazing into pools. Ignore the insects – they're an illusion to make you go astray."

"I don't like this," Cathy whispered, as they set off.

"Stick close to me," Alan told her, "and you'll be okay."

As soon as Alan stepped onto the path, a tremendous buzzing erupted around his head, as if several swarms of insects had decided to attack simultaneously. But, having faith in Lucky's assurance that it was only an illusion, he put aside all thought of the insects, and the noise soon diminished. However, once there was silence, he became aware of other distractions, such as exotic animals vanishing into the rushes. He stopped several times to take a closer look, but on each occasion Cathy, walking immediately behind, bumped into him and started him off again.

A number of deep blue pools appeared on either side of the path. Alan's eyes were drawn irresistibly towards them. The first pool was a kaleidoscope of colour. The second reflected starlight in a velvet sky. The third pool had a picture of two people galloping on horseback across a seashore. He was sure that one of the riders resembled himself and paused, but Cathy knocked into him once more so he kept going.

A large pool, too big to step over, lay across the path. Susan and Vicky cleared it easily. As Alan jumped, he glanced down at the water. An image of dashing seas and a tall masted ship caught his eye. He peered down, and instantly his knees came together, his legs stiffened and he fell deep into the water.

Chapter Six
THE WOOD OF WITCHES

Cathy screamed as Alan disappeared.

"Alan!'

Yvonne grabbed her jacket to stop her falling or jumping in after her twin.

"Let me go!" Cathy struggled to get free. "Alan's gone!"

The pool of water was shallow. She could see the sandy base, and a fish swimming between two large stones. Alan had vanished completely.

"Careful, Cathy." Yvonne's grip tightened. "I don't want you disappearing as well."

Vicky turned back and stood at the far side of the pool.

"What is it? What happened? Where's Alan?"

"He fell into the water." Tears rolled down Cathy's face but she barely noticed them.

Vicky stared into the pool. "I don't see him."

Susan appeared behind Vicky.

"Get out of the grasses, go back the way we came." Lucky

sparkled on Susan's shoulder. "We haven't come in too far fortunately."

Cathy didn't want to leave the spot where Alan had vanished.

"He's in there somewhere," she said.

"Yes, as a stone, or a reed or perhaps that fish is him," the Diamond said. "Let us get out of this place before anyone else falls in."

Cathy bent down. If Alan was the fish, she wasn't leaving. She stared closely at its golden scales and the expressionless eye, and tried to recognise something of her twin.

"I'm not leaving him."

"Don't worry, Cathy," Lucky said gently. "He's not going anywhere. And I won't forget which pool he is in, if that's what concerns you."

Yvonne tugged on her sleeve.

"Come on, Cathy. Let's hear what Lucky has to say."

Against her wishes, Cathy allowed Yvonne to turn her away from the water and lead her out of the reeds.

Back on the plain, a strong breeze had blown up, but the reeds stood straight and tall, unaffected by the wind. The dark blur of the wood loomed frighteningly near. Cathy hadn't realised that it was so close. Tears were still running down her cheeks when she turned to Lucky.

"What has happened to Alan? Why can't you rescue him?"

"Alan allowed himself to be distracted by the images in the pool. I warned you all about them."

"I didn't see anything when I jumped over it," Susan said.

"Unfortunately, Alan did. The marsh is magical, and the pool is a trap. If you leave the path, you will be caught."

"By who?" Yvonne said.

"By the witches who live in that wood."

"Witches?" Cathy's tears dried on her cheeks.

"Yes, which is why I wish to avoid the wood."

"Why aren't the witches in the Great Forest with all the other evil creatures?" Vicky said.

"That would be a suitable home for them," Lucky said. "But they wished to live in this little wood, and it was easy to fool the Nilkens into allowing them to do so. Nilkens are such trusting souls, but they can also be resolute. Some types of magic cannot cross running water. Once the Nilkens realised the truth, they diverted a stream to run around the trees and through the middle of the woods. Both witches, and there are only two, are now confined in their mischief-making."

"So what do we do now?" Vicky said.

"Someone must go into the wood and obtain the release spell," Lucky said. "I can't go. I am forbidden to interfere."

"I'll go." Cathy would do whatever was needed to get Alan back. Alan wouldn't baulk at anything to rescue her, she knew. She wasn't going to let him down, even if she had to face terrifying witches. She thought of Alan, imprisoned in the form of a stone, and longed to save him.

"You're too young, Cathy," Yvonne said. "You stay here, I'll go."

Cathy was about to object when Lucky intervened. "You

both should go. There are two witches, so let us send two warriors."

"Shouldn't we stick together and all go?" Susan said.

"No, you and Vicky stay here," Yvonne said. She looked at the Diamond. "What are we looking for?"

"One of the witches has the release spell, perhaps both. Hurry, you must leave now. There's not much time."

Cathy's heart beat faster. "What do you mean?"

"These evil traps rarely stay in one place for long," Lucky said. "If you're not back by this time tomorrow, the long grass and the magical pools will probably move elsewhere, taking our chances of rescuing Alan with it."

Lucky's words scared Cathy so much that she immediately started towards the misty blur that lay ahead. Yvonne called for her to wait, but Cathy walked grimly on.

Black mist wreathed about her ankles and she stopped, frightened, until Yvonne caught up.

"Don't go on ahead without me," Yvonne scolded. "We have to stay together."

Cathy was relieved to have her eldest sister by her side. "All right."

The mist shrouded the trees, and she could barely distinguish the trunks of the trees. She hesitated, afraid to enter such a frightening wood.

"Are you ready?" Yvonne whispered the words, as if afraid to be overheard.

Cathy nodded and plunged into the mist.

Darkness surrounded her and the clammy fingers of the

mist clung to her legs and touched her face. Strange wraith-like figures with bone-white limbs and ghostly faces rose before her and screeched silently.

"You're not real," Cathy said, remembering the trap that caught Alan.

Yvonne had grabbed hold of her jacket as she had stepped into the mist, but Cathy could no longer feel her. Her feet stuck to the ground and wouldn't move, but she thought of her twin.

"Alan, we're coming," she cried and stepped forward.

After a moment, the mist thinned, and she found herself among trees.

The wood was dark and stuffy, but there was enough light for her to make out the enormous boles of the trees, and the thick vegetation of the forest floor. The bark was dark and covered with lichen. The great branches of each tree stretched out and became entangled with their neighbours. Steam rose from the ground, and Cathy could not see below her knees. Snakes, lizards, little monsters, anything at all, could be lurking about her feet, waiting to trap or attack her.

"What a horrible place." Yvonne stood beside her and spoke in a whisper, as if unwilling to disturb the dead silence of the wood. "Urgh – look." She thrust a hand in front of Cathy.

Cathy looked at Yvonne's fingers and her face. Both were smeared with black.

"They're filthy." Yvonne sounded disgusted. "Your face is too. Must have been that mist."

Cathy didn't care. "Which way? I don't see a path."

"Well, we don't know where we're going, so what difference does it make?" Yvonne was suddenly cheerful. She took hold of Cathy's hand. "Come on."

Cathy allowed herself to be led through the thick undergrowth, weaving among the trees, ducking to avoid the low branches. The air remained thick and warm, and it was difficult forcing their way through the vegetation. Cathy soon became hot and tired.

"How will we find the witches?" Cathy said miserably. "Or get the release spell from them?"

"Don't worry, Cathy. We'll find a path soon, a sign that will lead us to those witches. Wait until I tell them what I think of their antics, leaving stupid magical traps carelessly around the place."

Cathy felt comforted by Yvonne's words.

Shortly afterwards, Yvonne grabbed Cathy's arm, pointed ahead and said triumphantly, "Look – what did I tell you?"

A few yards away, the vegetation was beaten down into a path winding among the trees. Cathy ran towards it, leaping over thick foliage, afraid the path would disappear before she reached it. As she gained the path, something flew through the air and blundered into her face.

Cathy shrieked, batting it away with her arms. Her fingers encountered something filmy and sticky but then it was gone.

"It's okay, only a moth," Yvonne said.

"Are you sure it's gone?" Shaken and close to tears, Cathy

felt her face and her hair. A gummy resin had been left behind. Disgusted, she tried to brush it off.

"Yes, it's over there." Yvonne pointed ahead.

An enormous moth, bigger than Cathy's face, rested on a nearby tree, its delicate wings vibrating gently.

Cathy shrieked again when she saw the size of it.

"It probably got a bigger fright than you did," Yvonne said.

Cathy rubbed her fingers against her jacket. She felt sick. "Yuk, yuk, yuk."

"We've found the path, come on," Yvonne said.

The path wove among the trees for a few minutes before ending abruptly. A new path appeared a short way off, and Cathy trudged after Yvonne to reach it. This trail looked more promising, but it too disappeared into the undergrowth.

"Are you sure this is right?" Cathy said.

"Yes, it must be – come on, I see another one starting over there."

Cathy traipsed after Yvonne again. Glancing back, she saw the first track had disappeared.

This pattern was repeated. Every time one trail ended, a new one began a short distance away, and all evidence of the previous pathway vanished. They were led deeper and deeper into the wood, with no way of finding their way back.

The undergrowth was filled with unseen life. Bushes rustled in an unfelt wind. Twigs snapped as if someone followed them, but other than the giant moths which frequently flew into her face or hair, they saw nothing.

Cathy lost track of time. Her legs were aching, and every

step was an effort, but she thought of Alan and kept going. The faint daylight faded, and they would have been in darkness only for veins of phosphorous which ran up the trunks of the trees, shedding an eerie light.

Yvonne stopped. "We have to rest. I'm exhausted and you can barely walk. Let's sit down for a while, and eat a few of those appley things."

Cathy didn't want to halt, but she was too weary to continue.

"Okay." A large grey boulder looked like a good seat. As she approached, the rock quivered and a huge mouth gaped open at the exact spot where she'd intended to sit. It made a horrible sucking, gurgling noise. She jumped backed several feet in fright.

"Better stand." Yvonne rummaged in her pack. "Here." She handed Cathy a bunch of small blue papples.

Cathy shook her head. "Not hungry."

"You have to eat, Cathy. And we have to find somewhere to sleep, if only for a few hours."

Reluctantly, Cathy accepted the fruit. For once the papple was tasteless in her mouth. She looked at the thick undergrowth, with its tangled vegetation. She didn't want to sleep anywhere near it.

"The trees are probably safe," Yvonne said. "They were here before the witches, weren't they? The bushes and rocks are evil because they are the witches' design, but the trees are good."

It sounded plausible to Cathy, and better than sleeping on the ground. She stood beside a huge tree with many broad branches. Yvonne tapped its trunk experimentally. Nothing happened to her.

"It's safe."

She sounded confident, and Cathy had no better idea. She climbed up the tree with little difficulty. It was so large she had plenty of room to snuggle up in one of the hollows where the branches joined the trunk. Yvonne used her belt to tie Cathy to a branch well above the underlying bushes, and climbed up to the one higher.

"Don't worry, Cathy," Yvonne said. "We'll find those witches in the morning and get the release spell. By this time tomorrow, we'll have Alan back again."

Cathy hoped Yvonne was right. For a while she stared at the surrounding forest. One plant grew much taller than the rest. Its great purple buds protruded above the undergrowth. In unison, the flowers turned towards Cathy. As their petals unfurled, a heavy perfume filled the air.

Cathy yawned, nestled into the branch and closed her eyes. Within a few moments, she was asleep. She dreamed of being immersed in water, unable to breathe, and struggling in vain to break free. The curious dead eyes of enormous sea beasts stared at her and she knew she was doomed to be trapped there forever.

When she woke, daylight had returned to the gloomy wood. She untied the belt and sat up.

"Yvonne?"

Her sister didn't answer. Cathy looked up at the branch where Yvonne had slept.

Nobody was there.

Cathy raised her voice. "Yvonne? Where are you?"

Silence.

Yvonne was gone.

Chapter Seven
CAGED

Yvonne was in the kitchen, scrubbing the counter. Yet, the more she scoured and polished, the longer the counter grew. This was infuriating, and she worked all the harder to make its surface gleam. When she came to the frustrating conclusion that she would never get it finished, she woke up.

She was lying on the floor of a large wooden cage, suspended from the ceiling. A sharp pain pierced her head, and her stomach felt sick. She should be somewhere else but, confused by the pain, she wasn't sure where. Grasping the bars of the cage, she peered at the room below.

Dreary daylight streamed through three round windows. The floor was alternating black and white tiles, and the furniture was striped to match. A roaring fire blazed in the hearth. Above it hung a glossy white cauldron.

A witch reclined on the striped settee. She was clad in loose fitting black trousers, her dark blouse edged with white, and a miniature pointed hat crowned a mass of slate-grey hair. She held a slender black stick from which a thin trail of dark smoke issued. Raising this to her lips, she closed her eyes and sucked loudly.

The pungent smoke made Yvonne sneeze.

The witch's lids shot open. "So, you're awake?"

"Let me out of here!" Yvonne shook the bars of her prison and sent the cage spinning. "You can't do this to me. Where's Cathy? What have you done with her?"

"Was there another? How annoying I missed her. Never mind, I'm sure I'll find her tonight when I do my rounds." The witch's eyes glinted at Yvonne. "You will be glad to be reunited."

"You've no right to keep me here. Let me out!'

"I have every right." The witch closed her eyelids. "You were in my wood. Now, silence please, you are disturbing my peace."

Yvonne shook the bars of the cage once more and glared at the witch.

"Let me out at once. You'll be sorry you did this to me."

"Shut up," the witch said, calmly.

Yvonne tried to control her anger. "What do you want with me?"

"Can't you keep quiet?" the witch said. "I haven't decided what to do with you. It's a simple choice. If I feel in good humour later, I shall merely eat you. I haven't eaten any decent meat in years – though, from the look of you, I probably won't fare too well. However…" The witch inhaled deeply on her black stick. "…should you annoy me – and I have a low tolerance for fools – I shall make you my slave. And that, I assure you, would be much worse."

"I won't be either." Yvonne kicked the cage to see if she could break the bars.

The slats of the cage remained solid, and her foot hurt.

"I told you not to make noise," the witch said.

"Set me free. You're cruel and wicked and I won't stay here."

"I shall not warn you again. I'll merely silence you – you won't be able to cry out with your lips sealed permanently together."

The witch's threat worked. Yvonne sat back in the cage and thought hard. She must have been snatched from the branch while she slept. Why didn't she wake up? She remembered the purple flowers and their fragrant scent– could they have sent her into a heavy sleep, ready to be picked up by the witch on her nightly rounds?

Luckily, the witch hadn't seen Cathy, who must be terrified and helpless, alone in the wood. Yvonne had to escape, get the release spell for Alan, and find Cathy.

She examined the cage. The bars joined smoothly together, above, below, and on all sides. Where was the opening? She felt for a catch and eventually her searching fingers found a tiny keyhole in one of the bars.

All she had to do now was to get the key to unlock it.

The witch's eyes were shut, although every so often she raised the cigarette to her lips. Yvonne noticed a bunch of keys hanging from the witch's belt. Surely one of them fitted the tiny lock?

If only she had a piece of wire, she could stretch her hand through the cage and tweak the keys off the belt of the witch once she slept. Yvonne searched her pockets but all she found was a handkerchief, a comb and two copper coins. Nothing else.

The chain about her neck swung clear of her blouse. She stared at the delicate key it held. What had Lucky said? Something about yet to find the lock her key fitted. Was it possible that this tiny key could fit the lock of her cage? It was a million to one chance - yet somehow Yvonne believed it would.

She had to wait for her captor to sleep. The witch's eyelids were shut, but the black stick still smouldered between her fingers. Yvonne waited. Eventually the black stick disappeared to a stub and fell from the witch's fingers.

The witch didn't stir.

Yvonne removed her chain. Stretching her hand between the bars, she felt for the lock. She almost dropped her chain as she tried to transfer it from her palm to her fingers but as if by magic the key slipped into the keyhole. With one twist of her wrist, the lock clicked and the floor of the cage fell open. Yvonne grabbed on to the bars in time to prevent herself clattering to the floor. For a moment she hung several foot in the air, clinging tightly to the cage as it rotated gently. She held her breath and let go, dropping lightly to the ground. The witch did not move.

The key remained in the lock. Yvonne was not leaving without it. She stretched her arm and jumped but her fingers couldn't quite reach.

"Come on, key, please," she whispered and leapt up again.

The cage spun lazily in the air and the key fell out with a musical tinkle.

She quickly bent to pick it up, glancing anxiously at the witch as she did so. A gentle snore broke the silence. Yvonne pocketed the key and looked around for a spell book.

Shelves flanked the hearth. Amid the mix of bottles and candlesticks, feathers and oddments, Yvonne spied a small, thick book, bound in white leather. Yvonne was sure it held the release spell for Alan.

Stepping as softly as she could, she approached the shelf. Something stirred by the hearth. It was a rat the size of a small dog. Yvonne hadn't noticed it earlier for its two-tone skin camouflaged it against the black and white tiles. Now she could see its sharp claws and bared teeth as it advanced towards her.

Yvonne stood still, gazing at the rat. Her hand reached out and felt for the book.

Instead of encountering leather, her fingers touched something furry.

Yvonne looked away from the rat towards the shelf.

A large white spider sat on the book, its fat, furry body and spindly legs embracing the cover. Malevolent red eyes stared at her.

She withdrew her hand.

The wall behind the shelf came alive. On every black tile a dark spider squatted, while a pale counterpart settled on the white sections. A hundred tiny red eyes glared at her.

Yvonne stepped away from the shelf. She needed a brush

to sweep the book free of spiders.

An angry squeak reminded her of the rat. She looked down. Now there were two. The second one launched itself at her but she managed to kick it away. It was back on its feet immediately.

Yvonne backed away. The first rat squeaked again and three more appeared beneath the table. All five ran at her. Yvonne turned and bolted for the door. She had almost reached it when she felt a heavy thump between her shoulder blades and a vicious stab of pain. She screamed and flung herself against the doorframe to dislodge the creature. It worked: she felt the sudden release of the rat's teeth. Ignoring the pain in her shoulders, she raced for the shelter of the undergrowth.

She crashed her way through the vegetation for a few minutes before she realised the rats were not pursuing her. Nor was the witch. Sinking to her knees, tears of disappointment stung her eyes. No spell, no Alan, no Cathy. She was hopelessly lost in this horrible wood, only a short distance from the witch who was sure to discover her.

After a brief rest, she got to her feet and headed away from the witch's cottage, determined to somehow find Cathy.

Chapter Eight
OLD SURU

Cathy remained sitting on the branch and waited for Yvonne to return.

But Yvonne didn't come back.

Tears stung Cathy's eyes and rolled down her cheeks. She felt for the chain around her neck and clasped her compass tightly in her hand.

Somehow she found enough courage to slip down the trunk. She had no food, but her water canister was slung over her shoulder. She buckled Yvonne's belt around her waist, and took a drink.

Which way did Yvonne go? The path that had led them to the tree the previous night had vanished completely. She stood alone in the undergrowth, listening hard.

The wood was dead, the silence overwhelming, and every direction looked dangerous.

She felt her compass warm against her palm. Unfurling her fingers, she popped open the case. The silvery dial of the compass glinted in the gloom. The words *The One True Way* were etched around it, glittering brightly; the golden tipped arrow spun around before pointing straight ahead. Without hesitation, Cathy set off in the same direction.

She was so sure that the compass would lead her to Yvonne that she dd not notice all the things that had scared her the previous day: the giant moths, the knotted vines, and the noises in the undergrowth.

Soon, she heard the gushing of water. Struggling through a thicket, she emerged beside a fast flowing river. Stepping stones marked a way across but they looked wet and slippery.

However, the compass pointed across the river, so Cathy carefully placed her foot on the first stone. It remained firm beneath her weight, so she made her way across.

On the far side, she struck a path that led to a clearing with a small thatched cottage. Its walls were smothered with roses, and smoke billowed from the chimney. As she drew close to the open doorway, she saw the roses were really purple flowers. Their petals rotated and made a hissing sound at her approach. Cathy halted.

"Is someone there?" a melancholy voice called.

Cathy looked through the door at a rustic kitchen with a wooden table, several chairs, and a dresser. A great black cauldron seethed in an enormous hearth. A witch sat at the table, her expression morose, as she leafed through a large leather-bound book. Yvonne was not in sight and Cathy felt a sting of disappointment.

The witch glanced briefly at Cathy before turning her

eyes back to the book. "Why are you bothering old Suru? What have I done to you?"

Yvonne wasn't there but maybe the release spell was in the book the witch so keenly read?

"Oh, can't you speak?" The witch looked up with sudden interest. "Are your lips sown together? Have you sold your voice to save a loved one? Or was it stolen from you by a grebbler?"

Cathy found her voice. "I'm looking for my sister, have you seen her?"

"Maybe the grebbler got your sister," the witch said. "I haven't seen anyone for years. I haven't seen a grebbler either. Maybe they are all dead."

"I'm here about my brother too." The witch did not seem threatening, so Cathy stepped over the threshold.

"Careless with your siblings, aren't you? I can't help you, I'm afraid. What's your name, my dear?"

Cathy was half way between the door and the table.

"Cathy."

"Old Suru doesn't bite, come closer."

Impish faces were carved into the furniture, their grimaces at odds with the comforting cackle of the fire and the pleasant voice of the witch. Cathy hesitated.

"It's been so long since I had anyone to talk to," Suru said mournfully. "Won't you stay a while? Perhaps you would like to have something to eat. I am about to cook a meal for myself." She flicked over a page.

Cathy pointed at the book. "Isn't that a spell book?"

"Perhaps I will whip up a meal from its pages. Come closer, I will show you."

Cathy didn't move.

"I have to find my sister. Are you sure you haven't seen her?"

"I'm sorry. Maybe my good neighbour has her. I'd like to help you, but a river runs between her side of the wood and mine. I cannot cross it."

The faces on the furniture sneered at Cathy. Something told her to retreat while she could.

"I'm so lonely." The witch's voice was sorrowful. "No one visits me. You're the first human child I've seen for many a long year. Although quite a miserable specimen."

"You don't look too happy yourself," Cathy retorted.

"What have I got to be happy about? I'm the wickedest witch in the east wood, but who cares? No one else lives in the east wood. Those pesky Nilkens, confining me here with their foul streams." She sighed heavily. "I used to have such fun too. Sowing discord was my greatest talent, how well it used to grow."

Cathy was not sure what the witch meant but it didn't sound good.

"Friends, sisters, young lovers – few could resist my charms. I had disappointments, some who opposed my good work. So I used stronger incantations, resorting to shape-changing when all else failed. If two sisters refused to argue over young men or clothes when I gave them the chance, they certainly couldn't argue at all after one of them became a chicken." She chuckled at the memory, before resuming her gloomy expression. "Not that it made me happy for long. Who cares about shape-changing spells? I need a greater challenge."

The pity Cathy initially felt had evaporated. The shape changing reference made Cathy certain she had found the right witch. Without thinking, she stepped a little closer.

"What about the traps you have in the long grass outside the wood?"

"Simple snares to catch me some food once in a while – a little meat never did anyone any harm."

Cathy looked in horror at the witch. "My brother is caught is one of those traps."

"That's unfortunate. Usually all I catch is a little quail or goose. And Fluff doesn't always bring them in for me in one piece." Suru turned a few pages of her book. "Little boy? Hmm."

"Couldn't you let him go? What do you want him for?"

"I could release him, but – I'm lonely. Unless you'd like to stay here in his place?"

"No." Cathy clutched her compass, hoping for help. An idea struck her. "If you're so lonely, why don't you leave the wood? Wouldn't you like to live in the Great Forest?"

A wave of longing crossed the witch's face. "Where wickedness runs through the sap of the trees, and the atmosphere is thick with malevolence. What bliss!"

"If you give me the release spell for my brother, I'll help you get there."

"How could a little girl like you organise that?"

"I know Lucky the Diamond. She could do it."

The witch spat on the floor. "That thing? She's the one who told the Nilkens to surround this place with running water."

83

"So she's the one who can end it." Cathy tried to sound confident, although she wasn't sure Lucky would agree.

Suru pushed the book away, and got up to rummage among the stuff on the dresser. Cathy glanced down at the open page. She couldn't read well, especially not upside-down, but she recognised the layout. A list of ingredients was on one side, instructions on the other. It was the page heading that gave away the recipe: *How to Cook Little Girls.*

Cathy was in more danger than Alan.

The witch returned to the kitchen table with a small, tattered book. Her movements disturbed a slight creature curled up by the fire. It yawned and stretched and rose to its feet.

"Oh, what's that?" Cathy said.

"That's Fluff, my cat."

Cathy looked at the creature's sorrowful brown eyes, short legs, and tail as it trotted past her towards the open doorway. "It's a puppy."

"It's a cat." The witch glared fiercely at her. "Every witch has a cat, and this is the finest cat in the wood. Ah, here's the release spell. Who did you say you wanted it for?"

"My twin brother," Cathy said.

The witch's hand paused, her long spindly fingers tapping the page.

"*She* won't be pleased with me. She's looking for human children."

"Who is?" Cathy said, afraid that "she" was Lucky's enemy, the one who had sent the half-grolsch.

"Queen Rose, of course. That's why we re-set the traps.

If I hand you and your brother over to her, she'll be delighted with me."

"If you give me the release spell, Lucky will be happy. And Lucky's the only one who can let you out of this wood," Cathy said desperately,

"You must give me something of value in exchange. A promise is not enough, what's that around your neck?" The witch's sharp eyes fixed on the compass.

Cathy found herself beside the witch, not knowing how she got there. The witch extended a claw towards her but Cathy shoved Suru away, ripped the release spell from the book and ran out of the cottage as fast as she could.

"After her, Fluff. Get her, Fluff," the witch screamed, as she sprawled on the floor. The dog, barking excitedly, chased out after Cathy.

Cathy tore through the shrubbery and back to the river. Halfway across the stepping stones, she realised that the puppy waited on the bank. It whined piteously, as if it did not know whether or not to follow.

"Come on, boy." Cathy bent down and extended a hand to encourage him. The dog grinned happily and stepped onto the first stone. Almost immediately it changed its mind, yelped and raced back in the direction of the cottage.

Disappointed, Cathy sat down on the largest stone in the middle of the river. Was she far enough from the witch? Hoping that the running water would protect her, she looked at the page crumpled between her fingers. The scrawled letters made no sense to her. Carefully smoothing out the creases, she folded the page once and slipped it into her pocket. After that, she opened her compass.

"What has happened to Yvonne? Please lead me to her."

The dial on the compass spun around in circles, not indicating any direction. It must want her to stay where she was.

It was hard to wait there, expecting the witch to come after her, but Cathy trusted the compass absolutely. Some hours later, the bushes on the far bank were forcibly parted and Yvonne staggered through.

Cathy had never been happier to see her sister. Yvonne looked distraught, but her face broke into a smile and she hastened across the stepping stones to join Cathy.

"Oh, Cathy, I've failed miserably. I met the witch but couldn't get the spell."

"I got it." Cathy patted her pocket. "My compass led me to the other witch. Can we go rescue Alan?"

"Which way?" Yvonne looked around helplessly. "I'm totally lost."

The dial on the compass swung southwest.

"My compass will lead us out," Cathy said. "Follow me."

Chapter Nine
RESCUE

Vicky watched Cathy and Yvonne disappear into the murky mist of the wood. Feeling disheartened, she followed Susan over to the quartet of Nilken fruit trees.

"Why did you send us through the marsh, Lucky?" Vicky wanted to blame someone.

"It's not Lucky's fault," Susan began, but the Diamond interrupted her.

"Yes, it *is* my fault. I didn't realise those old traps had been reactivated. I warned you purely as a precaution; I never thought it was needed."

"I didn't see anything strange there," Susan said.

"Me neither." Vicky already regretted her angry words. Lucky had warned them, why hadn't Alan listened?

"For some reason, your brother was vulnerable."

Susan frowned into the distance, as if mulling over Lucky's statement. "I've got my flute. I think it somehow protects me."

"Me too." Vicky slipped her telescope out of its pouch and hugged it. "My telescope, I mean, it's special. Yvonne and Cathy have their gifts too. But Alan doesn't, could that be the reason?" She had always felt her telescope was magical. It hadn't occurred to her before that perhaps the flute, the compass, and the key were too.

"Why doesn't Alan have a gift from your mother?"

"He lost it," Susan said, "though he won't admit it. He can't even remember what it was."

"Funny thing is, none of us can remember it either. Not even Yvonne. And she usually remembers *everything*," Vicky said, with feeling.

Susan sighed. "Will we ever see him again?"

"Of course you will." The Diamond shone a little brighter as she spoke. "May I see your flute again?"

Susan slipped it out of its velvet bag.

"It's beautiful," Lucky said. "Unusual craftsmanship. What do those symbols mean?"

Vicky leaned over to have a look. "What symbols? Where?"

"Don't you see them? Ah, it has a miasma attached," Lucky muttered.

Vicky exchanged a look with Susan.

"No idea what that is," Vicky said.

Lucky shone brighter for a moment, and Susan's flute was transformed from metal grey into the most beautiful shining silver. Symbols etched along its side blazed like fire for a moment before vanishing.

Susan gasped. "It's beautiful."

"Someone hid its true appearance under an unpleasant one," Lucky said. "Probably to keep it safe."

"What about mine?" Vicky held out her telescope, hoping her battered gift was also disguised by a miasma.

A spark from Lucky made the telescope as brilliant as the flute, the dents repaired, its metal so polished Vicky could see her reflection in it. If it were possible, she loved her telescope even more.

"If I had walked around Lowdar with this, I'd have been robbed," she said. "It's magic, isn't it, Lucky? The way I can see people far off, even when it's dark? With the telescope, I can hear them too."

"I see power in your mother's gifts." Lucky sounded uncertain.

"Our mother said the gifts would help us when we were in trouble." Vicky put the telescope to her eye and gazed towards the witches' wood. Tendrils of mist curled into shapes, crooked fingers and twisted claws. The sight made Vicky shiver. "Will Cathy's compass and Yvonne's key help them defeat the witches?"

"Perhaps. Don't forget that your sisters, like yourselves, are also resourceful," Lucky said. "Susan, why don't you play something on your flute in the meantime?"

Vicky expected to hear mournful, solemn music, in keeping with her mood, but instead a rousing, cheering tune filled the air. Vicky, almost unwillingly, felt optimistic about Alan's rescue. Surely Cathy and Yvonne would succeed, and Alan would soon be free.

Her hopeful mood lasted the rest of the day. Time passed slowly. They sat under the trees, mostly in silence. When the day drew to a chilly close, Lucky sent her to gather some firewood.

"Aren't you magic?" Vicky said. "Why don't you conjure up some wood and save us this trouble?"

Lucky cast an icy glance towards her. "You must learn to do some things for yourself."

It didn't take long to collect enough sticks for the fire. As Vicky arranged them, she happened to glance up. A large bird, high in the sky, flew some distance away. It abruptly changed direction and swooped towards the papple trees. As it approached, Vicky realised its massive size, and saw its cruel claws, stretching towards her as if she were its prey.

"Susan! Su!' Vicky called in an urgent whisper as she cowered on the ground. "Lucky?"

Then the bird was gone, speeding away into the distance.

Vicky fumbled for her telescope. Her hand shook but the bird was nowhere to be seen.

Susan appeared around one of the trees, holding an armful of papples.

"What is it, Vicky?"

"A bird. I think. Where's Lucky?" As the Diamond emerged from Susan's pocket, a suspicion crossed Vicky's mind. "Were you *hiding*?"

"I preferred the catchill not to see me."

Susan looked confused. "You said catchills didn't leave Peacemaker's Pass?"

"They don't. Nor should they be able to fly." Lucky sounded puzzled.

"I thought it was going to attack me," Vicky said, still feeling shaken.

"You were quite safe – catchills don't need to eat. Before you ask – yes, I am certain of that." As she spoke, Lucky sent a spark towards the fire which instantly ignited.

Vicky was not convinced but Lucky would say no more about it. They sat around the fire, and talked about happier days in Lowdar when their parents were alive. Afterwards Susan played a sweet lullaby, which made Vicky drowsy.

She woke to sunshine and a clear blue sky. Her first thought was of the traps.

The long grasses stood stiff and tall, unbending in the light breeze. At least they had not moved. Pulling out her telescope, she searched for any sign of her sisters.

Susan stirred beside her. Vicky tapped her shoulder.

"Susan, they're still not back."

Susan yawned. "Would they be able to find their way back in the dark? They probably decided to wait until daylight."

"It's long past daybreak now. Should we go look for them?" Not that Vicky wanted to, the sight of the wood filled her with dread.

Susan sat up. "What do you think, Lucky?"

The Diamond didn't answer. Susan slipped a hand into her pocket and withdrew the Diamond. She gave a cry. "Lucky!'

"What's wrong?"

For answer, Susan opened her hand. The Diamond lay dull and colourless, all the light gone.

"She's only sleeping," Vicky said, hoping it was like the time on the boat.

"Lucky?" Susan held her cupped palm close to her face. "Please wake up."

After a moment, a tiny gleam of light flickered in the Diamond's depths. It flared brightly, and Lucky stood up and spoke. "I'm sorry." Her voice came from far away. "I don't have much strength left so I am trying to conserve it."

Susan bit her lip. "Are you – are you going to die, Lucky?

The Diamond gave a faint smile. "Not yet. Not for a long time if I make it home in the next few days. I may have to go into hibernation before we reach Mount Slant. Don't worry, I will give you full directions for the remainder of the journey."

"That will make a change," Vicky said. Her joke fell flat, and both Susan and Lucky stared at her. "Sorry, I didn't mean it."

The ground trembled. Vicky turned her telescope towards the west to see a huge cloud of dust roll across the plain. Through the dust she caught glimpses of gleaming white and flashing gold, but nothing more substantial. She longed to know what the Demerai looked like.

"Lucky, are the Demerai like horses?" She kept the telescope to her eye as the dust cloud moved towards the horizon.

"Why do you ask me?"

"Because you know everything."

The Diamond laughed. "True, but if you wish to flatter me, at least sound sincere. Tell me, if you went to much trouble to become invisible, would you be grateful if somebody revealed your true appearance?"

"I suppose not," Vicky said reluctantly. She held up her telescope and once more scanned the wood. "Still no sign of Cathy and Yvonne."

"Keep looking," Lucky said.

"I am." Vicky could see nothing but black mist, but soon it cleared a little. "Wait, I see something."

"It's them," Susan said excitedly as two figures emerged from the wood.

"How do you know it's Cathy and Yvonne? Maybe the two warty witches have taken their place?" Vicky meant it as a joke, but couldn't help thinking that perhaps it wasn't really her sisters who approached. She was almost as relieved as Susan when Cathy and Yvonne finally arrived.

"We got the spell." Cathy beamed.

Vicky forgot her earlier doubts in her delight. "We knew you would."

Susan gave Yvonne a hug. "What happened to you, Yvonne? Your clothes are torn and there's blood on your collar."

"I'm fine," Yvonne said hastily. "Let's get on with saving Alan."

"Hear, hear," Vicky said, although she was dying to learn of their encounter with the witches.

This time Vicky and Lucky led the way into the long grass that surrounded the witches' traps, Cathy close behind. The pool they stopped at looked no different from any other: clear water with three or four stones lying on a sandy floor, and a fish with golden scales.

"Is that Alan?" Vicky said.

"Let us hope so." Lucky read aloud from the page Cathy held up. The words were ugly, even when uttered in the Diamond's silvery voice. Vicky couldn't understand any of them.

Lucky had barely finished speaking when, with a bright flash, a giant rook appeared before them. It reached Vicky's knees and she instinctively took a step back. It seemed dazed, stepped unsteadily sideways, stretched out its wings, and with a wink in Vicky's direction, rose up into the air.

"That wasn't Alan, was it?" Cathy cried.

"No. That was a rook," Lucky said shortly. "Let's try that large stone over there."

She repeated the words, light blazed once more and this time, although Vicky could see nothing, she had the impression that something quite substantial had materialised.

"Well, well." Lucky sounded surprised. "A Demera? I'd have thought you'd have more sense…but you're only a foal, I suppose."

A snort sounded in Vicky's ear, and she could feel warm breath on her cheek. It was as if the invisible Demera was bowing to or almost touching Lucky. Then came a rush of wind and Vicky knew that the creature was gone.

"Third time lucky," Lucky said, and again recited the spell. With an even more brilliant light, Alan stood in front of them. Cathy flung her arms about him.

"Wow!' he said. "What an experience."

"Aren't you glad to be rescued?" Cathy said.

"Yes, yes, of course. But I can't properly describe what happened, it was truly incredible."

"Cathy and Yvonne had to fight witches to rescue you," Vicky said. "We're all waiting to hear how they managed it."

"I'm sure they had a great time but I bet it wasn't as much fun as turning into a stone," Alan said.

"You're right." Yvonne shuddered. "Can we get out of here before someone else falls in?"

"What about that one?" Susan pointed to the remaining stone. "Aren't you going to release it too, Lucky?"

"Yes, I shall. I only hope it's not something that we regret releasing, like a Gorsch or a Haffinch."

These sounded like unpleasant creatures, so it was with trepidation that Vicky waited for Lucky to read the ugly words of the spell for the fourth time.

A boy stood in front of them. He had dark eyes, black hair, olive skin, and a proud, imperious expression on his face. He was slightly built, and looked about thirteen, Susan's age. His clothes were formal: jacket, shirt, waistcoat and trousers, all cut from expensive looking material.

"You took your time." His words were clipped and precise, his accent strange in Vicky's ears. He turned his head and gazed solemnly at each of them in turn, before giving a little bow. "I am Prince Paul Alexander Rovesvitch Ivan Kylovsky," he announced solemnly.

Chapter Ten
RETURN TO THE WOOD

Cathy found her voice first.

"*Who?*"

The boy ignored her.

"Lucky! It's you, I'm so glad to see you." His sudden smile faded to a frown. "What took you so long? I've been stuck there for months, fossilised and forgotten."

"I didn't know where you were taken, Paul. I was cast far from Mount Slant. I'm on my way back to the Rock now. We stumbled across you by accident."

Cathy had never seen a prince before, but she expected them to be arrogant and superior, like this one.

"Who are these children?" The prince spoke as if he had found them under a rock. He was even worse than Cathy imagined a prince to be.

"My friends," Lucky said. "I'll introduce you later. First, let's get out of here, this is a dangerous place."

"We've got the release spell now." Cathy was so pleased

she retrieved the spell she no longer feared the marsh. "Shouldn't we keep going?"

"The spell is about to expire," Lucky said. "I cannot guarantee we will still have it, if needed."

Cathy held out the sheet of paper she had stolen. "What do you mean 'expire'?

"This particular spell, away from its spell binder, will only last for a certain length of time, or a given number of uses, before it is worn out."

Lucky had hardly finished speaking when the scrawled words turned to black vapour and rose from the page. The paper ignited, purple flame quickly spreading. Cathy hastily dropped it before her fingers burned.

"Now *officially* expired," Alan said. "So, we cross the plains?"

"Too dangerous," Lucky said. "Unfortunately, we must go through the wood."

Cathy stared in shock at Lucky. She *couldn't* return to the witches wood, she'd prefer to be trampled by the Demerai.

"Neither Cathy nor I are going back into that wood again," Yvonne said firmly.

The prince cleared his throat. "And I won't take another step until I know who these people are. Where are my servants? Was no conveyance arranged? How am I to return to my palace?"

"Allow me speak, please," Lucky said.

Silence fell. Cathy gazed anxiously at the Diamond, who didn't sparkle as much as Cathy remembered.

"This is Paul, Prince of the Kingdom of Kyle, which

borders this country to the north. Paul and I were kidnapped at the same time. I was cast far away and Paul hidden in those traps. I am on my way home, thanks to the help of my friends." She introduced each of them to Paul.

The prince nodded graciously, raising an eyebrow at Vicky's leggings. Vicky noticed he only talked to Lucky, who stood on her shoulder.

"I never saw who attacked, Lucky. Who has the nerve to do so?" He fell into step beside Vicky.

"I do not know who would want to, but I can think of only one with the power to capture me," Lucky said.

Cathy was concentrating so much on the conversation that she barely noticed they were walking towards the wood. At the Diamond's request, Yvonne related their adventures.

"Sounds like you met Midea, Yvonne," Lucky said. "Nasty, but incompetent."

"If it wasn't for my key, I'd still be stuck in that cage." As Yvonne described her escape, she rubbed the back of her neck.

A spark flew from Lucky and settled on Yvonne's shoulder. After a moment Cathy saw it fly back to the Diamond.

"Its teeth went deep, but the wounds will be healed by tomorrow," Lucky said.

"What did you do, Lucky? My shoulders felt on fire; now they are soothed," Yvonne said.

"Don't you know that Diamonds have healing powers?" Paul said. Cathy caught a glimpse of his smug little smile.

"Of course we do," she said quickly.

"What happened to you, Cathy?" Vicky said.

"My witch was nicer," Cathy said, thinking back. "She *almost* handed me the spell but seemed too afraid. So I snatched it out of her hand and ran off."

"As I expected, very brave," Lucky said. "Both of you."

"Suru said someone called Queen Rose was looking for children." Cathy remembered the frightened look that had crossed Suru's face. "She couldn't be after us, could she?"

"She may call herself Queen, but she's *Witch* Rose," Lucky said shortly.

"You mean we now have a Witch Rose after us?" Yvonne's voice was sharpened by worry. "How could she know anything about us?"

"Colonel Thrand must have got word to her somehow," Lucky said. "But she's after me, and I'm ready for her this time."

"Isn't anyone interested in what happened to me?" Paul said.

"Later, Paul. Could we walk a little faster?"

Cathy did not want to re-enter the wood, and slowed her step as they drew near.

"Do we have to?" She stopped short of the mist that swirled around the wood.

"It will be easier this time," Yvonne said, taking her hand and pulling her forward.

Yvonne was wrong. Returning to the wood was worse. The thick mist felt twice as evil, and the stuffy air more oppressive and sinister than ever. The frightened faces of the others didn't make her feel any better, and Lucky was only a dim glow, as if the wood was sucking the life from her.

Before anyone could speak, a dozen tall plants with large buds thrust through the vegetation. Their buds began to unfurl, purple petals appeared and rotated. Cathy cried out.

"Lucky, those flowers…!"

"Cathy, can you take us to the river?" Lucky said quickly.

Cathy nodded. Eyes on her compass, she plunged through the scrub, ignoring the twigs and thorns that tore and scratched her. She pushed forward until she heard rushing water. Cathy was startled to see a crescent moon sailing across the sky. She hadn't realised it had taken so long to reach the river in the middle of the wood. The water glimmered silver but looked deep and dangerous, and she saw no way of crossing it. The compass had led her to a different part than before.

"What do we do now, Lucky?" Cathy spoke softly, afraid of attracting the attention of either witch.

"I hope to meet a friend here. He may be hiding, so if someone would stand on the riverbank and let me look…"

Alan obligingly stood at the edge of the river and extended his hand. Lucky stood on his palm and emitted a dazzling ray of light. Three times she did this, before requesting Alan stand away from the bank.

Cathy blinked, her eyes adjusting once more to the night, and waited in silence to see what would happen.

After a few minutes, she heard a new noise, a soft swishing, audible above the torrent.

Lucky smiled. "Here he is."

A dark shape moved through the water towards them. As it drew close, Cathy saw it was a large canoe. A happy face formed part of its wooden prow, and it smiled broadly as it pulled in beside them.

"Hop aboard," he called. "Plenty of room for you all."

"Children, meet Charlie Canoe," Lucky said, and quickly introduced the children as Cathy stared wordlessly at the canoe.

Chapter Eleven
CHARLIE THE CANOE

P aul pushed past Alan and clambered into the canoe.
"Hello Charlie."

"Hi Paul, what have you been up to?"

Alan followed the prince, the canoe rocking a little as he hopped in. Moving to the front, Alan noticed a large wooden foot gripping the bank, keeping the boat steady. On the other side, another foot gently treaded water. Alan looked back to see if two other feet existed at the rear, but he couldn't tell.

Cathy was last into the canoe, and she made her way to Alan's side.

"Pleased to meet you, Charlie."

"Pleased to meet you too, Cathy." The canoe couldn't turn his head but he gave a friendly wink all the same. Pushing off from the bank, he started to paddle upstream.

Lucky stood at the prow and lit up the whole canoe.

Charlie was right: there was more than enough room for

six children. His interior was cushioned, soft and warm, and Alan had a great view of the moonlit river seated at the prow.

"Are you taking me home, Charlie?" Paul sat on the seat behind Alan and raised his voice. "I'm sure many search parties are desperately seeking me."

"No, Paul, I haven't seen any. I came here to meet Lucky."

"This is extremely fortunate for us," Lucky said. "Charlie can carry us for many miles, and on the river we are safe from Suru and Midea's evil ways."

"So sit back and relax," Charlie said.

Alan was happy to travel along the river in a talking canoe. He smiled at Cathy but her face was anxious as she clung tightly to the canoe's rim.

The high banks of the river flashed by as Charlie moved smoothly upstream. He kept to the middle of the river, clear of the menace of the trees on either bank. Alan, straining to glimpse either of the wicked witches, was half disappointed not to succeed.

"Hang on," Charlie said. "We're coming to a waterfall."

Ahead, a cascade of water rose ten or fifteen feet into the air. Alan clung to the side of the canoe as they started to ascend. He heard his sisters squeal in alarm. A fine mist fell on his face as the canoe carried them higher. Through the mist, he saw Charlie grip the boulders behind the water with his large flexible feet and haul himself upwards. They reached the top and Charlie was once again sailing serenely on the river.

Alan released his breath. "That was amazing."

He glimpsed the corner of a smile on the canoe's face. "You should see the Rendleston Falls in Paul's land."

"No, thanks," Yvonne cried. "That was terrifying. I never want to travel up another waterfall."

Soon after this, the trees on either bank grew thinner. The black mist, which was greatest by the boundary of the wood, grew thicker. Moments later, they shot out into the open air.

Alan cheered, happy to be out of the stuffy wood. The air was fresh and the moon sailed high in a cloudless sky. The silver river snaked before them, and beyond the reeds that guarded both banks were the vast plains of East Nivram, bleached by the moonlight. A cold breeze blew, and Alan was glad to feel the warmth of the canoe's interior.

"Shall I keep going, Lucky?" Charlie said.

"As far as you can."

The canoe sped on through the night. Lucky remained a beacon of light at his prow, even if less bright than before. After travelling for some time, they came to a divergence in the river. Charlie hesitated.

"Go left," Cathy said.

Alan saw the compass clasped in her hand. "Go the way Cathy says."

Lucky nodded so Charlie ignored the broader tributary and took the more serene option. At first, scum clouded the surface of the river, making Charlie choke, but he kept going until he met cleaner water.

"I'll stop here," he said, pulling in to the riverbank. "We can rest for the remainder of the night."

Alan was disappointed their river journey had ended, but he curled up in Charlie's warm interior. The night was still. Not even a ripple disturbed the water, and no sound came from either bank. After a while he heard gentle breathing from his sisters as they slept. Alan didn't feel the least bit tired. His mind was full of their travels. He didn't know where their adventure would end, but he didn't care. It was exciting and dangerous, and that was enough.

Some time later, Lucky broke the silence. She spoke quietly, and Alan had to strain to hear.

"I was glad to see you turn up tonight."

"How do you think I felt?' Charlie said. "I've been searching for you everywhere. I got your message earlier, from a rook and a Demera, to head this way. What happened?"

"Witch Rose of Cassis kidnapped myself and Paul. Which of us she really wanted, I don't know, but she cast me outside our realm, far beyond Vitaria and Melchore, and hid Paul in one of those old traps by the witches' wood. It was by chance I found him."

"I have never been as far as Vitaria, nor would I survive being away from the Rock for so long. Let me..."

"No, Charlie, I won't disobey my father. If you bring us to the Great Road, I will be nearly home. I am weak but not extinguished. Tell me, did no one from Paul's country seek him?"

"I visited his palace after you disappeared. The regent was civil, as always, but not unduly concerned. Nor was I, at that point. I returned there recently. This time I was greeted with hostility. Afterwards, I discovered Witch Rose moved her castle into Paul's country, close to our border. She must have used Paul as a means to persuade the regent to allow her in."

"What is she up to this time?" Lucky sounded irritated.

"She has sent several deputations to the king, requesting a meeting."

"He will not deal with her."

"I believe he will meet her this time. You are not there to prevent him. Unfortunately, I can do nothing. Lucky, a meeting could turn out to be useful. We may discover what she's after."

Lucky didn't reply. Alan sensed her anger and could only be glad it wasn't directed at him. Witch Rose and her evil plans fascinated him. He longed to know more.

"Who are your young friends?"

"A half-grolsch picked up my trail in Lowdar. These kind children helped me escape. I would not have survived an encounter with the half-grolsch, nor would I have got this far without them. The children saved my life."

Alan was pleased, though surprised, to hear this. Lucky seemed so much in control it was hard to believe she could be so weak. His nose began to tickle and he fought to suppress a sneeze.

"Yet I wonder if it was a coincidence that I met Cathy…" Lucky said.

Alan sneezed. He couldn't help it.

A silence followed his sneeze.

Lucky broke it. "Alan? Are you awake?"

"Yes, Lucky."

"Were you listening to us? Don't you know it's wrong to

eavesdrop?" Her voice was edged with displeasure.

"I couldn't help it," Alan said, sitting up. "I couldn't sleep. And you mentioned Witch Rose and the half-grolsch."

"Go to sleep, Alan! And if you eavesdrop on me again, I will be extremely annoyed."

Alan said no more, and neither did Lucky or Charlie.

He woke up to an overcast day, with a chill wind stealing over the land. The river lapped gently against the canoe's side, and the mountains stood far in the distance. His sisters and Paul sat on the riverbank around a small fire while they ate breakfast.

"Morning Alan," Charlie said, as Alan jumped to shore.

"Thanks for the lift, Charlie."

"We're not done yet," Lucky said, from Susan's shoulder. "I thought you would like to stretch your legs before we continue."

"We're giving Charlie a rest," Vicky said. "We're too heavy. Last out of the boat has to stay behind, that's you."

"Ha, ha." Alan accepted a piece of toasted bread from Yvonne. The bread was burnt at the edges and hard in the middle, but it tasted delicious.

Susan peered into her rucksack. "We're almost out of papples."

"Good," Paul said. "The fruit is tasteless."

"I like them," Cathy said. "I love all the different flavours."

Paul gave a superior smile. "When you are used to eating the finest foodstuffs, delicacies prepared by the greatest of chefs, this fruit tastes so bland. I suppose you are used to plainer fare."

"Paul's rich diet is not good for anyone," Lucky said.

Paul sighed. "Ah, the palace banquets, beef, chicken, ham, peacock, wild boar, and other such delicacies. We have vegetables galore. And such pastries! Every delightful confection you can think of. You must visit my kingdom one day and I shall command such a feast the land has never seen."

The orange papple that Alan was eating grew tasteless at the mention of all the food, and he felt hungrier than ever.

"How wonderful to live in a palace," Yvonne said.

"It is an honour to lead my people."

Alan was more interested in breakfast. "Any more toast?"

Yvonne shook her head. "I'm afraid that was the last of the bread. When will we reach Mount Slant, Lucky?"

"In a few days. Charlie will carry us swiftly along the river, saving us many days' journey on foot. Are you ready to go?"

At her word, the fire went out, the last trail of smoke drifting away on the breeze. Within a few minutes, Alan sat once again by Charlie's prow while the canoe glided upstream. The left bank of rushes and reeds was open and without cover. The right bank was wooded. Graceful willows dipped their branches in the water, and Cathy pointed out moorhens and ducks to the others.

Alan sat beside his twin and, at a lull in the conversation, decided he would share his experiences as a stone. "First, my toes froze, my feet were next, and finally my whole body hardened. It was a kind of tingling sensation. When I changed back – it was like a block of ice melting in a rush."

"What was it like *being* a stone?" Cathy said.

"Relaxing, I felt half-asleep. Part of me thought I had been there forever. I could barely remember any other life. But when I changed back, it was as if it had only been five minutes. How long was it?"

"A day."

Alan was surprised he had been a stone so long.

"That's nothing," Paul said. "I was there years. How I longed to returned to my people and my home."

"How long was Paul there really, Lucky?" Vicky sounded sceptical.

"Less than three months."

"Tell us about your kingdom, Paul," Yvonne said.

Paul looked pleased. "It is an ancient and wonderful country, with deep valleys and towering mountains. The people are strong and hard-working, intensely loyal to the throne. Over the centuries, my family have led our people through famine and war. Now there is peace."

Alan only half-listened. He watched Charlie's feet thrust through the water, carrying them forward. Occasionally a bird, disturbed by their journey, flew up from the reeds. After a while the wooded bank fell away, and the central plains of the country stretched out on either side of the river.

Vicky held her telescope to her eye. "I want to see if the Demerai are running across... Oh, no. Lucky, the catchills are back."

Alan was surprised to hear the guardians of the pass had left their post.

"Vicky saw one yesterday," Susan told him.

"Charlie, somehow Colonel Thrand must have got word to Witch Rose that I escaped the half-grolsch," Lucky said. "I am sure she has sent some catchills to find me. She knows about the children as well – she seems to have told Midea and Suru to set the traps that caught Alan. They would never try them on me."

"Catchills, eh?" Charlie said. "They don't scare me. They move slowly."

"These ones can fly, and swiftly too," Lucky said. "We must keep moving."

Alan craned his neck. After a while, he could make out the dark specks of two catchills, coming at speed. Soon they were flying parallel to the river, maintaining a short distance between themselves and Charlie.

"Flying catchills above," Charlie said. "I don't believe it."

A short while later, the catchills dropped from the sky. Alan hoped they had given up and gone back to the Great Forest.

He was wrong. Half an hour later, the catchills flew alongside once more. After that, they disappeared on a regular basis, but always caught up with the canoe again.

"Are they stopping to rest?" Alan asked.

Lucky didn't know.

As the afternoon wore on, Alan began to tire of the journey. They stopped twice to stretch their legs and gather more papples, but the banks on either side gradually grew higher so he could no longer view the countryside. Above were only grey skies and catchills. As the light faded, the two birds veered away and flew out of sight.

"Good, they're gone," Charlie said. "I'll keep going. The bank here is too steep for you to climb out."

It was another hour before Charlie could pull up among the reeds and allow his passengers to alight.

"I'll start a fire if you gather some wood," Lucky said.

Alan picked up what brushwood he could find before the evening swallowed up the remaining daylight. Lucky glowed gently in the dark, and both Susan's flute and Vicky's telescope shone like moonlight. Yvonne toasted some fruit in the fire, and Alan discovered toasted papple was delicious.

"If I were in my palace now," Paul said. "I could sit before the great hearth where whole trees are fed into the flames. Such a fire warms not only the vestibule but all the surrounding rooms."

"How nice." Yvonne handed the prince a twig with several pieces of cooked papple.

Paul made a face as he tasted the fruit. "I'll never survive on this miserable fare. How much longer before I am home, Lucky?"

"You'll be returned at the earliest opportunity," Lucky replied.

"The ground is so hard. My clothes are filthy. It is cold." Alan had never heard anyone complain so much as Paul.

"Surely this is comfort after life as a stone?" Vicky said crossly. "Or maybe we should have left you there?"

"Life as a stone is very relaxing." Alan was happy to share his experience. "It's really comfortable sitting there, doing nothing…"

"It becomes tiresome after a few days," Paul said.

Alan couldn't dispute this, so he said no more. He wished Paul would stop boring on about his palace. Witch Rose was a much more interesting subject and he tried to think of a way of finding out more about her. Cathy, however, didn't want to talk about what Suru said. Alan was afraid to ask Lucky outright, in case she remembered he had eavesdropped on her and became cross again.

After he had eaten, Alan joined Charlie, who had drawn a little way from the fire. Charlie would be sure to tell him about Lucky's enemy.

"Charlie, what's Witch Rose like?"

"She's not someone you want to cross," Charlie said. "Why do you ask?"

"She sounds dangerous, and I want to be prepared," Alan said. Witch Rose had indirectly caused him to be turned into a stone, after all.

"Best ask Lucky," Charlie said.

Alan was disappointed but before he could ask anything more, Cathy pushed past the bushes and dropped to the ground beside him.

"Look." She held out her compass.

Alan couldn't bear looking at his sisters' gifts. He didn't want to be reminded he hadn't got one, but because Cathy was his twin, he took the compass and examined it. The dents were gone, and the case glowed a warm copper. When he pressed the catch to open it, the gold and silver surround blazed. Even the tiny star of the compass point shone, and the letters etched on the surround dazzled.

It was unrecognisable as Cathy's compass.

"It's amazing." He handed it back, feeling worse than ever about the gifts.

"Lucky said a spell disguised it so no one would know it was magical." Cathy slipped its chain over her head. "Charlie, would you like a papple? I brought some for you."

"I haven't seen Charlie eat anything." Alan suspected that the canoe wouldn't eat at all.

"Diamonds don't – I mean, canoes don't eat either," Charlie amended hurriedly.

"Are you a Diamond too?" Alan was amazed. He had imagined Charlie belonging to a race of canoe-folk living on the waterways of Nivram. In fact, he intended to visit them.

"Yes, but don't tell the others. And don't let Lucky know I told you. You see, being a canoe is a sort of punishment. I've been banished from the Rock of Diamonds for at least one hundred years."

Alan couldn't imagine Charlie doing something bad. In fact, Lucky gave the impression Diamonds were faultless.

"What did you do?" he said.

"The king took a dislike to me over something," Charlie said. "He's fond of banishing Diamonds. Catch him on a bad day and he'll exile you to the bowels of the earth. He's like that."

"He sounds horrible," Cathy said.

"Don't say that in front of Lucky. She's particularly close to her father. He's temperamental. He'll banish you for no reason one day, and be so remorseful that he'll load you with honours the next."

"But he didn't do that to you?" Alan said.

"He banished me for a year at first. But when he came to apologise, I was still too annoyed to forgive him, so he banished me for a hundred years instead. I told you what I thought of him, which included calling him a stubborn old-fashioned crystal so set against shape changing, that he said, 'Very well. Since you're so fond of shape-changing, you can spend your years of exile as a canoe.' Don't know why he picked a canoe, but here I am."

"Poor Charlie. How terrible." Cathy sounded quite upset.

"I'd say it's fun being a canoe." Better than being a Diamond, Alan thought, although he didn't say that aloud. "Sailing down the river, going where you please, and exploring the world. I wish I had been turned into a canoe instead of a stone."

"But a hundred years is *such* a long time."

"It's not so bad, Cathy. Besides, a hundred years out of a Diamond's life is nothing like a century out of a human's," Charlie said.

Alan was keen to find out how long Diamonds lived and how shape-changing worked, but Charlie wouldn't say.

"I've told you enough about me already. Remember, not a word to Lucky. Or anyone else."

"It won't go further than the three of us," Alan promised. Later that night as he curled up in Charlie's warm interior, he couldn't help being glad Charlie was a canoe.

The following morning was colder, with dark clouds scudding across the sky. The mountains were greyed out by a drizzling mist. After a quick walk to stretch their legs, the children were ready to go.

Charlie lined himself up by the bank. "Hop aboard."

Alan jumped in and took a place near the prow. He barely sat down when he heard a twang, a thud, and a little grunt from Charlie. Cathy screamed.

Inches away, an arrow protruded from Charlie's side.

Chapter Twelve
PARTING

A hail of arrows shot across Charlie, some clattering into the canoe, others falling directly into the water. "Lie low," Charlie shouted.

Alan dropped to the floor as an arrow whizzed overhead, barely missing him.

Through his sisters' shrieks, Alan heard Paul shout: "Mirehogs."

Another shower of arrows rained over Alan's head, most of them missing the boat altogether and plopping into the water.

Alan peered over Charlie's gunwhale. Partly hidden in the rushes on the far bank were a dozen creatures, each about seven foot tall, with leathery faces, and covered in orange fur. He could see arrows clutched in their paws. They raised their arms and a third wave of missiles flew across Charlie's bow. At the same moment, Charlie shot forward in the water.

"Stay down," Charlie said. "There may be more of them farther upstream."

Alan pressed his face to the floor of the canoe as stones and arrows fell around them, and their attackers yelled in fury. Soon their shouts faded, and Charlie told them it was safe to sit up.

"We've reached the point where the Aloe and the Reeve merge into one. We've remained on the River Aloe, which is the smaller of the two. Most likely the mirehogs haven't crossed the Reeve, so I think we're safe."

Alan sat up. A widening bank divided the rivers, with the other one growing more distant the farther Charlie sailed along the Aloe. Soon it would be out of sight.

"Is everyone all right?" Yvonne looked shaken. So did everyone else, but they all nodded. "Lucky, Charlie, who attacked us?"

"Mirehogs." Paul shuddered. "Huge, horrible, hairy beasts. They eat anything, dead or alive. They are only legends in my country now, but hundreds of years ago they terrorised my people."

"They're vicious, violent, and dangerous," Charlie said. "Do you know the tale of Princess Varya? These creatures were bred by her son in the Great Forest. Some infested Paul's country for a while before they were wiped out. They still inhabit the Great Forest but I am amazed to see them this side of the mountains. How did they cross Peacemaker's Pass?" Charlie sounded anxious.

"If the catchills have abandoned their post, it would be easy for mirehogs to leave the forest," Lucky said quietly.

"I never heard of them using arrows," Paul said. "Legends say that they tear apart a grown man with their claws before eating him."

Alan remembered the arrow embedded in Charlie's side. He had to pull hard to get it out.

"Did it hurt much?" he said, holding out the arrow for Charlie to look at.

"I'll live." Charlie squinted at the arrow. "That's strange. I expected it to be made of wood, but this arrow is fashioned from some kind of metal."

A few arrows were scattered on the floor of the canoe. Paul kicked them together with his foot, picked them up and dropped them disdainfully into the river. Alan slipped the first arrow into his pack. It would make a useful weapon. He wished he had a bow. Unlike the mirehogs, he wouldn't be able to fire an arrow without one.

Vicky held her telescope to her eye. "I can't see any more mirehogs. No catchills either."

Vicky checked at regular intervals throughout the morning, but spotted neither creature. The sky darkened and a light drizzle fell, but Charlie kept going. Not even Paul complained. Eventually, Charlie broke the silence.

"Lucky, this river will soon become too narrow for me. I'll have to leave you, but you'll be close to the Great Road, with only a day or so to Crocodile Lake."

"What's the Great Road?" Alan said.

Lucky spoke for the first time in a while.

"Varya's daughter, Scatherina, wished to build her home by Peacemaker's Pass, to be ready for the day when she and her brother made peace. It was to be a beautiful home for them to share. She also loved the sea, and wanted a magnificent road to run from her castle to the east coast so she could feel close to it."

"It's the straightest road in the world," Charlie said. "Runs the entire width of the country."

"Of course, she and Caralan never made peace. She died before her home was completed and her road even started. However, her children fulfilled her dream, half of it anyway. They built the roadway and finished the castle by the pass."

"Oh, she married?" Alan was surprised.

"Yes, and bore many children," Charlie said.

"What happened to them all?" Susan said.

"They lived happily in the castle for many generations," Lucky said. "Until one day the mirehogs came and wiped them out."

"Though there is a legend among the Nilkens that one daughter escaped," Charlie added, "and lived for a time amongst them. But we've never been able to ascertain the truth of it."

"What about the brother?" Alan said. "Did he marry too?"

"Not to our knowledge, but he shrouded his whole life in darkness so that we can't be sure. We believe not," Lucky said.

"Who *are* these Nilkens?" Cathy said. "Do they only plant fruit trees?"

"We'll be going through their territory soon, you'll meet them," Lucky said.

Alan watched out for the Great Road, but the terrain was hilly and he saw no sign of it. Ahead, the mountains drew near. The sky darkened. More rain was on the way.

A short while later, Charlie came to a halt. The river was

barely wider than Charlie, and Alan could see Charlie's large feet standing on the stony riverbed before the canoe clambered out of the water to the top of the bank

Lucky was at Charlie's prow, glowing faintly. "Time to get out."

Alan was disappointed to leave Charlie. He wasn't looking forward to traipsing over the land again.

"You too, Paul," Charlie said.

The prince looked up, startled. "Me? Surely you are taking me back to my palace? It's not fitting for me to travel by foot, you must know that?"

"Please take him, Charlie." Vicky clasped her hands in a pleading gesture. "It's not right to leave him with us."

Paul nodded. "Precisely."

"Sorry, Paul," Charlie said.

Paul frowned but didn't move.

"I don't want you to go home yet, Paul," Lucky said. "Whoever kidnapped you will know you escaped."

The prince gave a heavy sigh, got to his feet, and stepped out of the canoe. Alan, standing close to Charlie, heard the canoe speak in a low voice.

"Lucky, please come with me. I see how weak you are."

Alan hadn't noticed before but now he saw Lucky's inner fire was gone. The Diamond was like a clear crystal that light passed through.

"I'll see you in two days." Lucky jumped lightly from Charlie's prow to Susan's shoulder. Alan hurriedly stepped back in case Lucky thought he was listening to their conversation again.

"Very well." Charlie's usually cheerful face looked downcast. "I will return to Mount Slant and tell of your imminent return."

"And warn my father not to meet Witch Rose."

"I will tell him," Charlie said. "I'll watch out for you from the lake. Goodbye, children."

Alan held out his hand to say goodbye. Charlie looked both surprised and pleased, and awkwardly held up one large foot. The foot was many times the size of Alan's hand, but he managed to grip it briefly. Charlie's skin felt like smooth soft wood, firm yet flexible. When it came to Cathy's turn, she flung her arms about him and hugged him goodbye.

"Goodbye," Charlie said. "Take care of each other. See you at the lake."

Lucky gave a gentle glow of farewell. Susan turned and led the way over the hilly countryside. At the top of the first ridge, Alan glanced back. Charlie stood by the stream, watching them leave. Alan gave one last wave and ran down to join the others.

"How will Charlie get to Mount Slant?" he asked Lucky.

"Charlie is a flying canoe," Lucky said. "Although he prefers to travel by water."

Flying Canoe! Alan was impressed. "Couldn't he fly us to Mount Slant?"

"He is not allowed to take passengers when he's flying. Not even me," Lucky said. "Now, once you reach the top of the next hill, you should see the Great Road."

"From there we walk to Crocodile Lake, don't we?" Susan said. "Which will bring us to Mount Slant."

"And the end of our adventure," Vicky said cheerfully,

which made Alan think of the promised reward. Perhaps he'd ask the king of the Diamonds to change him into a flying canoe for a while?

After a few days in the canoe, Alan's legs were stiff as he clambered up the grassy slope. From the hilltop, he looked back on the plains, rivers, and woods that they had travelled through, drab as the morning. Ahead, at the foot of the hill, a wide paved road stretched into the distance in both directions. On the far side of the road, the undulating land was cultivated. Low stone walls marked boundaries between fields, but he could see no sign of any farmhouse.

"We passed many Nilken farmlands yesterday, but they were hidden by the river banks," Lucky said, in a tired voice. "Nilkens have farmed here for centuries; their land north of the Great Road is their oldest settlement. They are a simple, kind-hearted race, but extremely shy. They will help you if you ask them. I'm afraid I have been away from the Rock too long. My energy is drained. I shall be going into a deep sleep. You won't be able to wake me, but unless I conserve my strength in this way, I may not finish our journey."

"You will wake up again, won't you, Lucky?" Cathy said, her eyes full of unshed tears.

Lucky hesitated. "I hope so. Make sure you don't get lost or stray into the Great Forest, or anything. If you find yourself in the ruined city, you have gone too far east."

"Ruined city?" Susan said.

"The ancient city of the Goldener people, who fled here from the realm of Thule a long time ago," Lucky said. "They died out, and their city is derelict. From here, join the Great

Road and journey west. By this time tomorrow you should come to an ancient monument by the roadside. Turn north there, and after half a day or so, you will arrive at the Lake. Once I'm within glinting distance, I should wake."

"How will we recognise the right monument?" Vicky said.

"You can't miss it. It is the first, and I think the last, surviving monument on the Great Road. Among the many ancient symbols engraved on it, you will see a star emerging from a Diamond."

"Do not worry. We shall have no problems," Paul said.

"Good. If, by any chance, you reach Crocodile Lake before I wake up, do not go near the northern shore."

"Why not?" Alan was curious.

"I don't know what kind of a reception you'll get, so be sure to wait for Charlie. Now, who's got the warmest, snuggest pocket?"

Chapter Thirteen
HARKY

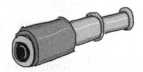

Susan's pocket was the one Lucky picked for her hibernation. As Susan slipped her away, Vicky noticed how lifeless the Diamond looked. Without her interior fire, Lucky appeared to be no more than a piece of glass, dulled by time. Vicky wasn't sure if they would make it to Crocodile Lake in time for Lucky, so she started down the slope towards the road, skidding a little on the grass.

A few drops of rain spattered the ground as she reached the Great Road. She could see how it had gotten its name. Broad marble slabs, cracked and broken, stretched at least twenty feet across. Weeds pushed their way between the paving, which must have once been covered with pictures, but the images were so faded she couldn't make them out.

"It's beautiful," Susan said, joining her.

"Once," Vicky replied. She slipped her telescope out of its pouch. West was towards the mountains, she knew, but better to check if there were any mirehogs or catchills around. By the time she was happy their way lay clear, Yvonne, Paul and the twins had joined them.

The twins immediately tried to guess what the pictures represented.

"No time for that," Yvonne said. "Let's go."

The road was wide enough for all six to walk together. Vicky, however, preferred to walk on top of the wall bordering the far side of the road. From there, she saw field after field, recently tilled, and marked out by low stone walls. She wanted to find the Nilkens before they discovered her.

"You'll fall," Yvonne said disapprovingly.

"No, I won't," Vicky said, and to prove it, ran along the uneven surface of the wall.

They hadn't been walking for long before the rain started. The wall became slippery so Vicky reluctantly abandoned it. Large puddles formed on the road. Vicky splashed her way forward, ignoring the fact she was getting wetter every moment.

"We could ask the Nilkens for shelter?" Paul said. He looked miserable, his clothes streaked by the rain and his hair plastered to his head.

"Oh, yes," Cathy said eagerly. "I'd love to meet them."

Vicky wasn't so sure. Having seen some of the inhabitants of east Nivram, or *not* seen, in the case of the Demerai, would they even be human? She took out her telescope once more and scanned the fields but could see no sign of any home.

"We better keep walking," Yvonne said, marching on. The others groaned.

"Walk! Walk! Walk!" Paul muttered. "I'm so sick of it. Walk until we drop."

"Any better suggestions?" Vicky said sweetly.

"It's all very well for you but it's different for me."

By mid-afternoon, the rain finally eased off, and they sat on their packs and leaned against the wall and munched on some fruit.

"Somebody's coming," Alan said, pointing.

"Nilkens!" Cathy and Paul said in unison.

Vicky could also see some movement on the road ahead, although it was too far away to make out what it was. When she put her telescope to her eye, she realised two figures approached on horseback. Or rather, on ponies, and while the riders seemed the size of small children, both were grim-faced, dressed in dark uniforms, and heavily armed.

"What do you see, Vicky?" Yvonne said. "Mirehogs?"

"Soldiers," Vicky said. "With swords. Like the town guard, but kind of tiny."

"Nilkens are human-like, though little, and always smiling," Paul said. "They are *never* armed. Not even those that serve the Diamonds."

"Let's not meet them until we are sure," Yvonne said. "We'll hide behind the wall until they pass."

Paul started to protest, saying he would hide from no one, but Vicky scrambled over the wall and dropped down to the ground. She was in a large field, partly tilled. Not far off a pair of miniature ponies, with golden brown coats and cream manes and tails, pulled a minute plough. At their heads walked a young female, smaller than Cathy, with a round face, spherical blue eyes, and a button nose. Two long dark plaits hung down her back and she was dressed simply in a cotton shirt and skirt. Walking behind the plough was an old man, much smaller than his companion, but with the same round eyes and wide smile on his face.

Nilkens.

She heard a squeal of delight as Cathy, followed by Alan, landed beside her.

"They're so cute." Cathy ran over to pat the ponies, who only reached her shoulder.

"Pilkens." The old Nilken said in a slightly high-pitched but pleased voice. "That's what they be, Sasha."

Sasha smiled shyly but said nothing.

"Human pilkens. Never seen them before." The old Nilken's eyes widened as the others scrambled over the wall. "Six. Soldiers are looking for human pilkens. You best hide, you don't want to be seen."

Yvonne looked flustered. "What do you mean?"

"Who cares?" Paul turned to the Nilken. "I'm cold and wet and my clothes are filthy. I haven't eaten for days. My companions are exhausted. Could you provide us with a few hours shelter so we can dry off?"

"We'd be pleased to." The Nilken's smile was broader than ever. "Sasha will finish the ploughing."

"Yes, Harky." Sasha's lips were still curved in a smile

but a slight frown lingered in her eyes. She held up a hand. "Listen."

At first all Vicky heard was the snorting of Sasha's ponies, but she soon caught the distant clip-clop of hooves along the paved roadway. She crouched against the wall, next to the twins, pulling Susan down with her.

Sasha resumed work, helping the ponies pull the plough through the sodden earth. Sheltered from view by the wall, or so she hoped, Vicky pressed her eye to a gap in the stonework. A couple of ponies trotted into view, halting immediately in front of Vicky. Two uniformed Nilken sat on their backs. One of the Nilkens addressed Sasha, his voice hard and severe.

"Have you seen strangers in this area?"

Sasha didn't pause in her work. "No."

The ponies moved a few steps along the road.

"We expect six human pilkens to pass this way. If you see them and fail to report to us, the penalty is death."

"If you say so."

"If you assist these travellers in any way, the penalty is death. If you provide food and water to these travellers, the penalty is death," the soldier continued, kicking his pony to keep pace with Sasha as she moved through the field. "If you provide shelter of any form…"

"I know," Sasha said. "The penalty is death."

"The penalty is death." He continued as if she hadn't spoken. "If you attempt to hide the travellers, the penalty is torture and death."

Sasha had drawn some way down the field, and the

Nilken soldiers followed along the road. Although still in sight, their voices became indistinct.

Harky put a finger to his mouth, and jerked his head in the opposite direction. Vicky exchanged glances with Yvonne, who nodded. In a single line, they all crept along the wall after Harky until they crossed into the next field. There, Harky straightened up and trotted northwards. He led them through a series of fields, some recently ploughed, while others had early shoots pushing their way through the soil.

The rain started to fall once more as the day grew steadily drearier.

Sasha was long out of sight by the time Harky led them into a field where the grain grew shoulder-high. Vicky followed him through the crop towards a large mound in the centre of the field. A thin trail of smoke rose from it. To her surprise, it was a cottage, with small round windows and a bright red door. The rear and roof of the building were covered by the crop. From a distance, other than the giveaway smoke, it was impossible to tell that the cottage existed.

"Why are crops growing on the roof?" Vicky said.

"Security," Paul said. "When Nilkens become anxious, they cover one gable with turf and plants. They hide the other next and the back of the house in a similar manner. Finally, in extreme emergencies, they conceal the front. Sometimes they do it so well they forget where they've hidden their homes. On occasion they have buried their families alive."

"How do you know?" Vicky said.

"Lucky told me."

Vicky shuddered, imagining Nilkens trapped under vegetable and fruit plants.

"What else do you know about them, Paul?" Yvonne said.

"Pilkens are Nilken children," Paul said. "The females are called Milkens. They are friends of the Diamonds."

Harky stood by his door, his hand on the latch. His round face still wore a smile, although his eyes were anxious.

"This is my home," he said. "You will be safe here."

"What about the soldiers?" Alan said.

"We will not allow them to find you. Please, come in." Harky threw open the door.

"Thank you, Harky," Yvonne said gratefully. "We won't be any trouble."

Harky's cottage was bright and noisy, cluttered with furniture, and dominated by a fire that roared in the hearth. Tiny Pilkens ran around the table, laughing as they played. Three or four Milkens were busy with various tasks. One of the Milkens, about the same height as Harky but twice his width, bustled over to greet them. A few strands of grey ran through her dark hair. Her face expressed no surprise at seeing them, only a warm welcome.

"You're early, Harky," she said, smiling.

"Look what I found by the Great Road, Misha." He nodded at the children. "Wet, hungry, and lost."

"Who are these poor strays, Harky?"

"Human Pilkens that foolish General is after." Harky turned to Yvonne. "This is my daughter, Misha."

"The poor things, so wet and miserable." Misha beamed at them.

A strong smell of cooking permeated the cottage. Vicky's eyes fell on a large pot, bubbling gently over the fire. She had never smelled anything so good.

"Come." Misha led her towards the fire. "Supper will soon be ready."

"I don't think I'll want to leave here," Vicky said, as she joined the others trying to dry off. Harky's cottage was the nicest place she had ever been in.

Shortly afterwards, Misha returned with an armful of clothes, and offered to dry their wet ones. The Nilkens' soft cotton shirt and breeches were clean and fresh, and fitted the twins but looked slightly ridiculous on the prince.

"I would like my attire washed and pressed," Paul said, as he handed Misha his silken outfit. "Be careful, the fabric is extremely delicate."

Yvonne and Susan were both too tall for any of the clothes to fit, and Vicky refused to even try them on.

"I'll stick with my leggings. They'll dry quickly," she said.

Supper was served shortly afterwards. The Nilkens didn't speak as they ate. Vicky was silently enjoying the best meal she'd ever had. Yvonne looked anxious, but the rest were far too busy eating to speak. Only Harky made the occasional remark, usually about the weather or the work due for tomorrow.

"We'll finish the west gable tomorrow. All needed to complete the job," he said, several times.

Beneath their warm welcome, Vicky detected unease, maybe fear. No wonder, too, if they were caught sheltering humans, Harky and his family would be in a lot of trouble

After supper, Harky moved to a stool by the fire, and beckoned the visitors over. A couple of the Pilkens ran over and hugged Harky's knee.

"Grandoc, play with us," one of them begged.

Harky ruffled the hair of the tiny Pilken.

"I'll play for you, little Baley." The thin reed that Harky had in the corner of his mouth now moved across his lips. Harky's cheeks filled out, and a merry little jig began to play. The Pilkens laughed in delight, and jumped and danced around the fire. Even Misha and another young female, more grown up than the Pilkens, joined in, holding their skirts out and tapping their feet.

When the music stopped, the human children all clapped.

Outside the wind moaned and the rain rattled against the small, round windows. Inside, the fire flickered merrily, and coloured lanterns cast playful shadows while the Nilkens abandoned themselves to a carefree caper.

In the middle of the wildest dance, the front door flew open, a blast of wind buffeted the room and rattled all the hanging lamps. The music stopped abruptly. Vicky tensed.

The pretty Milken from the field blew in with the wind, and, shoving her shoulder against the door, just managed to close it.

"Here's Sasha now," Misha said. "She's late."

Sasha still wore a smile but her eyes were worried. She removed her cloak and a pair of muddy boots, and crossed over to the hearth.

Sasha sat down on a three-legged stool. When she spoke, it was slowly and softly.

"Berry was there, as you saw, warning that we should not help any strangers. He left eventually, and I continued the clod turning until darkness fell. Something stirred in the hedgerow, startling Sweetness and Sugar. It was Grisha from Ubark. He came to warn us."

Harky held up a hand. "This news will sound better once the little ones depart. Misha?"

Misha nodded and delivered supper on a tray to Sasha, before rounding up the Pilkens and herding them to bed through a door at the far end of the room.

Harky waited until Sasha had finished her supper before asking her to continue.

"Yes, Harky. Grisha said that all northern territories have been raided."

"Raided?" Yvonne said sharply. "What's going on?"

"A few days ago, some Nilkens turned up at our door, clad in black and bearing swords." Harky's smile was gone. "I have never seen such a sight. They took away my son and grandsons, Misha's husband and sons, Sasha's brother, the pilkens' father and uncles. All gone."

"Why would they do such a thing?" Paul said. "I have never heard of Nilkens carrying weapons."

"Someone calling himself General Cable is organising Nilken soldiers," Sasha said. "We do not know why."

Vicky could guess. It was bound to be another ploy of Witch Rose to catch Lucky. The soldiers were looking for six children – which meant Witch Rose also knew about Paul. The catchills were definitely spies.

"Bah," Harky said, his blue eyes angry. "I call him General Fool." He spat into the fireplace. "Berry has been bewitched."

Sasha looked sadly into the fire and did not reply.

"Where did the soldiers take them?" Yvonne said.

"Grisha says there is a large training camp in the Ubark area."

"How did he evade capture?" Harky said.

"He was returning home from visiting friends and spotted the soldiers from far off. He hid in the mud pond until all danger was past. He said it is not safe to travel, and even less so to shelter strangers."

The reed whistle in Harky's mouth moved from one corner to the other. "Grisha tells the same tale as the soldiers. It does not worry me."

Cathy looked frightened. "Have you a mud pond to hide us?"

"We better move on," Yvonne said. "Before the soldiers find us here."

"And we have to get to the lake as soon as possible," Susan said, in a meaningful way.

Despite the warmth of the fire and the tasty food, Vicky had not forgotten about Lucky, but it would be worse for the Diamond if they were caught by Witch Rose's soldiers.

"Remain safely here tonight," Harky said. "Leave at first light."

Yvonne hesitated. "We *do* need sleep…"

"It's too dark now, we'd only get lost," Vicky said.

"Very well." Yvonne nodded. "But what if the soldiers come?"

Vicky looked around for a hiding place, or even a back door to make a quick exit. Of course, half the cottage was buried under the crop, so a rear door wasn't an option. The room was brightly lit, and the wooden table and chairs provided no cover.

Harky pointed to the wooden beams above his head, and at a short ladder propped against the wall.

Alan dragged the ladder into position. Vicky couldn't see an opening but she watched Alan run his fingers carefully along the wood until the trapdoor fell open, narrowly missing his head.

"Take care, lad," Harky said.

Alan climbed into the loft. He stuck his head out a moment later. "It's perfect."

"Good night, good night." The old Nilken looked tired, his eyes rimmed with red, and seemed anxious for them to hide in the loft immediately. "Sleep without fear."

Vicky followed Cathy into the attic. It smelled of straw, and gaps between the ceiling planks allowed light to filter upwards. The roof was arched and low; only a Nilken could stand upright. The loft ran the length of the house so there was plenty of room. Yet she had grown used to sleeping in the open air under a star-filled sky. The attic seemed stuffy and cramped in comparison.

Paul was last to clamber up the ladder. He stopped at the top, and sniffed.

"I don't like this place," he said. "It smells, and I don't want to sleep on straw."

"Sleep by the fire, and be the first one caught by the soldiers, if you wish," Vicky said. "But get off the ladder so we can close the trapdoor."

"That's the most sensible thing I've heard you say," Yvonne said approvingly. "Come on, Paul: it's not Charlie-comfortable, but at least it's dry and warm."

Paul reluctantly crawled into the attic, and picked a spot away from the others. Once Alan shut the trapdoor, the sounds downstairs were muted. Vicky caught the rattle of a chain and the scrape of a bolt as the front door was secured. A murmur or two passed between Misha and Harky, and then all was silent below. The lamps must have been doused for the attic plunged into darkness.

Susan took out her flute and it shone like the moon, allowing the children to unroll their blankets and find a place to sleep.

"We better stay quiet," Yvonne said in a loud whisper.

"And try and get some sleep. We have a long walk tomorrow."

Vicky kept one hand on her telescope in case the Nilken soldiers came, but her eyelids grew heavy and she soon dropped off to sleep.

Chapter Fourteen
THE GREAT ROAD

Cathy slept badly that night, certain that soldiers would torture Harky until he confessed to hiding them in the loft. Every time she woke, the cottage was quiet, even the wind had died down. Eventually it was morning, and a delicious smell of freshly baked bread filled the loft. Shortly afterwards, she heard the ladder being put in place, and Harky opened the hatch.

Downstairs, Misha handed the travellers their clothes, washed and ironed. Cathy reluctantly accepted her bundle; she much preferred the soft cotton Nilken clothes.

Breakfast was waiting: porridge and toast.

"I'll never be able to eat again." Vicky put her spoon down in an empty bowl and leaned back in the chair.

"You certainly managed to put enough away," Yvonne said. "Three helpings?"

"Only two and a half. I wanted to make sure that I could last the whole journey, but now I'm not sure if I can walk at all." She made a comical face and Cathy laughed.

Alan finished his third bowl. "Where's Harky?"

"He checks the Great Road for soldiers," Sasha said.

She had barely finished speaking when the front door opened to admit Harky. He went straight to the small fire that burned in the grate and warmed his hands.

"I saw no sign of any patrol, but it would be best if you journeyed separately."

"We could travel in twos," Vicky said. "And meet at Lucky's monument."

Cathy was pleased that she and Alan were chosen to set out first, to be followed an hour later by Vicky and Susan, with Yvonne and Paul bringing up the rear.

"Wait for us at the monument," Yvonne said.

Cathy nodded.

"Don't go on without us," Yvonne said. "We'll be a couple of hours behind you."

"All right," Cathy said.

"Keep yourselves hidden while you wait for us." Yvonne fiddled with her chain. "If something happens and we don't turn up at all, continue on towards Crocodile Lake."

Vicky drained her glass. "How will we know if something has happened to you?"

"If we don't turn up for three or four hours after you get to the monument."

"Do we assume you've been caught by one of the patrols?" Vicky said. "Shouldn't we come and rescue you?"

Yvonne shook her head. "Go and get Charlie."

Cathy shouldered her rucksack, which included food

from Misha for the journey. "See you at the monument."

The sky was overcast but the rain held off. Harky led the twins through the fields to the Great Road. Climbing onto the wall, he checked both directions before pronouncing it safe.

"Goodbye Harky," Cathy said. "And thank you."

"Come and visit when the troubles are over," the old Nilken said, waving farewell.

The Great Road was elevated, and though it gave a good view of the surrounding countryside, Cathy feared she was equally visible to everyone in the area.

"The soldiers will see us if we stick to the road," she said.

"We'll see them from miles off," Alan said. "We'll have time to hide in the fields."

Cathy checked her compass. Although she knew the direction they should be going in, she was cheered to see the dial pointing towards the dim blue-grey of the mountains.

"Do you think it's raining on the mountains? What will we do if the catchills find us?" She imagined their cruelly curved beaks tearing her to pieces and shuddered.

Alan laughed. "First the town guard chased us. Next the half-grolsch. Then the catchills. Now the Nilkens. Everyone is after us and we've escaped them all."

Cathy didn't find it funny. "It's scary."

"Look, Cathy." He pulled the metal arrow out of his jacket pocket and showed it to her. "If any catchill gets close to us, I'll make it sorry."

"I hope it doesn't." She was not as brave as Alan.

"I'll only threaten it. Scare it away." He slipped the arrow back into his pocket. "Let's play Drubble."

"Yes!" Cathy loved this game of their own invention. No one else understood the obscure rules, a combination of word associations, rhyming schemes, and private jokes. "I have one for you: feather light."

"Hmm." Alan frowned in concentration. After a few minutes, he got the answer. "Mount Slant. My turn now."

Cathy didn't notice the time pass, and she even forgot to watch out for Nilken soldiers. The level surface of the Great Road made walking easy, and the cooler temperatures pleasant. They stopped several times to rest and eat before continuing onwards. Eventually Cathy wearied of their game and wondered if they were nearing their destination.

"I'm tired," she said, dragging her feet. "I wish we could meet Charlie and finish our journey by boat."

"Me too, but we must be nearly there by now."

Cathy lifted her eyes from the paving. She had been so intent on their game that she hadn't noticed that the countryside had changed. It was desolate now, barren of life apart from a few sickly grasses and the occasional dying shrub. Even the papple trees, which had been so abundant earlier, no longer grew along the roadside. The only one Cathy saw had been wrenched out of the earth and was completely withered. The mountains were near, and the land, no longer cultivated by the Nilkens, seemed hostile.

Cathy walked more slowly, not only because she was tired, but also to give the others time to catch up. But no matter how long she stared at the road behind, Cathy could see no sign of anyone at all. Her only comfort was that her compass continued to point due west. She gave a small sigh and wished Lucky had warned her of the long walk to the monument. The sky began to clear and the Blackhand Mountains were rimmed with gold. Sunset was not far off, and Cathy knew they would never find the monument in the dark.

The twins trudged on, eyes on either side of the road seeking that elusive monument. All they saw was the low stone wall fallen into disrepair, even collapsed in many places.

"It looks as if some giant hand pulled the wall to bits and threw the stones over there." Cathy pointed at the large piles of rubble strewn beyond the wall.

"Someone tried to destroy the road as well," Alan said. Huge chunks of the roadway had also been torn up. "Hey, could we have walked past it already? Maybe the same people destroyed the monument. What does the compass say?"

Cathy looked at the compass for at least the hundredth time that day. "We're going the right way."

Ahead, the mountains were dark and menacing against the evening sky, but she could make out a narrow gap between the nearest mountain and its neighbour. It had to be Peacemaker's Pass.

"We should stop here," Alan said. "It's too dark, you could trip on those rocks." He kicked at one of the upturned stones that blocked his path as he spoke.

Cathy followed him to an intact part of the wall, and hoisted herself up beside him.

"Here." He handed her a papple. Misha's food pack had

been devoured earlier. "Tasty and refreshing."

She wasn't hungry but the juicy papple quenched her thirst. She dropped the core over the wall, hoping that it would sprout and take root and feed other hungry travellers in years to come.

Alan found a dry patch sheltered by some broken rocks, and they shared their blankets. Stars appeared in the night sky, and Cathy shivered in the chill breeze. It was the first night she had spent in the open without Lucky or Charlie to warm her.

As they huddled together, Alan talked of long-distant childhood days.

"Do you remember the country walks we used to go on? And how we always had to rush back to Lowdar before the gates closed? One time, we were a few moments too late, but Papa climbed over and persuaded the gate-keeper to let us in before the beasts got us, remember?"

"No."

"Of course, you always stayed at home. You were too scared of the forest monsters to leave town."

"Flying monsters who drank the blood of little children?" Cathy sat up, offended. "I wasn't scared. I was *wise*."

Alan yawned. "I think Vicky made those stories up."

"What about the mirehogs?" Cathy didn't like being so close to the mountains and in sight of the pass. "They're real."

"The compass wouldn't send us into danger," Alan said, with another yawn.

Cathy believed this was true, but the image of the Great

Forest monsters lusting for her blood wouldn't disappear. She tried to think of something else. "The stars are coming out. Charlie was teaching me their names."

Alan didn't answer.

Cathy gazed admiringly at the velvet sky. She loved clear nights where the stars were displayed in all their glory. That bright star was the North Star, she knew. Immediately below, and a little to the east, two shining stars shimmered. The Twins, Charlie had said, named after Princess Varya's children, Prince Caralan and Princess Scatherina. Alan thought they were silly names, he said Scatherina sounded too similar to scatter-brained, and as for Caralan, surely that was a girl's name? Cathy didn't agree. Being a twin herself made her feel close to the Diamond princess's twins.

For a while she stared at the sky, trying to remember the names of the other constellations before finally closing her eyes.

She was drifting off to sleep when something cold and rubbery touched her face. Her eyes flew open. A huge shadow loomed over her, blocking out the starlit sky. She screamed and clutched Alan's arm.

"Go to sleep," he murmured.

Several more large shapes appeared. Cathy opened her mouth to scream again, but a huge hand plucked her from the ground and flung her onto its shoulder. Her mouth was pressed against its fur so tightly that she could scarcely breathe. She struggled, but the monster held her firmly in its grip. She heard a startled shout from Alan as her captor lurched into a run.

Her worst nightmare had come true. She had been caught by the blood-guzzling child-devouring creatures from the Great Forest: mirehogs.

Chapter Fifteen
CAUGHT

"My stables are beyond compare," Paul said. "My stallions prized throughout the northern lands, and their trainers the envy of my neighbours." He patted the pony's neck so she would not feel jealous.

"I'm sure you're a wonderful rider," Yvonne said. She looked unhappy. Her fingers clutched the reins, and her body slipped from side to side as Sweetness plodded along the Great Road. "But I wish I hadn't agreed to this."

It had been Paul's idea, of course. Better to remain later in Harky's cottage and borrow Sweetness and Sugar to catch up with the others at the monument. Sasha had agreed, and promised that the two ponies would walk in a straight line without stopping until they reached the rendezvous.

They had overtaken Vicky and Susan hours earlier, but despite Yvonne's pleas to halt, Sweetness had walked on without hesitation. Whatever Sasha had whispered into the pony's ear before they left had greatly impressed the pony.

"It's more fitting," Paul said. "Someone in my position should not be tramping along the road like a commoner. We will soon reach the monument where you may rest."

The words were not long out of his mouth when he spied a stone edifice ahead. It was not what he expected, for it reached no higher than the pony's head, but something about it made him certain it was Lucky's landmark.

Sugar came to a halt and he slipped off her back.

Yvonne dismounted as well. "Where are the twins?"

Sugar neighed and shook her head, and both ponies turned and trotted away, their task completed. Paul was sorry to see them go. From what Lucky had said, several hours journey still lay ahead, and he was not looking forward to walking across the country.

"Alan and Cathy must have stopped for a rest. We probably passed them while they hid out of sight." He ran a hand over the rough surface of the stone. The images that once decorated it were worn away, and the monument itself looked broken and damaged.

Yvonne sat next to the monument and closed her eyes.

"We better keep watch," Paul said. Barely had he said these words when five ponies, each carrying a Nilken soldier, appeared on the Great Road only a short distance away. They must have come over the fields, otherwise he would have seen them earlier. Before Paul could think of a plan, he was surrounded. The Nilkens were dressed in dark green livery, embroidered with a black rose, and used their mounts to block Paul's way.

Paul put on his grandest manner. "Kindly remove your animals from our path."

The Nilkens dismounted, but the ponies did not move.

"Human Pilkens," one soldier said. "Two of the six. Seize them."

Before Paul could react, his hands were bound and his feet tethered.

"This is an outrage." He was so angry he could barely speak. "How dare you touch me!"

Two Nilkens lifted him off his feet and flung him over the back of one of the ponies like a sack of grain. He saw Yvonne pummel the Nilken tying him to the saddle.

"Run, Yvonne! Save yourself," he said.

Yvonne was dragged away, and a few minutes later he glimpsed a similarly trussed Yvonne draped over another horse. The sight made him even more furious.

"Release me, at once!" he yelled.

A gag was shoved in his mouth, silencing him. The horse moved, and for the next few hours Paul only saw the ground as he was bumped across rain sodden fields. His stomach hurt, his head was dizzy, and he was unable to comprehend this dire treatment.

Hours passed before one of the Nilkens finally broke the silence.

"Our camp."

Paul tilted his head back to see pinpoints of light flaring up in the gathering dusk. Some time later, they reached their destination. The horse came to a halt, the rope binding him to the saddle was untied, and he was dumped on the ground.

Limbs still bound, Paul struggled to his feet. Torches illuminated rows of tents stretching into the distance. At least a hundred, he calculated.

His arm was grabbed and he was propelled forward through the maze of tents to one that was larger than the rest. A dozen soldiers guarded the opening, but two dark shadows immediately beyond the entrance caught Paul's attention.

Catchills.

Yvonne, trussed up and gagged like he was, was shoved next to him. He gave a nod to reassure her.

"Move." One of the guards prodded him to enter the vestibule.

Beyond the canvas curtain, he heard a high-pitched nasal voice speak.

"We decamp at noon and should reach our destination by nightfall. Attack at dawn the following day. The catchills will secure our victory. What? Bring them both in."

The tent was warm and cluttered, filled with boxes, candles, and other paraphernalia. A large table took up the centre, covered with papers, pencil holders, and glasses. It took Paul a moment to notice the small figure perched in a high leather armchair behind the desk.

He stared at Paul, piercing eyes in a withered face. The hand holding a quill was so wrinkled and spotted that it was barely recognisable as a hand.

"This is General Cable, leader of the Nilkens of the Rose, loyal subjects of Queen Rose," one of the soldiers intoned. "Make your obsequies."

Paul shook his tied hands angrily and attempted to spit out the gag. General Cable made a sign and the gag was removed, although Paul's hands were not freed. He spluttered in anger.

"Do you not know who I am? I demand you release me at once. In which case I shall prevent Reece, my Regent, taking any further action against you for laying hands on my person."

"So you are His Highness Prince Paul?" General Cable's voice was dry and flaky. "Travelling without your retinue in eastern Nivram. Is this normal behaviour for a prince of your country? I hardly think so."

Paul shot a cold glance at the general. "I was kidnapped by an evil witch, and am now on my way home."

The general smashed his hand on the desk. "Are you plotting against her most supreme majesty, Queen Rose?"

Yvonne's gag was also removed. "We're not plotting. Against anyone…" she said unsteadily.

"Do you deny being an enemy of her majesty? Are you allies of Queen Rose?"

"No." Paul put as much loathing as he could into his answer.

"Therefore, you must be her enemy. To be the Queen's enemy is punishable by death."

"We have done nothing wrong," Paul said fiercely. "You have no right to hold us prisoners. Release us immediately."

"I find you guilty of being enemies of her majesty. I hereby sentence you to death at first light."

The impertinence of General Cable stunned Paul into silence.

"But we don't know your queen," Yvonne said. "How could we be plotting against her?"

"The only hope of reprieve is if you make a full confession." General Cable picked up his quill. "Take them away."

"Wait!" Paul raised his bound wrists for silence. "Why kill us? Your queen searches for us. She will not be pleased if anything happens to us."

For a long moment, the general fastened his eyes intently on him. Finally he nodded. "You are right. I will leave my queen to pass judgement. Prepare the catchills at dawn to carry the prisoners to her majesty. Take them away and secure them for the night."

"What?" Yvonne said.

She sounded outraged but Paul was pleased. His clever strategy had saved their lives.

"Why did you say that?" Yvonne's voice shook as they were bundled outside. "Now we will be sent to Lucky's enemy. She will kill us anyway, more painfully. I know what witches are like."

"It bought us time." He turned to the guards as they led him away. "I am Prince Paul of the Kingdom of Kyle. Release us at once."

The Nilkens did not reply. Instead, they pushed the prisoners into a nearby tent and tied them to chairs, making sure both wrists and ankles were securely bound before leaving them alone.

Outrage and anger struggled for domination in Paul, but he recalled something his regent had once told him: *Keep cool in times of crisis. Focus your mind, not your heart. The time for anger or revenge will follow.*

He swallowed his rage, and tried to focus on the important thing.

"We must escape tonight. I am not exactly sure how. I've never been in this situation before."

"Neither have I," Yvonne snapped. "Sorry, but I want to escape too. I need to know the others are safe."

"I am sure they are. Otherwise, they'd be here." He tested his ropes but the Nilkens had tied the knots well. He attempted to inch his chair away so he could face Yvonne. Maybe his fingers could loosen her ropes. But the chairs were too heavy to move.

"Could we…?" Yvonne said. "No, it wouldn't work. I only hope Charlie will see the catchills flying us to Queen Rose."

"He won't. We will escape before that." Paul was determined. What would Reece say to see him so helpless? His regent had ruled the country at sixteen. Surely the future king could escape from a few Nilkens? "Let me think."

Yvonne interrupted his thoughts with a loud cry.

"Help! Help!"

Two guards rushed into the tent.

"Sssh," one said.

"The general does not like noise," the other said.

Yvonne yelled again. Paul couldn't help being peeved that she was acting up like this. He shot her a look that said *Leave the plan to me* but she didn't seem to understand.

The second guard was agitated "The general will be angry."

"I don't care. I'm tired and hungry and tied up. The last thing in the world I care about is the general," Yvonne said.

The two Nilkens conferred in low voices. Then they faced the prisoners.

"We will bring food and water."

A few minutes later the Nilkens returned with some bread rolls and a jug of water. Paul's right hand was untied so he could eat. He pondered on escape plans as he ate.

"Finished?"

"Don't tie us up again," Yvonne said. "The ropes are too tight. Especially for the prince. I think he'll die."

Paul played along with a shuddering groan. "Don't tie my wrist. I've lost feeling in my hand. My ankles are in agony."

The Nilken hesitated, fingering the rope.

"I am Paul, prince of the Kingdom of Kyle, and I will never walk again."

"Hurry," the other Nilken said, as he trussed up Yvonne once more. "We have no time for this nonsense."

"Your queen won't be pleased with you if the prince is damaged," Yvonne said.

"Argh." Paul raised his voice. "Such pain I have never before experienced."

"Be quiet or we will gag you," the second Nilken said.

This silenced Paul. He couldn't bear to have the gag thrust into his mouth again. As the guard tied his wrist, he met those empty eyes and caught a glimmer of emotion. It vanished so quickly he wasn't sure it had existed at all.

Yet once the guards left, Paul felt the rope securing his arm to the chair was slack. Yvonne's idea had worked. He glanced at her with new respect.

"The rope is loose."

Within a minute, he worked his right arm free. It was an easy matter to untie his left, and then his ankles. He knelt by Yvonne and pulled at the cords which bound her.

"Was that luck?" Yvonne said. "That he didn't tie it properly, I mean."

Paul was indignant. "Luck? That was your strategy and my execution."

Yvonne smiled. "My strategy was luck."

Once he had freed Yvonne, Paul walked over to the tent entrance and peered between the flaps. "Two guards outside the tent. Pacing."

"Could we sneak out the back?"

Paul tried to prise open a gap large enough to slip under but the canvas was pinned firmly to the ground.

"No good." He stood up, warm from exertion. "I need my sword."

"You have a sword?" Yvonne squeaked.

"Of course. My fencing master says he has never seen so adept a pupil." He returned to the tent entrance. "I'll keep watch. We may get a chance to slip out later."

"Could we lure the guards in and tie them up?"

Paul had considered that earlier. "Yes, but their cries would alert the whole camp."

Yvonne paced the tent anxiously. "We need to leave before dawn."

"Give the camp time to settle for the night before we make our escape." Paul wasn't happy with his plan but it was the best he could come up with. Yvonne had no better suggestion, so he kept watch by the flap. After a couple of hours, the two guards began to yawn. One left, perhaps to get relief, while the other sat down and closed his eyes.

It was the chance Paul had been waiting for. He called Yvonne, and together they slipped out of the tent. Paul led the way, grateful for the torches at each tent which cast sufficient light to find a path. A series of small fires marked the camp perimeter. Guards warmed their hands and stared silently at the flames. Beyond the fires, the night was very black.

Paul selected a spot mid-way between two sentry posts and walked straight out into the darkness. Nobody noticed. Confidence was everything, he knew.

Yvonne, keeping close, spoke softly. "Which way? I haven't a clue."

"I have an excellence sense of direction. Follow me."

He stepped across the grass, concentrating his senses on the way ahead. It was a trick one of his tutors taught, to discern obstacles in total darkness. Almost immediately his foot stubbed against a rock, and he smothered an exclamation of pain. At least he had performed well in astronomy, and by the position of the stars was able to pick a path across the hilly terrain that led roughly north-east.

"We need to get as much distance from those catchills as possible," he said.

They walked without stopping for what remained of the night. When dawn came, Paul was disappointed not to see Crocodile Lake in sight.

Yvonne lay down on the grass. "Let's stop for a few minutes."

In the distance, a terrible cry sounded. No doubt a catchill, although there was no sign of it in the sky.

"The hunt has begun," Paul said grimly.

Yvonne got to her feet without a word. The sky darkened and a few drops of rain fell. Paul hoped it was enough to keep the catchills from finding them.

After a few hours, the rain cleared and the sky brightened, and they crested a hill and saw the peculiar shape of Mount Slant. A long strip of deep blue lay at its base. It was miles away but Yvonne grinned and danced in delight.

"Crocodile Lake," she said. "We made it!"

"We're not there yet," Paul said severely, although he

was secretly thrilled by the sight. He calculated it would take them an hour to reach the lakeshore.

That was before he heard the cry of the catchill once more. This time, it didn't sound so far away.

Chapter Sixteen
MIREHOGS

Cathy's mouth was full of thick, coarse hair, and mirehog stench filled her nostrils. The creature was at least seven foot tall. It started to run, a shuddering loping stride that jarred her as it sprang across the ground. Forcing her head back from the mirehog's chest, she managed to gulp a little air. She called Alan's name but all she heard was the thundering of feet across the earth.

Paul said mirehogs ate human flesh. Cathy quailed at the thought of ending up as dinner for these beasts.

After some time, the pace changed. Cathy was shoved higher, and she peered over its shoulder at the moon-flooded valley below. The creature climbed uphill and shifted its grip again. Cathy slipped from its hold, head first towards the ground, but with a snarl, the mirehog hauled her back into its arms. Her brief glimpse of rocks and a boulder-strewn hillside was swallowed up by its fur, grey in the star light.

"Ugh." Her mouth was full of hair as she was jolted and

shaken once more. When the mirehog eventually slowed, Cathy managed to turn her head. She expected to see hungry mirehogs waiting among the trees of the Great Forest. Instead, she faced a smooth marble wall, glimmering faintly in the moonlight. The mirehog easily scaled it, although several times Cathy slipped from its grip. She desperately grabbed tufts of its hair as its long arm reached for her again.

The climb only took a minute, but every second felt the most terrifying of her life. Reaching its destination, the creature lunged forward and dropped Cathy onto a cold floor. She took a mouthful of hair-free air, and looked up at the mirehog: huge and hairy, with beady black eyes in a leathery face, fangs protruding from a large mouth. Cathy shuddered at the sight.

At least she wasn't in the Great Forest. The mirehog had taken her to a large room, its ceiling high above her head. The floors and walls were marble, veined with gold. Eight enormous arched windows lined one wall. At the far end of the room she spied a huge hearth and a pile of broken furniture. Several heaps of branches and leaves were scattered across the floor but otherwise the room was bare.

A moment later a dark shape blotted out the moonlight in one of the windows. Something slung over its shoulder was dropped to the ground beside her.

Alan.

"You were right, Cathy," Alan said, sitting up. "Imagine, beasts from the Great Forest finally caught us." He sounded thrilled rather than terrified.

"We must be in Princess Scatherina's castle," Cathy whispered. She'd wanted to see it ever since Lucky mentioned it, though she wished the mirehogs weren't with her. One of them touched her face and made a crooning noise. Cathy screamed and batted away its leathery paw.

"See how different they are," Alan said, as if he were looking at puppies rather than child-eating monsters. "My one has a stripe of white fur down its back."

Cathy looked more closely at their captors. Their faces were different too, one was smaller and grey, the other scarred and coloured like its fur. The grey-faced one pulled a couple of vines from a heap of sticks, and the two mire hogs sat down and chewed some leaves.

Cathy began to breathe a little easier. She didn't seem in immediate danger of being eaten. As it chewed, the grey-faced mirehog kept its eyes on her, so she was afraid to move. Then, it made a choking noise, spat mushy green pulp into its palm, and held it to her mouth.

"Ugh," Cathy said. It smelled as bad as it looked. She shook her head and pushed away the paw.

The creature's deep-throated growl made Cathy wriggle closer to Alan. Before the mirehog did anything further, three more burst into the room, yammering loudly. They loped across the room, sat on their haunches, and stared at Cathy and Alan. One leaned forward and prodded Alan in the stomach. Cathy had seen women in the market prod bread for its freshness in the same way. Another of the newcomers kept pulling at Cathy's hair, even though she shouted at it to leave her alone.

The grey-faced mirehog screeched loudly. A brief vocal argument, loud and discordant, broke out among all five creatures. The opposing sides circled around the room, glaring at each other with wicked eyes.

One creature dived at another. Both fell to the floor and rolled away, biting and snarling. Cathy made herself as small as she could to avoid the snapping jaws as the mirehogs fought perilously near her. Then the slighter of the two broke free. It scurried towards the door, closely followed by the larger one. The grey-faced mirehog seized something from the floor and flung it after them. An arrow lodged in the shoulder of one but it didn't stop them fighting. Cathy could hear them scuffling and growling in the corridor.

"Come on," Alan said. "While they're not looking!"

Cathy bolted after him to the pile of furniture and squirmed under a broken chair. Maybe the mirehogs would forget her if they couldn't see her.

The pale light of dawn filtered into the room, so Cathy crawled further in, trying not to dislodge anything. The remaining mirehogs looked puzzled. Noise broke out in the lower part of the castle. Three mirehog heads shot up, and two of them bounded from the room. The third one snuffled along the floor. Cathy bit her lip. The mirehog was tracking her.

It didn't take long for it to reach the broken furniture and stretch its arm under the chair, inches from her. Cathy was grateful to whoever had stacked the furniture like a maze of tunnels. The mirehog was far too large to follow. She crawled after Alan. She reached the backwall and sat under a table next to her twin.

'Here." He handed her one of the metal arrows.

Cathy looked at it in disgust. She wasn't going to stab

any creature, even a mirehog, but something clattered to the floor, followed by another crash. The mirehog *was* following her, but knocking down the tunnels as it went. She could hear it panting and growling as it came close.

Alan held his arrow out like a sword, its metal shaft glinting in the growing light.

Crash!

The mountain of furniture continued to collapse. Now Cathy could see its face, deep purple with tufts of orange fur surrounding its eyes. It snarled, showing its sharp fangs. Cathy picked up the arrow and clutched it tightly.

Somewhere nearby came a shout, and with a mighty roar, the mirehog rose to its feet, scattering the furniture like matchsticks. Cathy screamed. The mirehog fell forward, smashing through the table and landing on top of her. Almost immediately, its body was dragged away and a stern, bearded face gazed down.

Shrieks and howls came from the corridor.

"Wait here," the bearded man said. "I got some beasties to get rid of."

Cathy scrambled to her feet to help Alan, who was pushing part of the table off his legs.

"Who was that?" Alan got up. He seemed unhurt.

"I don't know." Cathy looked at the fallen mirehog with a knife sticking out of its back. She wished she was still with her sisters and Lucky.

Alan nudged the mirehog with his foot. The creature did not stir. "It's dead."

Cathy shivered. "I don't want to stay here."

She went to the doorway and peered into the corridor. Two men stood at the top of a flight of stairs close by. Elsewhere in the palace, the shouts and cries were fading into running footsteps and distant voices. One of the men at the stairs turned and stared. Cathy withdrew into the room.

It didn't take long for the bearded man to return. He was accompanied by a tall, clean-shaven man, with a kind face and sad, dark eyes.

"Where are your Nilkens, Bardey?" He broke off abruptly on seeing Cathy and Alan. "Nilkens? They're children." He said the last word with an effort, as if he had difficulty remembering it.

"Aye, so they are," Bardey said. "What are children doing here?"

"Well?" The tall man looked at Cathy with a friendly smile. "What are you doing here?"

Cathy couldn't think of anything to say in reply.

"Just leaving," Alan said, slipping his arrow behind his back.

"I see." The man looked amused. "Wait here. Bardey will keep you company until I return." He strode quickly from the room. Cathy could hear him shouting orders: "Remove those carcasses. Post scouts."

The twins waited silently with an equally taciturn Bardey, who eyed them suspiciously. Cathy had no doubt that he would foil any attempt to run off. The tall man returned within a few minutes, followed by half a dozen others. Like Bardey, they were all squarely built and bearded. Ignoring Cathy and Alan, they set about sorting out the heap of broken furniture, while Bardey and another dragged away the dead mirehog.

The tall man, who seemed to be chief, flung himself into a chair that had been re-assembled.

"Destructive beasts," he said. "We've had quarters here for almost a month, but three days ago a large force of them drove us out. See how they have smashed up our furniture and torn up segments of the roadway? All to no purpose."

"Where have the mirehogs all gone?" Cathy said timidly.

"Is that what you call them? We know them as marvinlings, after the orange fruit with the furry peel. But tell me, what are you doing here? Surely you have not come from the Great Forest?"

Cathy shook her head. "No, we travelled here through east Nivram." She bit her lip. She shouldn't have said so much.

"Indeed? What brought you here? How long have you been in the castle?" he said.

"The mirehogs brought us here last night." She gave a yawn.

"Interesting, I look forward to hearing more. But you look tired. Sleep now for a few hours, and we will talk later. Bardey, some blankets for our guests." He rose to his feet. "My men will be close at hand so you will be safe."

Bardey produced a couple of rough blankets for the twins and showed them a corner of the room where they could sleep.

Alan looked as tired as she felt. "Let's rest for a bit before we say goodbye," he said.

Cathy could barely keep her eyes open. She curled up with the blanket and yawned again. Alan was already asleep.

She woke to sunlight and the sound of sweeping. A man with a broom worked nearby. Alan was already up, looking out of one of the windows.

"I can't see the Great Forest from here." He sounded disappointed.

A message arrived at that moment from their leader, requesting the twins' presence. The twins obediently followed the messenger along a wide passageway to a door set in one of the castle's turrets. Narrow stone steps led to the roof.

"The children, Tremere," the messenger announced.

The tall man standing at the parapet beckoned to the twins. "Come, there is a fine view from here."

He was right. From the roof, the undulating countryside spread below. Cathy saw the hills and the valleys, the plains and the rivers all sparkling in the morning sun. The Great Road stretched like an arrow into the distance, and the Blackhand Mountains towered behind the palace.

"Are you the leader?" Alan said. "Is Tremere your name?"

"That is what they call me. It is an ancient term for leader."

"Don't you have a name of your own?" Cathy said shyly.

Tremere shook his head. "All these men, and we total over one hundred, are exiles from northern lands. They endured terrible ordeals in the Great Forest before finding safety in the caves near the pass. Almost three years ago, they found me, feverish and near death. They saved my life, but I have no memory of who I am or how I got there. Tremere really means Lost Leader."

"But you're their chief?" Alan sounded surprised.

"It is their tradition. The latest arrival is leader. It seems strange but has some merit. The newcomer is likely to be fitter and stronger than those who have spent more time in the forest. I shall be leader only until another joins us."

"Do you live in the Forest?" Alan said. "I didn't think *anyone* could."

"The trees are thin by the mountain pass, and we can defend the caves from attack," Tremere said. "I doubt if anyone going deeper would survive."

"Are all the marvinlings dead?" Cathy said.

Tremere smiled at her. "Sadly, no. We are under constant attack from them. They usually strike in small groups, never more than half a dozen. That was why they took us by surprise when they drove us out of here, for there were almost fifty of them."

"Do you live here in the castle now?" Cathy couldn't understand why the men would stay in the forest when they could leave by the pass now that the catchills were gone.

"Not yet," Tremere said. "It will be hard for many of the men to adjust. We also need to be sure we are welcome here."

Alan bent down to retrieve something lying on the ground.

"What is it?" Tremere said.

Alan held up an arrow, its shaft glinting in the sunlight.

"Some marvinlings attacked us a few days ago with these," Alan said.

"It must have been a raiding party from here, using our

arrows." Tremere gazed at them curiously. "Tell me about your journey. It is unusual to meet such young travellers."

Cathy looked doubtfully at Alan. Tremere seemed kind, but he was still a stranger, and although she liked him, she was reluctant to tell him anything.

"Could we have some food please?" Alan said. "We lost our packs yesterday."

Tremere nodded. "I already requested breakfast to be brought here for you."

As if on cue, two men walked onto the roof. One was the messenger who had brought them up to the tower, the other was shorter, winking at Cathy as he set down a pitcher and two goblets on the parapet. The messenger placed a basket before Alan.

"Go ahead," Tremere said, after thanking the men.

"Aren't you eating?" Cathy said.

Tremere shook his head. "I ate earlier."

The basket was filled with slices of dark bread, thickly smeared with paste. Alan picked up a piece and bit into it. Cathy waited for his reaction. He made a face, as if to say *not bad*, so she chose a piece also and munched on it. The bread was tough and chewy but not unpleasant, and the yellow paste quite tasty.

Tremere poured some water, and waited until they had finished before asking again about their journey. Alan was good at dealing with awkward questions so Cathy left it to him.

"Our parents are dead and we had to leave Lowdar. So we sailed around the mountains to east Nivram." Alan looked pleased with himself for telling the truth without giving away Lucky or their sisters. "We're making our way to Mount Slant."

"We walked and walked," Cathy told Tremere with feeling. "Last night the marvinlings caught us and took us here." She looked up innocently at him.

"Hmm," Tremere said. "And why are you going to Mount Slant, is that your name for the mountain yonder?"

"We heard the Kingdom of Kyle is a great country to live in," Alan said. It wasn't a lie; Paul said so many times. "It lies beyond Mount Slant."

"We're looking for somewhere safe," Cathy added, which was also true.

"The Kingdom of Kyle is far from being a safe place," Tremere said, "if the tales I hear are true. It's also much too dangerous for people so young to travel alone in these parts. But for us, the marvinlings would be now digesting their favourite breakfast. You must stay here, for the moment at least."

He spoke with an air of finality. Cathy's mouth fell open in consternation. She didn't want to stay in the castle, and what would the others think if they never arrived at Mount Slant? They would have to make a plan to escape, she thought, and tried to express it with a grimace. Alan nodded understandingly.

"I must go about my business," Tremere murmured. He lingered, however, looking at the sunlit scenery, as if he found the children's company more congenial than his men's. "I have to return to the caves for a short while.

Perhaps you would like to accompany me?"

Before Cathy could express her dismay, Alan enthusiastically agreed.

Tremere got up. "We leave later today. I can show you the castle now, if you wish?"

The castle was the most beautiful building she had ever seen, with grand staircases and spacious rooms. High ceilings were carved into graceful arches, and faded mosaics everywhere reminded Cathy of the Great Road. Magnificent views of the surrounding mountains and valleys were had from every window. The mirehogs had soiled many of the rooms during their three-day occupation, and Tremere's men were working hard, cleaning the beautiful marble and repairing the damage.

As they walked down a flight of stairs, a commotion broke out on the landing below. Above the shouting and banging came the sound of terrified squealing. Cathy, Alan, and Tremere ran down the steps to find that a tiny, orange-furred creature was halfway up a window. It clung desperately to a torn curtain, looking fearfully down at Bardey. A couple of men joined Bardey as he vainly tried to dislodge the little creature with a broom handle. Finally, Bardey drew a blade from his belt and prepared to throw it. Cathy flung herself at him and dragged down his arm, crying "No!"

"It's a mirehog," Alan said.

"Aye, and the last one on the premises," Bardey growled.

Cathy looked at the huge, dark eyes in a frightened little face and burst into tears. "It's only a baby."

"She loves animals," Alan said.

"Animal? It's a murderous beastie," Bardey muttered.

Tremere put his arm around Cathy. "What would you have me do? It's only a baby now, but its teeth will soon be sharp. It will grow big so fast that it will become a threat to us all."

Cathy raised her eyes beseechingly. "*Please* don't kill it."

Tremere hesitated, threw a helpless look towards Bardey, and shrugged his shoulders. "Very well. You can look after the creature for the moment, but at the first opportunity, we shall release it into the Great Forest, where marvinlings belong."

"Oh, thank you, thank you." Cathy was delighted, her tears instantly ceasing.

"Bardey will help you feed the creature," Tremere said. "But you must excuse me, I see Henchant has ridden in from the caves and needs to speak with me." He stepped away to converse to a grim-faced man standing silently by the stairs.

Bardey nodded at Cathy and said in a surly tone: "I'll see about food for the… thing."

The men left, and Alan also withdrew, leaving Cathy to coax down the scared animal. Eventually, it descended and jumped into her arms, where it clung tightly to her. Cathy patted it and murmured soothingly, and thought it looked much happier. When Bardey came back, the little creature whimpered and shrank back, but Cathy accepted the cup of warm milk and retired to a corner to feed it.

A short while later, Alan returned.

"I think he trusts me, Alan," she said. "The poor thing is

starving. I'm going to call him Marvin, after Tremere's name for them. Look at his snowy white face and paws. Bardey says mirehog skin should be tanned and leathery. Isn't he cute?"

"Right," Alan said. "Listen, Cathy, Tremere wants to leave now for the caves. A man came to say that a new leader has turned up in the forest, and Tremere wants to meet him."

"What about Lucky and the others? Aren't we going to Crocodile Lake?"

"When we come back. The caves are only a couple of hours away, I think. It will be really interesting. Anyway, we don't have a choice: Tremere is not going to leave us behind."

Cathy knew he was right about Tremere. She dreaded the thought of entering the forest, that place of nightmares and monsters, but if the Forest men lived there, perhaps the place wasn't so bad? Or so she told herself.

A narrow path led from beyond the castle to the mountain pass. Cathy perched on Tremere's horse, clutching the baby mirehog. Alan shared Henchant's mount, and a third rider, Bentam, brought up the rear.

"Since the castle was attacked, we guard the pass. There is absolutely no danger," Tremere said, guiding his horse along the stony slope.

The rocky path up the steep mountainside grew narrower as gradually the sides of the mountain edged together. Cathy's courage began to falter but she refrained from begging Tremere to turn back.

They reached the beginning of the pass, the gateway to the Great Forest.

Chapter Seventeen
THE RUINED CITY

"Aren't Nilkens lovely?" Susan said enthusiastically. "So kind and friendly…"

"Good cooks, too," Vicky said. They were sitting on a wall, eating their lunch. A few clouds scudded across the sky, but otherwise it was a fine afternoon. After walking continuously for over three hours, Vicky felt entitled to a long rest. "I've never eaten such tasty food."

"Their faces are so sweet," Susan went on. "And they have the happiest smiles."

"I wonder if that monument is much farther?" Vicky kicked her heels against the stonework. "The twins must be walking fast – not a sign of them ahead." Even Yvonne and Paul, who had overtaken them about an hour earlier, were only visible through her telescope.

"Perhaps they've reached the monument by now?" Susan said.

"I suppose we better start walking again." Vicky jumped

down from the wall but landed awkwardly. A stab of pain shot through her leg, and she collapsed to the ground.

"What's the matter?" Susan said, rushing to her side.

"My ankle." Vicky groaned, blinking back tears. "I've twisted it, I think."

"Rest it for a few minutes," Susan said.

Resting didn't make any difference. Vicky attempted to stand, but it hurt too much to put any weight on her leg. Susan couldn't find anything to serve as a crutch, so she tore a strip from her skirt to bind Vicky's ankle. Vicky was able to hobble, leaning heavily on Susan's shoulder.

Day turned into evening before they arrived at a shoulder-high, weather-beaten rock. Among the worn engravings was something that could have been a Diamond rising out of a star.

Susan helped Vicky lower herself to the ground but remained standing, staring into the gathering dusk. "Where are the others?"

"They've gone on without us," Vicky said in disgust. "What shall we do now, Su?"

"I don't know," Susan said. "Why didn't they wait? Perhaps this isn't the right place?"

"Has to be," Vicky said. "It has Lucky's emblem." She couldn't help feeling envious of Yvonne and Paul travelling by horseback. Perhaps they had already reached the Lake?

Susan sat beside Vicky and leaned against the cold stone of the monument.

"I really can't go any farther tonight," Vicky said, unable to ignore the painful throb of her ankle, swollen beneath the swathe of binding. "Should we light a fire?"

"Won't it draw attention to us?" Susan said.

Vicky sighed, but she didn't want to attract Nilken soldiers. The clouds cleared as the evening deepened about them, and stars emerging in the sky. Silently thanking Misha, Vicky shared out most of their remaining food, and they huddled together to keep warm.

"Play something, Su," Vicky said, shivering.

Susan's flute gleamed silver in the starlight as she raised it to her lips. A beautiful tune Vicky hadn't heard before floated softly into the air. The notes seemed to wrap themselves around Vicky, spreading a comforting warmth so that the night didn't seem so cold after all.

Susan woke Vicky at daybreak.

"Need another hour of sleep," Vicky muttered, but with a groan, she pushed herself upright. The eastern sky was tinged with pink and gold. "The sun isn't up yet."

"We have to get Lucky home as soon as possible." Susan handed Vicky a couple of papples. "How's your foot?"

Vicky gave her ankle a tentative waggle and felt no pain. She pulled off the bandage and discovered the swelling had completely subsided.

"It's amazing." Vicky got to her feet and walked a few steps. "Like magic." She watched Susan check the pouch for her flute. Vicky couldn't remember the tune which had haunted her dreams, but was it possible that Susan's flute had cured her ankle? She decided she'd ask Lucky later.

The day brightened as the two girls started off. Vicky didn't need Cathy's compass to head north, for Mount Slant, with its distinctive drooping summit, was clearly visible on the horizon. The problem was there was no clear path to follow, only a series of fields to cross. They skirted around each crop rather than plough through the grain, but Mount Slant grew no closer. It looked like they were travelling more east than north.

The sky clouded over and a cool breeze blew around them, bearing a spatter of rain. They had been walking for some hours, with only a brief mid-morning break, when Susan, leading the way across a wall gave a startled exclamation. Vicky followed and dropped down, not into another field, but onto a narrow, overgrown path.

"It must lead to the lake," Susan said, smiling happily,

Vicky was more pessimistic. "Or back to the Great Road."

The path twisted in several directions before joining a broader roadway, equally overgrown and unused-looking. This, in turn, led to the ruins of a city. Houses without roofs, crumbling stone walls, and everything half buried by moss. No wonder the road was wild and unkempt. They wandered through the maze of streets, admiring what must have been a beautiful city, although now its atmosphere was one of intense sorrow.

In the central square, a huge monument was erected.

"To Goldie, Hero, Sage, and Champion," Vicky read. Above the words, a statue had once reared, but it had long since crumbled to dust. "I wonder who he was, and what happened here?"

Susan ran her fingers over symbols etched along the base of the monument.

"This place reminds me of my flute," she said.

"I see no resemblance at all," Vicky said. "Unless this has a what-do-you-call-it – miasma cast over it too?"

They walked on, passing sad houses and gardens run riot. The street sloped upwards, heading towards a grassy hill.

"We'll get a good view from up there," Vicky said excitedly, and broke into a run. She heard Susan shout out something but didn't stop.

That was until, with a clap of wings, a catchill landed on the street in front of her.

The catchill towered over Vicky, its ruby eye the only bit of colour in its stone-grey plumage. The cruel beak turned towards her could shred flesh, and its talons pin her to the ground. It eyed Vicky curiously, and for a wild moment, Vicky thought it was surprised. Until it raised one claw, ready to seize her.

Soft music stole through the air. The catchill retracted its claws, folded its wings, and tucked its head away.

Vicky backed into Susan, who played her flute for a few moments more. The tune ended and she put the flute away. Vicky looked at her in silent amazement.

"It's asleep," Susan said. "For several days, I think."

"How... who... *when* did you learn to do that?"

Susan shrugged. "I had an urge to play."

"Is there anything else you can do?" Vicky fell into step beside Susan. "You cured my ankle, sent the catchill to sleep – what other magic can you work?'

"It's not me, Vicky. It's the flute, and I don't know if it can do anything more. Ask Lucky, if you like."

177

Vicky intended to. She had always guessed the flute was special, like her telescope, but she had no idea it was so magical, which made her wonder what else her gift could do.

The grassy hill levelled out into a plateau, providing a good view of the countryside. Blue-grey in the distance were the Blackhand Mountains. Much nearer, slightly to the northwest, rose the cragged Mount Slant. At its base streaked a gleam of dark blue. In between were many fields and a winding river.

"Nearly there," Vicky said. "Let's follow the river."

It didn't take long to reach the river. For a while, they walked along its bank, enjoying the sound of rushing water. Vicky expected to hear birdsong too but the birds were silent. Perhaps the flute had sent all flying creatures to sleep? Hoping her telescope had also developed new powers, she held it to her eye, but everything seemed much the same as usual. Slightly disappointed, she put it away again.

After it seemed like they had walked forever, leaving behind the cultivated lands of the Nilkens, the river disappeared underground. The land was hilly and uneven, covered in short thick grass occasionally punctuated by a shrub or tree. Cresting another hill opened up a clearer view of the mountain.

"Crocodile Lake," Vicky said, impressed by the great expanse of water at its base.

At the same moment, sparkling brightly, Lucky emerged from Susan's pocket.

"Lucky!" Vicky exclaimed in unison with Susan, as the Diamond resumed her place on Susan's shoulder.

"Yes, I'm quite recovered now that I am within sight of the Lake. But what's been happening? Where are the others?"

Vicky and Susan briefly filled her in on the events of the past two days.

"Take my eye off you for a couple of days and disaster strikes." Lucky sighed.

Vicky was indignant. "It's not our fault…"

"By the way," Lucky said, cutting across Vicky. "I meant to thank you for being kind to Paul. His life has not been the easiest."

"What – amid all the wonders of his palace?" Vicky said sarcastically.

"His mother died in childbirth, and his father was murdered shortly afterwards," Lucky said.

Vicky's cheeks grew warm. "I didn't know…"

"How awful for him," Susan said, her eyes softening with sympathy. "Has he got any family?"

"None of his siblings survived infancy. His people have a violent and bloodied history," the Diamond said. "Fortunately, his regent – who took command of the country shortly after the king's death – was able to prevent the land erupting into civil war. Now there is peace, but Paul has been brought up to value strength and courage as the prime virtues."

"Aren't they?" Vicky said.

"They are good things to have, but you must also know mercy and justice. Wisdom, prudence, kindness and many other good qualities – all these we are trying to teach Paul so that when the time comes for him to be king, he will rule wisely."

"He has a few other things to learn also," Vicky began, but her voice trailed off. Susan looked at her in amazement, and she added lamely: "Joke."

Lucky changed the subject once more by saying, "I always forget how long it takes humans to cover distance. For being so large, you certainly move very slowly. At this rate, it will take us a couple of hours to reach the lake."

Three hours passed before the blue streak widened into a vast expanse of dark water. The ground grew marshy as they neared the lake, and the far shore could only be guessed by the position of Mount Slant. The deep blue of the lake reflected Mount Slant and the late afternoon sun in its depths.

"How beautiful," Susan breathed.

"It's huge," Vicky said, awed. "Lucky, why is it called Crocodile Lake?"

"I told you that the Diamonds were given stewardship of these lands. The ancient ones retired to rest below the lake, with crocodiles as their sentinels."

"Will they come back?" Susan said.

"We were told never to disturb them. Their rousing will mark the end of our tenure as guardians. It will be the end of the world for us. Perhaps for everyone. The years of our stewardship are limited, we know that some day they will end, but we do not anticipate that it will occur for many millennia. Any sign of Charlie?"

Vicky slapped her telescope to her eye, and, after a few moments, spied a dark shape on the water speeding towards them.

Chapter Eighteen
THE GREAT FOREST

The way to the Great Forest led through a long, narrow channel cut into the mountain.

"Usually there are rockbirds preventing us entering the pass," Tremere explained. "But about three weeks ago, they disappeared – so a few of us walked through and found the abandoned castle."

Alan didn't bother telling him the rockbirds were actually catchills, or that Witch Rose had called them away to find Lucky. Entering the Great Forest was something he'd longed to do his whole life. He wished Cathy was as excited about it as he was. The tangled mass of trees at Lowdar's gates had always called to him, so how could he turn down the chance to enter the forest? Besides, as he had said to Cathy, they had little choice.

It was hot between the rocky walls of the pass, and Alan was glad to reach the end of it. Beyond lay a completely different world. Trees, dark and menacing, blocked out the sunlight. A heavy, stuffy atmosphere, threaded with evil, soaked the forest. Tremere and his men were stern-faced as they moved among the trees. The only one of the group who did not appear conscious of danger was the baby mirehog. The tiny creature looked happy and reassured. It still clung tightly to Cathy, but Alan saw it raise its head and peer around.

"We must keep silent," Tremere said quietly. "Marvinlings may be close by."

Tremere led them to a small clearing, where he gave a low whistle. The thicket rustled, and eight men surrounded them. Like Bardey, they were stocky and bearded. They stood tense and alert.

"Good," Tremere said. "Three of you, take the horses. The rest, follow me." He disappeared into the bushes that grew by the rockface.

"Go on." Alan gave Cathy a shove and followed her into the thicket. Leaves and branches brushed against his face as he saw Cathy disappear into a crack in the rock. A hidden entrance! No wonder Tremere's men felt they were safe in the caves. Alan entered a dark and narrow passageway. Cathy was immediately ahead of him, and he heard Tremere's voice further on, reassuring them, as he felt his way forward. The tunnel twisted and turned before opening into a brightly-lit chamber.

Torches flared from brackets on the walls and a small fire crackled in a corner. Several other exits led from the cavern, and a dozen men sat around a table. One of these, a young man in his mid-teens, rushed over to greet them.

"Tremere, it's good to see you home. You retook the castle?"

"Without loss," Tremere said. "Other than Bardey missing a good night's sleep and being grumpy in consequence." The young man laughed at this. "But what news from here, Tom?"

Tom's face clouded over. "Only a few hours after you left, Jensen found a stranger wandering about, half delirious. He claims to be from a town down south, who banished him to the forest. Says he has wandered about for years, encountering untold dangers, and by sheer luck, escaping on each occasion."

Tremere raised an eyebrow and gave a slight, amused smile. "Why don't you like him?"

"It's Jensen really," Tom blurted out. "He wants this Serand made chief."

"So I hear. Where are they now?"

"Hunting. Serand is showing off his expertise." Tom seemed to notice Alan and Cathy for the first time. "What are these?"

"A couple of strays I met along the way. Tom, meet Cathy and Alan. Tom will show you around. I must meet Serand. Cathy, I advise you to keep your pet hidden. He won't be welcome here."

Tom did not look pleased but he took the twins over to the fire and offered them some food. As they ate, he questioned them closely, his manner cool and unfriendly. Alan kept to the tale he told Tremere.

Strangely, this seemed to soften Tom. A smile

brightened his face.

"So you didn't find your way here through the Forest?"

"No, and we can't stay long either," Cathy said.

Alan nodded. "We only came to see the caves. How long have you lived here?"

"I am the youngest survivor of the Great Forest," Tom said proudly. "I was only seven when my father was exiled, and he would not leave me behind. I have been here eight and a half years – I think. It's hard to keep a close reckoning on time, isn't it?"

"Wouldn't you like to go back to your own country?" Cathy said.

Tom shook his head vehemently. "No, it would not be safe. There is still a price on my father's head. Even if I went back without him, they would probably kill me in his place. It's a matter of honour."

"I see." Cathy looked totally mystified.

Alan wanted to see the caves. "Can you show us around?"

Tom nodded. "Yes, of course."

"Why isn't the cave full of smoke?" Cathy said, gazing at the fire. "Is that a real chimney?"

"It's a natural air vent in the rock," Tom said. "These twist so much that the smoke emerges some distance away and totally confuses the marvinlings. We used to live in caverns far from here, under constant attack. Tremere insisted we inhabit these ones instead. He also set up all our scouting systems. We've never been attacked in the caves since he became our leader."

"Who was leader before Tremere?" Alan said.

"My father was." Tom laughed. "I wasn't too pleased at first when Tremere arrived. Come this way, and I'll show you around." Removing a torch from its wall-mount, he led the way towards one of the exits. "You must be careful. We only occupy caverns near the entrance, but hundreds more extend to the heart of the mountain. If you were lost in them, you could spend the rest of your life searching for your way back."

A short walk led to a small chamber, with four passageways leading off it. Tom chose the nearest exit. This also ended in a round chamber with tunnels leading off from it. Alan lost track of the different passages and caverns Tom led them through.

It was a fascinating journey. The caves were not merely black rock, as Alan assumed, but were veined with shining substances. Blues, reds, greens and yellows all glistened in the torchlight, like gems in an ebony setting. Some of the caverns had lodes of silver and gold snaking through the walls.

In one of the caves, great slimy creatures, like growths swelling on the floor, obliterated the sparkling stones shining in the rock.

"Ugh! Let's go," Cathy cried. "They're disgusting."

"They hate the light. You're quite safe." Tom waved the torch to demonstrate. At the same moment, one of the slimy blobs slid across the floor towards Cathy. She screamed and ran out.

"We use them for soap," Tom said, following Cathy out.

Alan would have loved to find out more about them, and how the Forest men used them for soap.

"Do you like living here?" Cathy said, as they turned back towards the occupied caverns.

Tom's eyes lit up. "It can be exciting, pitting your wits against the marvinlings, searching for food. We don't go far among the trees – there are much worse things there. Some years ago, a large group left here to explore the forest. None made it back. What's that?"

Marvin, the baby mirehog, stuck his head out of Cathy's jacket. Tom jumped back against the wall, fists clenched.

"It's all right," Alan said quickly. Cathy cradled the mirehog and glared at Tom.

"It's one of them," Tom said. "What are you doing with it? It can't be here – it will kill us."

"Tremere said I could keep him," Cathy said hotly.

Tom relaxed his fists. "He did? That makes it all right with me."

Alan kept a close eye on Tom for the rest of their tour, in case he changed his mind. Once assured of Tremere's approval, however, Tom seemed quite cheerful, and even got some milk for Marvin once they returned to the main cave.

Tremere was waiting for them and they sat by the fire while Tom entertained them with stories of fire-breathing monsters and battles with mirehogs. Alan was sorry when the tales were interrupted by the noisy arrival of a dozen men. The centre of attention was a tall gaunt man with a hooked nose and penetrating eyes.

Something about the man seemed familiar.

Tremere stepped forward and held out a hand. "You must be Serand. Welcome."

"And you must be Tremere. Thank you." Serand shook Tremere's hand vigorously.

Alan watched the two men appraise each other. Both were tall, and though the newcomer was bearded and ugly, whereas Tremere was clean-shaven and handsome, in some respect they looked alike. It took Alan a few moments to figure it out. Both men had authority. Both seemed accustomed to command. The newcomer was no lost, terrified wanderer. He appeared strong and confident, despite his shaggy exterior. Tremere inspired Alan with trust and liking. Something abrasive and unapproachable, even disturbing, radiated from Serand.

A burly man held up a dozen dead birds. "Thanks to our new friend, we shall eat well tonight."

"I'm happy to help, Jensen," Serand murmured.

Jensen nodded at Tremere. "I have told Serand of our customs, especially the important ones."

"You mean the leadership law," Tremere said. "If it is the wish of the men to abide by that, I raise no objection…"

"How could you? You abided by it when it suited you."

"On the other hand," Tremere ignored Jensen's interruption, "if you wish me to continue as I have, I shall do so."

"Hear! Hear!" Tom shouted. He stood a little apart, arms folded and chin jutting out. He looked set for a fight. Alan and Cathy exchanged glances, and both rose to their feet, ready to run.

Jensen thrust himself forward aggressively. "You were content to follow our laws three years ago. Why not now? Has power gone to your head? Give our new friend a chance."

"It should be a vote," Tom said.

The new arrivals stood between the twins and the cavern exit. Alan wasn't sure they could slip past unnoticed.

"The council members are all here," Jensen said. "We'll put it to them now. Who's for giving Serand a chance?"

A low murmur of agreement ran around the room. It seemed to be the feeling of the majority, even though one or two of the men stared at the ground and remained silent.

"Very well," Tremere said and left the chamber.

The atmosphere changed with Tremere's departure. Jensen congratulated his friend and called for refreshment. A flagon was passed from hand to hand, and the mood of the group became convivial. Only Tom stood aside, muttering loud enough for Alan to hear: "It's not fair. Tremere helped us escape from a marvinling raid and led us here *before* we made him leader. What has this man done?"

"Merely provided us with the best dinner for months,"

one of the men said, overhearing Tom.

Tom clenched his fists. Alan waited for something to happen but after a moment, Tom turned away.

"I don't like him." Cathy petted the little mirehog cowering inside her jacket. "He looks wrong. Serand, I mean."

A little squeak, as if in agreement, came from Marvin.

Cathy stroked his head soothingly. "Let's keep out of his way."

Alan thought this was a good idea. "We'll all do that."

Soon afterwards a delicious smell of roasting meat filled the chamber. Tom sat beside the twins and told them one of the adjoining caves was used for preparing food.

"Where's Tremere?" Alan said.

"He is talking to the men." Tom kicked the rock beneath his feet. "I hate Jensen. He always makes trouble."

Supper was served at a long table that stretched the length of the cave. Tremere did not return. Alan was glad Tom was with them, for it was difficult to put up with the stares of the Forest men. Fortunately, Serand, seated at the far end of the table, took most of their attention with his talk. Alan didn't care that the men hung off Serand's every word, but Tom complained of it throughout the meal.

After supper, Tom brought some blankets and straw, and made beds by the fire. Cathy curled up and immediately went to sleep, the baby mirehog inside her jacket. Alan meant to ask Tom more about the caves, how far into the mountains the passages extended, and how a hundred men living in the forest managed to feed themselves, but instead he drifted off to sleep.

When he woke, it was to the sound of Tom calling their names loudly and cheerfully. "Wake up, sleepy heads. Breakfast."

Faint threads of daylight filtered into the caves through the air vents, and cast a pale grey hue over the cavern. All the men were gone, the fire was a pile of glowing embers, and Tom was placing food on the table.

Alan sat up groggily. "Is Tremere back yet?"

"He has gone to the other caves, beyond the pass, to talk to the rest of the men."

Cathy scrambled to her feet. "When will he be back?"

"He didn't say," Tom said. "Could be days."

Alan decided they better not wait for Tremere. He had seen the caves, and the forest was not as interesting as he hoped. It was time they caught up with Lucky.

"We'll be leaving today. Tell Tremere sorry we couldn't wait."

"You won't get back to the pass without him, or me, to guide you." Tom said. "You'll get lost among the trees and probably be eaten by marvinlings."

Alan didn't worry about getting lost, not when he had Cathy with him. "We'll find the pass ourselves."

"But you'll never get *through* the pass. Without giving the code words, you'll be dead the moment you step inside the gully."

Alan remembered Tremere speaking to some men guarding the pass. At the time he was busy wondering what they would do if the catchills came back. He couldn't imagine the guardians of the pass being easy to defeat. "Won't you tell us the passwords?"

"Nope. Tremere would kill me if I did. He told me to look after you."

Tom would not budge from this. Alan didn't think any of the other men would be helpful, so it looked like they would have to wait for Tremere's return. He sat at the table and munched thoughtfully on some bread.

"Why don't you take us through the pass yourself?" Cathy said.

Tom shook his head. "Not unless Tremere tells me to. I'll take you to see more of the caves, if you like?"

Not even Alan was interested in doing a return tour.

"I wish Tremere was back," Cathy said. "I'm afraid for Marvin."

Tom took them for a short walk outside instead. He wouldn't allow them go far from the cave entrance, but the few minutes outside perked everyone up. Especially Marvin, who skipped out of Cathy's arms and jumped among the branches of the trees before returning to her.

Unfortunately, his little run in the open air increased his confidence so much that he ran out at meal time, scampered over the table and stole a piece of meat off the plate belonging to Serand.

"Marvin! Come back!" Cathy said. "*Please.*"

The little mirehog darted back to her arms.

"*What* was that creature?" Serand demanded.

His question was met with silence.

Serand stared at the twins, his eyes so cold that Alan shivered. "Get rid of it. Or I'll have it served for supper."

Cathy immediately burst into tears, but there was no softening the new leader's face. Alan dragged his sister away from the table. Marvin peered out from Cathy's jacket. It was less than two days since they had found him, but the mirehog had already increased significantly in size. Alan doubted if Cathy could still close the buttons.

"We better let him back into the wild," he said.

Cathy's lip trembled. "He's too young."

Alan led the way outside. Marvin clung to Cathy but as they walked farther into the forest, he raised his head and looked around with great interest. A dozen yards from the caves, the trees grew thickly together, their branches so closely entwined the darkness was almost total. The air felt dead, as if it had been sucked dry of oxygen. Alan shuddered. He felt suffocated.

Cathy did not appear to notice the oppressive atmosphere. The tears coursed down her face as she said goodbye to her friend.

"It's not safe for you in the caves, Marvin. Go and find some of your own kind. But I'll never forget you."

Marvin took a few steps into the darkness, came back and gently touched Cathy's face with his soft white paw, as if he understood. Then he dashed off into the freedom the trees offered.

"It's for the best," Alan said.

"I know." She sniffed. "That horrible man would eat him. Alan – I want to go home. I don't like this place. I want Lucky and Yvonne and –"

"Me, too. Why don't we find Tremere, wherever he is, instead of waiting for him to return?"

"Let's take Tremere with us. They don't like him here."

Before Alan could reply, a sound of a dead branch being snapped in two broke the silence of the forest. He laid a warning hand on Cathy's arm, and she nodded nervously.

Something big was moving among the trees. They had strayed too far from the entrance to the caves, and were in the territory of the fire-breathing beast and the hideous fanged monster of Tom's tales. Alan's heart thumped loudly as he pressed himself against the bole of a tree and tried not to make noise. Whatever the thing was, it came to a halt on the far side of the tree trunk.

Cathy squashed herself against the trunk beside him. He knew what she was thinking, and held out a hand to restrain her. He wanted to run as well, back to the caves and Tremere and even Serand and the other Forest men. But if either of them moved, the monstrous beast might lunge forward and snap them up in its jaws.

Another agonising moment passed.

Alan had to know what fiend waited on the other side of the tree. Slowly he inched around the tree trunk until he could glimpse the monster.

It was worse than he thought. On the far side of the

tree was a great beast. It reached over six foot in height and its ribbed body stretched among the trees, glowing an evil, phosphorous green as it snaked its way into darkness.

Chapter Nineteen
MEETING AT THE LAKE

"Charlie!" Vicky jumped in delight and waved her arms. Charlie, his smile broad enough to split his wooden face, reached them a few minutes later. Lucky blazed with light, and Vicky and Susan cheered.

"Hop aboard," Charlie said. "Careful, the ground's a bit damp there."

As Charlie paddled away, Vicky said, "Where are the others, Charlie? Didn't you meet them?"

"We thought they'd be with you," Susan said in distress.

"No, but don't worry – I know where they are." Charlie smiled. "Yvonne and Paul are making their way here even as we speak. The twins are with the Forest men."

"Who are the Forest men?" Vicky said, imagining trees like the ones in the Wood of Witches coming to life.

"Exiles from Kyle, Suella, and other lands, who live in the Great Forest," Charlie said.

"Cathy and Alan in the Great Forest?" Susan paled. "Isn't that terribly dangerous?"

"No, no," Charlie said soothingly. "A few of the Forest men have taken up residence in Scatherina's castle. That's where the twins are – quite safe, I assure you."

Vicky was stunned to learn that anyone could survive a day in the Great Forest, let alone live there.

"How is it possible to live in the Forest?" she said.

"Peacemaker's Pass is near Mount Slant and the Rock of Diamonds," Lucky said. "For most evil things of the Forest, this is far too close for comfort. Which means the fringes of the forest beside the pass are not as dangerous as the rest."

"Which is where the Forest men live," Charlie said.

"Did you get word to my father?" Lucky said.

"Unfortunately, no," Charlie said regretfully. "The king had already agreed to meet Witch Rose to listen to her grievances, whatever they may be. They're erecting a place for the conference close to Mount Slant. I thought you would be exploding with anger at this news. I know you disapprove of your father meeting the witch."

"No use crying over split planks," Lucky said calmly. "At least I will be able to attend it."

Vicky glanced at Susan. She didn't like the sound of Witch Rose coming anywhere near them. Lucky and Charlie remained silent so Vicky told Charlie the story of their adventures since they parted.

Charlie whistled in dismay when he heard about the Nilken soldiers.

"Nobody mentioned anything to me," he said. "It sounds bad."

"Another ploy of Witch Rose, no doubt," Lucky said.

Vicky took out her telescope to scan the shore. It wasn't long before she spotted Yvonne and Paul farther along the lakeshore. Charlie hastily paddled over to meet them. A short while later, Charlie and his five passengers sailed across the lake, the deep blue of the water reflecting the boat and the landscape yet hiding its own depths from their scrutiny.

Paul was full of their adventure and his brilliant strategy.

"Otherwise we would have been carried off to Witch Rose first thing this morning," he said. "Yvonne is owed much of the credit too."

Yvonne smiled, but she still looked anxious, despite Charlie assuring her that the twins were safe.

"Didn't the catchills come after you?" Vicky said.

"We heard one, quite close, but we didn't see it," Yvonne said.

"We met one," Vicky recalled with a shudder. "Susan sent it to sleep – I wonder if it was the same one?"

"Sent it to sleep? You didn't mention that before," Lucky said.

Vicky hadn't included that part in the abbreviated version she had told earlier but she was happy to relate it now, and even included her belief that Susan's flute had cured her ankle the previous evening.

"That is an incredible flute, Susan," Charlie said with a smile. "Look after it well."

Lucky didn't make any comment, which surprised Vicky.

"Incredible," Paul said. "But you are likely right with your surmise, Vicky. I could not understand why the catchill, which seemed so close, never reappeared. It was fortunate for us. Now I must warn my agent of the impending attack by General Cable."

"Why do you think Witch Rose is sending her army into Kyle?" Lucky said.

"Where else?" Paul said.

"It's more likely Witch Rose is lining up a Nilken army in case she doesn't get what she wants from my father," Lucky said drily.

"I hate to think of Nilkens fighting each other," Susan said.

Lucky nodded. "They'd never get over it, if that were to happen. But I cannot imagine Nilkens fighting anyone. They simply are not up to the task – not even when they're enchanted. I am surprised at Witch Rose using them in this way."

"Maybe she has got more powerful in the centuries since we've seen her last?" Charlie said. "Perhaps she *can* galvanise the Nilkens into fighting this time?"

Lucky did not reply to this.

As they talked, Charlie had been steadily approaching the farther shore, where Mount Slant began to loom large. A lot of activity was taking place on the lakeside and Vicky raised her telescope to have a closer look.

"They look like tents." She could see Nilkens hurrying between them. "With loads of colourful banners and flags flying in the breeze."

"They're called lopseys," Charlie said. "Specially prepared for the king. This is the first time in centuries he has left the Rock. The meeting is scheduled for dusk."

"Why so late in the day?" Susan said.

"Evil likes to flourish in the dark," Paul said dramatically.

Charlie laughed. "So do Diamonds."

"Oh no," Susan cried. "Diamonds are – well, like starlight captured live. They *shed* light."

"Aren't Diamonds descendants of stars?" Paul said vaguely. "Or is it the other way around?"

It was Lucky who answered. "A kinship exists, though very distant."

"Do you realise," Yvonne said, "that once we reach the shore, we'll have fulfilled our quest, returning Lucky to her home."

"What shall we do once we get across the lake, Charlie?" Vicky said. It was almost an anti-climax to complete their mission. She looked forward to getting their reward, of course, but she hadn't actually thought about what they would do next or where they would go. She didn't want to return to Lowdar. She didn't want to leave Lucky and Charlie. She forced a smile. "Say goodbye and fade into the sunset?"

"At the very least, you need to be reunited with the twins first," Charlie said. "I'm sure Lucky will want you to stay for the conference too."

"You cannot leave until Witch Rose is defeated," Paul said, which made Vicky feel much better.

"Here we are," Charlie gently touched the shore and

grasped some reeds to steady himself. A couple of Nilkens ran towards them but, recognising Charlie, relaxed their grip on their swords, and greeted him cheerfully.

"Tawley," Charlie said to one. "Could you relay a message to the king? Tell him that his daughter, the Most Royal Princess Lucky, is here, accompanied by Prince Paul of the Kingdom of Kyle, and Yvonne, Susan, and Vicky of Lowdar."

Both Nilkens bowed and ran off, returning promptly, bearing the king's reply. Briefly, he requested the presence of Princess Lucky and Prince Paul, but he did not know any Yvonne, Vicky or Whatsit, and anyway he was far too busy to talk to any stranger. However, they could return in a month if they had any serious claim on his time, but he doubted if he could see them even then. Nilkens, being literal creatures, repeated his answer verbatim. The unwelcome visitors were taken aback, but Lucky merely laughed.

"Don't mind that message: you're all to come with me now," she said.

Charlie bid them a cheery farewell. Vicky looked with interest at the half dozen lopseys of various sizes already erected. Each structure was built from smooth, dark, bark, and seemed lopsided. Perhaps they were meant to mimic the shape of Mount Slant? The largest carried a flag that was so ruffled by the breeze that it could not be read. Lucky disappeared into this one, taking Paul with her.

The others remained outside, feeling rather forlorn, not knowing what to do. Nilkens guarded the lopseys, armed, but nonetheless looking happy, quite unlike those Yvonne had spoken of. They obviously were not expecting trouble, and carried their weaponry like toys.

Paul reappeared a few minutes later without Lucky. "It is nearly time for the council. The King has asked me to represent my people."

Vicky was disappointed. "Oh, can't we all be there?"

"I've no wish to go. I don't want to meet her," Yvonne said with a shudder.

Other than wonder what the twins were up to, there was little to do but wait for the conference to commence. Lucky sent a young Nilken to bring them some food, and they sat by the lake in the sun. The Nilkens, as always, were generous with food, but even Vicky had eaten her fill long before anything happened. They were left to hang around disconsolately for several hours, hoping that Cathy and Alan would soon show up, and wondering what Witch Rose was like. Finally, distant trumpets were heard, and Paul was called away.

"Let's watch for the witch," Vicky said. "From a safe distance."

It was late afternoon, and away in the hills a long cavalcade slowly approached. As it came nearer, Vicky could see numerous unsmiling Nilkens, all clad in green uniform, and bearing furled banners. In the midst of them, as if riding on the crest of a wave as she towered above her Nilken servants, came a strikingly beautiful young woman. Black chiffon floated and swirled about her, like the mist surging around the Witches' Wood. Her long black hair flowed down her back, and dark eyes flashed beneath soaring brows.

Scarlet lips curved into a smile. She held herself regally, a proud and beautiful queen. Her Nilken escort glumly scattered flowers – black rosebuds that fell on the fresh green grass like coals – before and after her. Vicky and Susan shrank back as her shadow passed, but she did not spare them a glance. Her arrival had been marked in advance, and she marched imperiously to where the King of the Diamonds waited.

After the witch entered the lopsey, Susan wandered over to examine the scattered flowers. As she reached for one, a young Nilken standing by exclaimed. "Don't!"

Susan's fingers touched the stem. "Why not?"

The Nilken shrugged. "She is wicked."

Susan laughed and picked up the flower.

"Look, nothing happened. It's so pretty." She held the rosebud up to her face and inhaled. As she did so, its petals started to unfurl and drop off. Susan stared, fascinated.

"Su, come over here," Vicky said. She was sitting close by the lopsey where the council was taking place. "Maybe we'll hear what's going on."

Chapter Twenty
THE BEAST IN THE FOREST

Alan swallowed hard. Ripples of movement ran through the sickly green beast, while a bright light flared at its head, weaving crazily from side to side. The front segment detached itself from its body, leaving the remainder to crumple to half its height. Alan didn't know if the creature was dying or giving birth, but the segment that disengaged was still huge and could easily swallow himself and Cathy. It moved through the trees, leaving a wisp of trailing green mist dissipating into the blackness of the trees. The other part of the monster remained where it was. As quietly as he could, Alan stepped back behind the tree trunk.

Cathy looked like she had not taken a breath since they had first heard the monster.

"It's huge," Alan said in a whisper. "It split in two, and even the small part is massive. We've got to race back to the caves before it can eat us."

Cathy looked frightened, but she nodded. Moving as

quickly and as quietly as possible, they made their way to the caves. The monster didn't pursue them, but an unpleasant surprise awaited them. Men clad in the uniform of the Nivram National Army stood in the clearing by the hidden entrance.

The twins ducked behind the bushes.

"What should we do?" Cathy said.

Alan could not imagine what soldiers were doing in the Great Forest, but he had spent too long dodging the town guard in Lowdar to consider walking past them.

"Do you remember that other cave Tom showed us?" he said.

Cathy nodded. "Where they keep the arrows and Tremere sometimes goes to be alone?"

"Yes. Let's wait there until the soldiers have gone."

The cave he meant was not far from the main one. A steep and narrow passageway led upward, and as Alan felt his way along the passage, he saw a gleam of light ahead. Hoping a friendly face awaited, he hurried on.

He got his wish. Tremere sat on a log, writing or drawing something on a piece of bark, but he smiled at the twins when they burst in upon him.

"I wondered where you were," he said. "And where's your little friend?"

"I let him free in the forest," Cathy said breathlessly. "But there's a monster."

"Soldiers too," Alan said.

"Please take us through the pass," Cathy begged. "Please come with us."

"Or at least give us the secret codes," Alan said.

"Before the monster gets us all," Cathy said at the same time.

"Hold on," Tremere cut across them. "You've seen a monster in the trees? What kind of creature?"

"A huge one," Alan said. Its segmented body reminded Alan of a caterpillar but he didn't say so, afraid Tremere wouldn't take it seriously. He hadn't seen the monster's mouth but he was sure it was full of fangs. Or maybe this monster used poison to kill or could crush and absorb its prey? "Evil, surrounded by a green mist."

"What is it doing?" Tremere got to his feet, buckling on his belt. Alan noticed for the first time the long sharp knives he carried and saw how grim his face could look. "It's unusual for anything other than marvinlings to venture this close to the pass. You mentioned soldiers?"

"Nivram National Army," Alan said. "Outside the main entrance."

"Good timing, perhaps," Tremere said. "They can help defeat this beast."

"They mustn't find us," Cathy said, clutching Tremere's sleeve. "They'll take us back to Lowdar."

"Is that where you come from? These soldiers sailed around the mountains and walked through East Nivram, like you did?"

Alan shook his head. "Couldn't have. They must have come through the forest."

"Impossible."

"Serand did it," Cathy said.

Tremere checked the fastening on his boots. "One man, perhaps, might pass through the forest unnoticed – though I doubt it – but not a battalion."

"Not without powerful aid." Alan thumped Cathy's arm. "Isn't that what Lucky said?"

"I thought she meant *magic*," Cathy whispered.

"Yeah – I bet those soldiers used magic to get through the forest. I bet they… I bet they disguised themselves as that horrible green monster." It all made sense to Alan now. Beneath the magical green mist, a group of soldiers left the troop to go to the caves, while the rest sat on the ground to wait. No wonder he and Cathy had so easily escaped a forest monster!

"I have no idea what you are talking about, but something underhand is going on," Tremere said. "Come, let us seek out the council and discover what's happening."

He strode purposefully from the cave, and the twins followed. The soldiers still waited at the main entrance but Tremere walked straight past them. Alan and Cathy kept close behind him.

"Thirty soldiers," Tremere muttered. "Well armed."

In the main chamber, Serand, Jensen, and four others sat at the council table engaged in earnest discussion, which ceased abruptly on Tremere's entrance. Several of the men shifted uncomfortably in their seats.

"Is this a high council meeting?" Tremere said brusquely. "Why was I not summoned?"

"It's nothing of importance," Jensen began, but Serand interrupted.

"If we could have found you, you would have known. Come, join us. Something has come up that we must discuss."

"Indeed?" Tremere remained where he was, although

Serand indicated an empty place at the table.

"A short while ago, two of our scouts apprehended a stranger who followed them down from the pass. He asked to speak with me. It appears he wishes permission for himself and his companions to proceed through the mountains."

"How does he know we hold the pass?"

"He watched it for some days. He says he is captain of a small unit of the Nivram National Army. While on an exploratory mission, they were attacked, and most of the troop lost. He believes it would be safer to travel home on the far side of the mountains, rather than return through the forest."

"It is remarkable they survived the forest this far," Tremere said. "I would give much to learn their secret."

"No secret but being well-armed, and having sufficient numbers to look after themselves, I warrant," Serand said. "Either way, they are here now, and I see no reason why we should not allow them passage."

"I advise caution," Tremere said. "Find out more about these men, and what their purpose is. We have lived as outcasts for many years, how can we be sure we will be left undisturbed?"

"Purpose?" Serand sneered. "What purpose could they have other than their stated one?"

"I do not know. But my lack of imagination should not mean we abandon sense."

"I believe they had some means of disguise to penetrate the forest," Serand said vaguely. "What we must decide now is whether or not to grant their request. I say let them through. This is our first contact with people other than criminals and exiles. If we obliged these men, they could be invaluable to us – obtain pardons, help us return home to our womenfolk and our families."

A murmur of agreement came from the table. Alan wanted to warn Tremere that the soldiers were lying but he could see Tremere didn't believe the story either.

"Let us put it to the vote." Serand raised his hand, his sleeve falling back. The dark smudge on Serand's wrist looked familiar but Alan couldn't think where he had seen it before.

Tremere was the only one who voted in favour of a delay. He shrugged. "I am taking these children to the castle. I shall warn Bardey of your decision." He ushered the twins out of the council chamber. When they were several paces away, he said, "I will accompany you on your journey. For a while, at least. I have grown weary of the forest. We shall take Tom with us as far as the castle and leave him with his father. Come, no time like the present."

Tom agreed to go with them, and soon all four they were ready to leave. The soldiers waited patiently by the cave entrance. Ignoring them, the travellers made their way through the forest. The spring sun was warm as they emerged from the trees and started the steep ascent to Peacemaker's Pass.

Alan stopped, half-way up the slope. He remembered where he has seen Serand's tattoo before.

"Serand is an imposter," he said. "I *knew* we'd met Serand before – and I've just remembered where. The army uniform reminded me. He's that colonel from Lowdar."

Cathy gaped at him. "Are you sure?"

"Certain. He has the same tattoo of a black rose. Which means he works for Witch Rose – *she* gave him the magic disguise."

"We've got to tell Lucky." Cathy's voice shook.

Alan agreed. "As soon as possible."

Tremere waited for them at the top of the slope.

"It's that horrible man," Cathy blurted out.

"Serand?"

Cathy nodded vigorously. "He's lying."

"He hasn't been lost in the forest for years," Alan said. "He was in Lowdar two weeks ago – we saw him."

"Are you certain it was Serand?"

"His name is Colonel Thrand. He has a tattoo on his right wrist," Alan said.

"I knew he was a bad 'un!" Tom said, delighted.

Tremere looked thoughtful.

"If this is the case, we will not let those soldiers enter the pass until we know the truth," he said. "Tom, go and tell the watchers on duty to let none but ourselves through. And continue to the castle and inform Bardey."

Tom nodded, taking Tremere's horse as well as his own, and hurried ahead.

"Now we confront Serand." Tremere turned but before they had gone many paces, he stopped. Soldiers moved among the trees. "Back to the pass."

Returning to the start of the pass, Tremere pointed to where the gully above his head was broken into several ledges. "Hide up there and stay out of sight."

Alan easily scrambled up to one ledge, positioning himself so that he could see without being seen.

"The soldiers are coming up the slope towards Tremere," he whispered to Cathy, who hadn't got his vantage point. "The soldier saluted Tremere and asked to enter the pass."

"I'm not deaf," Cathy said.

Tremere's reply rang out. "I cannot allow you do that."

The soldier's expression changed. "We have been given permission by the Forest men."

"That permission has been revoked."

The soldier glared at Tremere. His gaze shifted to the rocky channel of the pass, came back to Tremere, and finally rested on his own troops.

Alan tensed. Tremere was one man against thirty. Even if a couple of scouts hid in the pass, Tremere hadn't a chance. And what could he and Cathy do if it came to a fight?

The soldier took a step forward.

"Perhaps we are outnumbered." Tremere spoke softly, and Alan had to strain to catch the words. "But it is death to the first man who crosses into the pass without my permission. You may tell that to Serand, your leader." On these words, he withdrew into the pass.

"What happens now?" Alan said to Tremere.

"Now? We wait and see."

Serand was fetched. He walked arrogantly up to where Tremere had recently stood.

"You're making a mistake, Tremere." He took a step closer. With a whiz, an arrow shot through the air. Alan jumped. He hadn't noticed the scout somewhere among the boulders above. He still couldn't see him.

The arrow landed so close to Serand's foot that the leather at the tip of his sole was split. He took a hasty step backwards.

Tremere stood at the head of the pass.

Some of the soldiers drew their swords, and a dozen men raised bows.

Tremere remained where he was. "Any attack on me means Serand's death." Serand at once motioned them to lower their weapons. "Serand, I know you are a spy in our midst. Explain yourself."

Serand took a moment to answer. "Not a spy. I entered your camp solely to help my friends and in the nation's interests. We only wish to pass through the mountains in safety."

Alan didn't believe a word Serand said, and waited in trepidation to see what Tremere would do.

"Why the subterfuge?" Tremere said. "Why not just ask us?"

"I did not realise men of vision lived among the forest folk. But you are one, Tremere." Serand spoke eagerly. "This is an opportunity for all men to grasp. You have heard, no doubt, of Queen Rose of Cassis?"

Tremere shook his head.

Crouched behind the boulder, Alan nudged Cathy. "I *knew* it."

"She has hired a large portion of our army. Indeed, I answer directly to her, rather than to our own leaders."

"You are some kind of mercenary?" Tremere said.

"It is the way the army has operated for years. An ample source of revenue for the country."

"And for what purpose does this queen hire you?"

"What does the reason matter? We are to be well compensated for our pains. The quickest route to join her is through the pass, and we are already running several days late." Serand lowered his voice slightly. "I can make it worth your while."

"Explain."

"Total pardon for your crimes, for a start. Also, a share in our reward: a substantial cut of the income generated from working mines in these mountains. I had been told that they were laden with precious metals, but your caves alone hold more riches than I'd imagined."

"You plan to mine our mountains?"

Serand nodded, his eyes glinting. "Why not?"

"Mercenaries one day, miners the next," Tremere murmured. "Not for me, thank you. I trust you not, Serand, and I cannot allow you travel through the pass."

"You fool!" Serand shouted angrily after Tremere's retreating person. "You'll live to regret this. Stedson."

One of the soldiers stepped forward. "Yes, Colonel?"

"Mount a guard, Stedson. We'll drive them out yet."

Back in the gully, Alan heaved a sigh of relief. "Did you hear that? Tremere is not fooled by Serand."

"I knew he wouldn't be," Cathy said.

Tremere approached, and Alan said, "What happens now? Can you hold them back?"

Tremere smiled reassuringly. "We are perfectly safe. Two scouts watch each entrance to the pass. We can organise relief and supplies from the castle. We can hold out indefinitely, unless he is willing to sacrifice many men to conquer our few. Let us wait for a little while to see what he does next."

Alan fidgeted at the delay. Lucky needed to know about Serand but they couldn't leave the pass without Tremere. At least Serand was stuck on the wrong side of the pass. For now. Alan waited uneasily to see what Serand would do next.

Nothing happened.

Tremere and his scouts stood at the lookout post, and a guard of twenty soldiers watched from the forest edge. Alan and Cathy sat on the ledge and waited. It was hot and stifling in the pass; the shade disappeared with the afternoon sun.

Finally, Alan had had enough.

"Let's go. We'll find a way past the scouts."

He didn't realise that Tremere was within earshot.

"I'll take you to the castle now, if you are ready. I should have sent you down with Tom and Firefly," Tremere said.

Alan was relieved. He wanted to tell Lucky as soon as possible that the Nivram army was working for Witch Rose.

It was a long hot walk with another unpleasant surprise at the far end of the gully. One of the lookouts there approached Tremere and said, "I was about to send for you. Look."

On the grassy slopes below the pass, dozens of Nilken tents were spread, while many more were in the process of being erected.

"They've come to meet those soldiers in the forest," the guard informed them. "They were not pleased to find us, but we chased them off all right. Now they're laying siege."

The Nilken camp lay between the pass and the castle.

"I thought Nilkens were peaceable folk?" Tremere said. "I've heard Bardey speak of them as such."

"These ones are under a spell," Alan said.

Both Tremere and the lookout looked up at the interruption.

"Magic?" The scout gave a short laugh. "I've yet to see such a thing."

Alan could have told him of all that he had seen in the last

213

two weeks but he didn't care whether the scout believed him or not. He had more important things on his mind.

"What do we do now?" he said

Tremere gazed towards the castle. "We may be caught between the Nivram army and the Nilkens, but the Nilkens are also between us and Bardey. Supplies from the castle will not get through without a fight, but Bardey should easily rout them."

"Aye, but this is Nilken country," the scout said. "Bardey won't want to attack."

Alan started to count the tents. It seemed an awful lot of tents, even for Bardey's fighting skills.

"In that case, our sojourn here might be longer than anticipated," Tremere said. "What are your supplies like, Rasor?"

"A day or so," Rasor said. "If we ration them."

"Better start rationing." Tremere glanced at the twins and gave a faint smile. "Don't worry, Tom will have made it to the castle by now and filled in Bardey on recent events. He will take appropriate action."

Alan was doubtful. The Nilken force below them was growing larger; at least several hundred troops were amassing. Bardey had, at most, a couple of dozen. It seemed an uneven fight.

"In the meantime," Tremere said, drawing the twins aside, "I'd like to hear a bit more of your story. There's more to you than meets the eye."

Chapter Twenty-One
THE COUNCIL

Paul took a deep breath and entered the wooden tent. A long narrow table ran the length of the lopsey. A dark blue object, about two feet high and with several steps carved on it, was placed at the top.

Halfway up the box, on the uppermost step, the King of the Diamonds sat enthroned. Slightly shorter and broader than Lucky, he sparkled in such an agitated manner that it was far more difficult to determine his expression than his daughter's. Lucky stood on the step below her father, and below her, on each subsequent level, were two Diamond courtiers.

On either side of the table, stemming from the makeshift throne, and reaching half way down the table, was a line of Diamonds, a guard of honour, Paul knew.

The second half of the table was left free for the Witch's retinue. A Nilken stood on either side of the entrance. Above each, a torch burned, but this was the only artificial light.

The Diamonds were light in themselves, pure silver light that more than outshone the torches.

Paul was dazzled by the spectacle of so many Diamonds together. He slipped onto a chair placed at the top of the table and said nothing.

"Rose, Regent of Cassis," the sentries announced.

Witch Rose floated into the tent in a swirl of darkness, and the Diamond light seemed to dim. Paul hadn't expected her to be so beautiful. Her scarlet lips curved into a sweet smile. Her eyes were pools of darkness reaching deeply into Paul. He tore his gaze away lest she should harm him.

She was accompanied by two Nilkens, empty-eyed and uniformed. She seated herself at the foot of the table, and her Nilken guards stood behind her chair. Paul shivered from a sudden chill. He wished he had selected a seat other than one directly opposite the witch.

The king greeted his guest, welcoming her on behalf of a long list of names that Paul had never heard of.

The Witch rose to her feet to reply. Malice oozed from her but when she opened her lips, her voice was low and melodious.

"You referred to me as Regent of Cassis when I am, in fact, Queen. A small realm, I acknowledge – but mine own. In whatever name, however, I thank you for my welcome. I thank you also for granting me this audience, which I so long sought."

"Our pleasure," the King murmured.

The king, in Paul's opinion, was far too polite. Paul itched to denounce her for kidnapping him, for having him transformed into a stone, leaving the Kingdom of Kyle bereft of its leader. Until he looked at the Witch, and then he longed to slink away from the lopsey before she noticed him again.

"That this long-sought audience," the witch said, with only the slightest emphasis on *long*, "would be so public, I had no notion." Her gaze passed over each Diamond, lingering a few seconds on Lucky before turning to Paul. Her eyes bored into him once more. This time he was unable to look away as she probed his mind.

Warmth radiated from the Diamond throne and the spell was broken.

The King stirred impatiently, and the witch hurried into speech, reverting to her urbane tone. "But no matter. My reasons for seeking an interview…"

"Yes, yes, what's on your mind?"

"No light matter, King." Witch Rose's eyes flashed. "It concerns Nivram, its sad history and glorious future."

This seemed to catch the King's attention.

"Continue, please," he said.

The witch went on in her sweetest tones. "We are all of us familiar with the tragic tale of Princess Varya, daughter of the most gracious Diamond king, and how she lost her heart to a human who caused her death, leaving behind a legacy of twin babes. These children grew into adults, and to Princess Scatherina was given Eastern Nivram, and her brother Western Nivram. We know much about the young princess, how she loved birds and animals…"

Listening to the soft cooing voice, pictures of verdant

leaves, dappled by warm sunshine, and lambs gambolling on green pastures floated through Paul's mind. He could even hear larks singing. He knew he was being bewitched but couldn't help staring raptly at the witch as her persuasive voice continued.

"When she died…" A wave of sorrow engulfed Paul at the thought of Princess Scatherina's death, "…the world mourned, and rightly so. But of her brother, Prince Caralan, little has been learned. He retreated into the forest of mighty oaks and magnificent trees he had nurtured and tended and watched mature."

Paul saw tall trees bending in the breeze, and could almost hear the music of the leaves as the wind played them. Lucky and the other diamonds seemed far away, almost forgotten.

"He lived the lonely life of a hermit." The Witch's words struck Paul as being the saddest he had ever heard.

The trees were bare now and stark in the winter chill, but from the north came a faint beam of light, of hope.

"Although he welcomed all and sundry to his land," the witch said sorrowfully, "he may as well have been a leper, for no one visited. Until one day he met a girl from the north who had strayed into his domain. Unknown to the Diamond king, he now had a companion to share his burden, and they lived blissfully together for many years. Long was his life, far longer than is generally thought, but the shadow of death extinguished it in the end. Yet, they were happy years, and glad I am to relate it." She paused, and Paul, though he tried to fight it, was conscious of an upwelling of happiness also.

"You think that I speak with emotion? You are right, but I have reason: I am the offspring of that union."

Paul gasped. The Diamonds did not make a sound.

"Yes." The witch seemed to grow taller and more imposing as she spoke. "I am the descendant of Prince Caralan, and therefore the sole surviving heir of the royal twins. I have come to claim my inheritance."

With a light laugh, Lucky broke the silence that greeted these words. "*You*? In kinship with Diamonds? Ridiculous."

Relief swept over Paul. Lucky was not going to be fooled by such an evil creature.

"Preposterous," the King said hastily. He glowed brightly, dispelling some of the darkness emanating from the witch. "Unbelievable."

"I do not expect you to be overjoyed by the relationship," the witch said, with a sneer. "I ask only for justice. Although some may have thought you would be glad to learn that Caralan's descendants live, considering that Scatherina's line ended."

"What makes you so sure of that?" Lucky said.

"The castle was attacked, all occupants killed. Unless you believe that foolish tale of a daughter who survived the attack and lived in hiding among the Nilkens. Even if true, she must be long dead."

"I believe Scatherina's heirs still live," Lucky said firmly. A startled tinkling of Diamonds echoed through the lopsey. Paul straightened in his seat. Lucky had never told him this part of the story. "Therefore, your claim can only be for half of Nivram, at best."

The witch's brow darkened, and the black haze swirling about her expanded to engulf the room. Paul gripped the arms of his chair. His country's honour was at stake, and if the Diamonds did not flee, neither would he, no matter how terrifying the Witch was.

The King shone even brighter in response, and the vapour retreated and Paul breathed again.

"Prove it," the witch demanded harshly. "Prove that such an heir exists; produce the heir for my inspection. Where is your evidence?"

"How dare *you* ask *me* for proof of anything I say!" Lucky said indignantly.

"It *is* impertinent," the King agreed. "I would rather ask *you* – er – Queen Rose, for some good reasons to support your claim. Evidence for your sudden and unexpected connection to us."

"Sadly, I recall little of my early life." Witch Rose sat back in her chair, her voice dripping with melancholy. "As a babe, I was sent to my mother's country to be brought up by her family. It is only more recently that I have realised the significance of who my father was."

"I look forward to learning the details," the King said politely, but clearly in dismissal.

"Very well." The witch rose to her feet. "I shall return tomorrow at noon with my proofs. But if *hers* do not outshine mine, I shall claim the whole country."

On these words, she departed.

The lopsey grew bright, the Diamond light no longer challenged by darkness.

Paul shook himself, as if by doing so he could rid himself of the witch's impact.

"She means it," Lucky said.

"She might well be entitled to it," the King said mildly. "I may have to allow her to take possession. After all, daughter, yours is so tenuous a theory."

The Diamonds turned to each other to discuss the situation, and under the cover of their musical silvery voices, Paul spoke to Lucky.

"I don't believe she has any Diamond blood inside her veins. Why do you tolerate her? Cast her down before she uses a magic spell to take Nivram. She is wicked, through and through." And she would make a dangerous and evil neighbour for his kingdom, he thought, if the Diamonds allowed her take control of the country.

"She doesn't have that power. Only the King of the Diamonds, as guardian, can hand over Nivram to the control of another."

"Why does she want Nivram?" Paul couldn't understand it. "My country is much more beautiful."

"And perhaps many other countries are also. But we won't let that happen," Lucky said. "My guess is that she is motivated by her hatred for the Diamonds. Her own realm is tiny, and perhaps she would like the Nilkens as her slaves."

"She is a danger to the world." Paul could not understand why Lucky was so calm. "Why don't you crush her?"

"We are guardians, not executioners," Lucky said coldly. Then she smiled. "Guardians of the land and those who live on it, even the witch herself. We wish to stop her trampling over others. Otherwise she is free to do as she chooses. Now, I see my father is ready to leave – go and join the others. The Nilkens will look after you well tonight."

Paul swallowed his anger and exited the lopsey.

Chapter Twenty-Two
SIEGE

Cathy told Tremere everything, from the moment she found Lucky to when the mirehogs captured them. She hadn't meant to, but he managed to draw it all out. He seemed to believe everything she said too.

"I've learned enough to know that things are not always what they seem," he said. "And that sometimes the unlikely, even what seems impossible, is true."

"So, you'll let us join our friends at the Lake?" Alan said.

"Of course. Your family must be worried about you."

"And yours too," Cathy said impulsively. "Lucky will help you find them."

"If I have any," Tremere said.

The hot afternoon melted into cool evening. Tremere decided to return to the forest side of the pass. Serand's men had made a couple of half-hearted attacks, easily beaten off, according to the scout who made the report.

"He may be waiting until tonight for a real attack," Tremere said.

"What about the Nilkens?" Alan asked.

"We don't have many men in the pass – four, plus myself. I need to be where there is most danger. The men must sleep as well. Perhaps you would assist in keeping watch over the Nilken camp?"

Alan nodded eagerly. "You can count on us."

The scout called Rasor woke the twins for the second watch. It was still several hours to dawn. The Nilken camp was well lit with torches and bonfires, but Cathy couldn't see anyone moving. Princess Scatherina's castle glimmered in the starlight, but everything else lay in darkness.

Cathy yawned. Keeping watch had sounded exciting but was really boring. She wondered why Alan had been so keen to do it; he had already fallen asleep beside her. She yawned again and rested her head back against the rock.

When she opened her eyes next, the morning sun warmed the mountains and the valleys below. Alan was still fast asleep, his arms flung out and his head resting on a large boulder.

"Oh." Cathy remembered they were meant to be on lookout. She shook Alan's arm and looked around guiltily. The Nilken camp was still below, the enchanted Nilkens carrying out some army manoeuvres.

"Mmm," Alan said sleepily.

Already the sun was creeping into the pass. Cathy didn't want the scouts to find him asleep, so she shook Alan's arm more vigorously and cried, "It's a half-grolsch!"

Alan sat up. "Where?"

"Do you think someone will be here soon to relieve us?" Cathy was stiff and sore, hungry and even thirstier, and didn't want to do lookout duty again.

"Been here the last two hours," a voice above them said. Cathy looked up. A man was perched on a narrow ledge beneath an overhanging rock. "Didn't want to disturb you."

"Thanks," Alan said. "Where's Tremere?"

The scout jerked his head back towards the forest.

"Let's find him and see what's happening." Alan scrambled down from the lookout post. Cathy, trying to hide her embarrassment, followed.

Even at this early hour, the heat in the gully was building up between the walls. Alan set a fast pace, but it still took over an hour to reach the other lookout post. Tremere was with the scouts. He gave the twins a warm smile, although he didn't interrupt his discourse.

"We need to get supplies. Either from the castle or from the caves. Any suggestions?"

"Nilkens might be easier to get around," one of the scouts said. "Those soldiers look dangerous."

A shout from the forest interrupted him. Jensen stood at the entrance to the pass.

"Tremere," he shouted. "Have you gone mad? Why

won't you let these men through?"

"Because they are mercenary soldiers hired by a foreign queen," Tremere said. "Serand himself admits to being an impostor."

"Impossible." Jensen looked shocked. "I don't believe it."

Serand stood behind Jensen. "It's true. I am Colonel Thrand of the Nivram National Army. But come, I have a proposition for you."

Cathy watched Serand draw Jensen aside. Jensen nodded and clapped Serand on the shoulder before descending through the trees again. Cathy's heart sank.

"I fear he has convinced Jensen to join with him," Tremere said, voicing her thoughts.

A short while later, Jensen returned. To Cathy's surprise, he shouted out: "We have you surrounded, Serand. Throw down your weapons."

Dozens of the Forest men stepped out from the trees, with bows and swords drawn.

"This is foolish." Annoyance saturated Serand's voice. "My ally, General Cable, and a large force awaits me on the far side of the pass. I have several other units of troops waiting not far off in the forest; these men you see are only a part of my army. I do not want to see you all slain. I thought you were my friend, Jensen. See sense."

"I do not like to be fooled, and I will not betray my true friends. We shall take our chances with your army." Jensen's face was grim. "Put down your weapons."

Several of the Forest men came forward and disarmed

the soldiers. Once they were disarmed, Jensen called to Tremere.

"What would you have me do with them?"

"I'd like to send them back the way they came: through the forest."

"You can't do that," Serand said. He stood unresisting while his arms were bound behind his back. His confidence made Cathy nervous, like he knew something the Forest men didn't. "You'd send these men to certain death, unarmed in this forest."

"They've already survived it successfully," Tremere said.

"So they did," Jensen said. "What about that wonderful disguise ability you all have?"

"It won't work anymore, we've run out," Serand said. "We'll die."

"*We?*" Jensen repeated. "What makes you think you'll be joining them? We'll be keeping *you*."

Serand seemed faintly satisfied. Cathy did not trust him. "Don't forget, other soldiers are waiting in the forest," she reminded Tremere. "We saw hundreds of them."

Tremere summoned Jensen up to the lookout post.

"I'd rather Serand did not overhear every word. Most of his soldiers wait in the forest. More of them than us. Serand is too confident: he probably expects them to attack and rescue him."

Jensen groaned. "What can we do? Can't let this lot go in case they attack us. We'll need every man among us to watch the prisoners we have, and where can we hold them?" He glared at Tremere. "Why don't we let them through the pass? Let them go about their business and leave us alone?"

"They're not going to leave us alone," Tremere said quietly. "They'll kill us, either now or later, when they come back to mine these mountains."

Jensen hit his fist against the rock, and grimaced. "What should we do?"

"A Nilken force waits to attack us at the other side of the pass. I think we could surprise them tonight if you could hold Serand's people, and send me some men. If we clear the route to the castle, there's plenty of room to hold the soldiers there until we decide what to do with them."

"I'll see what we can do."

Jensen was about to turn away, when Tremere said, "Also please send some food and water, we're almost out here."

Jensen nodded and left.

Cathy was glad when Jensen returned a short time later with food and drink. She drained the canister and started on the bread.

Some way into the forest, a sudden commotion broke out. Shouts and cries for help erupted, loud and fearful enough to be heard by those in the pass. Cathy dropped her breakfast.

"What's going on?"

The soldiers began to mutter, and the Forest men

watching them looked unhappy.

"Are we being attacked?" Tremere left the lookout post, and ran out of the pass towards Serand. Grasping him by the collar, he shook the colonel.

"Are your soldiers attacking the caves? Answer!"

Cathy could see the sneer on Serand's face even from a distance. "What do you think?"

An explosion echoed among the trees. Cathy clutched Alan's arm.

"That's the emergency signal." One of the soldiers said, his face white. "The unit has met some hideous beast." He turned to Serand and began to shout. "You didn't leave them any protective potion. You left them to die!"

"Don't be ridiculous!" Serand bellowed.

Cathy watched the Forest men fall into argument among themselves, Tremere trying to calm them. "What will we do, Alan?"

"Let's get out of here," Alan said.

Cathy followed Alan through the pass, glad to be away from the forest and whatever monster was attacking the soldiers. Maybe the mirehogs were responsible, maybe something worse.

The castle-end of the pass came into sight. She could even see the green of the fields below, but as she got nearer, a scout raced towards her, buffeting her.

"Nilkens," he wheezed. "The... The Nilkens... are attacking. I'll get Tremere."

Then the scout was gone.

Cathy and Alan were left alone to defend Peacemaker's Pass from the Nilken army, swarming up the rocky slope towards them.

Chapter Twenty-Three
OVER THE BORDER

It was almost dusk when the witch emerged from the tent like a black shadow, and floated away, accompanied by her Nilken escort.

"I wonder where she's off to?" Vicky said.

"Lucky says her domain consists of a castle and its gardens and nothing else," Yvonne said.

Paul exited the lopsey and joined them in time to overhear. "Yes, but it is a floating realm. She can move it wherever she wishes as long as she has permission."

"Has she nowhere of her own to leave it?" Vicky said.

"I think it's a punishment," Yvonne said. "I'm not sure. Lucky wouldn't say anything more. What happened at the council, Paul? What did Witch Rose want?"

Paul opened his mouth to reply but at the same moment Current, the Nilken Lucky sent to look after them, came to announce supper was ready.

"I will tell all later," Paul said.

Yvonne was itching to hear but knew Paul was right to be discreet. The Nilkens had given them a cottage to stay in, one of several nestled at the foot of Mount Slant. Nilken-style, they were half-buried in the earth, and covered with grass and early spring flowers. Behind them, halfway up Mount Slant, a circle of stars were pressed into the mountainside. They shimmered beautifully. Current told her the stars marked the lower entrance to the Rock of Diamonds, home of the Diamonds, which was part of Mount Slant itself. Yvonne longed to have a closer look but she knew it was forbidden.

The main room was furnished with a couple of armchairs, a low table, and some cushions scattered on the stone floor. Despite the warm day, the evening was chilly so Yvonne was pleased to see the small fire burning in the grate. If only the twins were there, everything would be perfect.

Current waited on them at supper, supplying an abundance of food. Afterwards, the Nilken removed the table, the guests sat about the fire, and Paul related in detail what had taken place at the council.

"She wants to take over Nivram?" A shiver ran down Yvonne's spine, though she couldn't help but ask, "Why?"

"She claims it is her birth-right," Paul said. "If she was after my country, I could understand better."

"Your country must be beautiful," Yvonne said.

"You must visit, once Lucky gets rid of the witch and it is safe for me to go home," Paul said graciously.

Vicky stirred the logs in the fire, sending sparks flying up the chimney. "If she kidnapped you and Lucky, why don't the Diamonds arrest her, or something?"

"Lucky cannot prove it, and though the witch stared with hatred at us, she did not show her guilt at the council."

"What happens next?" Yvonne said.

"The witch is to bring evidence of her claim tomorrow," Paul said.

"I wish the twins were here," Yvonne said. She couldn't help being anxious about them.

"Charlie said the twins were safe with the Forest men," Vicky said. "They're escaped convicts, maybe from Paul's country – isn't that what Charlie said, Su?"

"In that case, I will grant them all a pardon." Paul gave a regal wave of his hand. "When I am king," he added, less grandly.

Vicky counted on her fingers. "How long is it since we left Lowdar? Is it a week or a month?"

Yvonne couldn't tell. The horrible, grimy town seemed so far away. She had almost forgotten she had ever lived there.

"It is five days since I met you," Paul said. "I have kept careful count."

"It's bedtime, for me anyway." Yvonne nudged Susan, who had been staring silently into the hearth all evening. "What about you, Susan?"

Vicky gave a great yawn, which set everyone else off.

The cottage had only one bedroom, which Yvonne insisted Paul should take. The rest curled up by the fire on bedding provided by Current. After the nights spent in the open air, the mattress by the fire was luxury, and Yvonne soon fell asleep.

Something woke her in the middle of the night. By the light of the glowing embers, she saw one person asleep on the floor and glimpsed a shadow slipping through the doorway. Yvonne pushed aside her bedclothes and hastily dressed herself.

Susan had been acting strangely all evening. She had not spoken a word, and simply gazed blankly at anyone who addressed her, almost as if she were in a trance. At the time Yvonne put it down to exhaustion, but now, as she left the cottage, she thought differently.

The moon was almost full and shed an eerie light on the landscape. Susan picked her way over this strange terrain as if she knew exactly where she was going. She proceeded initially for the Nilken lopseys, before cutting behind and beyond them, towards Paul's land. Scrambling along after her, Susan's destination dawned on Yvonne, and a cold terror gripped her.

Susan was heading for the witch's castle.

"Susan! Come back. Now." Yvonne called but Susan was either too far ahead to hear or too deeply enchanted to heed her.

Yvonne ran on, determined to drag Susan back.

But no matter how she hurried, Susan always remained ahead.

The land was hilly, with gentle slopes that rose imperceptibly until Yvonne, glancing back, was concerned to see how far Crocodile Lake was below them. She lost all track of time but guessed three or four hours had passed before they crested the final hill and began to descend.

She was grateful for the moon, for the north side of the Little Hills descended steeply down to a rocky ravine. Yvonne paused to catch her breath.

On the valley below, a shining black pyramid rose menacingly from the ground. Halfway up each side, small towers protruded like horns, their angry red turrets matching the huge red arch that was the yawning entrance. Witch Rose's domain, castle, and gardens, filled the width of the valley. A high hedge formed its boundary, with a wide opening facing south towards Nivram.

Susan, her head held high, walked towards the entrance, holding the stem of a dead rose before her.

The sight of the witch's abode filled Yvonne with terror. She sank to the ground, covered her head with her arms and groaned. "No, no, I don't want to go in there. I can't."

A hand touched her shoulder, and she jumped in fright. Turning her head fearfully, she gazed into Vicky's eyes.

"Saw you leaving and followed you," Vicky whispered. "What's going on?"

"I think Susan is under a spell," Yvonne said. "She's gone into Witch Rose's castle."

Vicky bit her lip. "So Susan's rose was enchanted after all. What are we going to do?"

"We'll have to go in after her and bring her back."

"But the witch will catch you as well."

"We have no choice." Yvonne was absolutely certain of that, although she dreaded following Susan into Witch Rose's domain.

Vicky stared at the ground. "Perhaps I'll stay here as

lookout? Or should I go back for help?"

Yvonne said nothing for a moment, bitterly disappointed. The last thing she wanted to do was to go any closer to the cruel turrets and fiery entrance of the pyramid. She didn't think she could enter it without Vicky. As she stared at the evil dwelling, Susan disappeared through the hedge. Yvonne made up her mind.

"Go back and tell Lucky." She felt sick at the thought of going in alone, but at least Vicky would be safe. "Do me a favour? Mind this for me." She removed her chain and key from about her neck and pressed it into her sister's hand. One witch nearly got hold of the tiny silver key, and she had no wish for another to do better. Hastily bidding farewell, she rose to her feet and started down the rubble-strewn slope that led to the barren vale below.

She passed through the broad gap in the thorny hedge without hesitation. Everything inside the grounds was a grey hue, from the exotic flowers to the statues dotted on the colourless grass. The black triangular castle loomed above her. Susan had melted from sight.

The huge, arched entrance cast a dull, red glow on the nearby plants. It was not a normal gateway, opened and closed by the human hand. It was rather a living curtain of flaming red, which vibrated and pulsed and even hissed. Yvonne's heart quailed as she drew near it. The thought of Susan, already within this fortress, drove her on. She took a step forward and passed through the roaring red curtain.

She expected fire. Instead, a bitingly cold substance froze her blood, but almost immediately Yvonne found herself on the far side, and she gasped with relief. She was in a huge black hall whose steeply sloping sides met in a vaulted roof. It was lit only by the red glow from the curtain and two crimson torches mounted high on the walls. The floor and the walls were all made of the same black metal as the exterior of the pyramid. It was deadly cold, causing Yvonne to shiver violently. The sound of echoing footsteps caught her attention. She peered through the gloom and glimpsed a figure disappearing into the darkness at the far end of the hall. It had to be Susan. Yvonne forced herself onward.

At the back of the hall was a small doorway, opening into an unlit passage. Yvonne moved cautiously along it, arms outstretched, feeling her way. It had been too easy to enter the witch's home. The sensation of walking into a terrible trap grew stronger, and she felt the witch's malevolence dripping from the walls.

Turning a corner, Yvonne entered another chamber, similar in dimensions to the first. This room was crowded with shadowy figures. At first, Yvonne took them for people, until she noticed the variety of shapes and sizes. Some were human and others inhuman. She didn't dare breathe until she realised that only statues, interspersed with pillars, thronged the room.

A flash of colour caught her eye.

Susan.

Yvonne slipped among the silent grey figures after her sister.

Susan headed to the far end of the room, where an imposing triangular throne was flanked by two enormous hearths. Fires roared in both of these, but Yvonne's attention was drawn to where Queen Rose sat waiting for Susan. Roses were fastened in the witch's hair and covered her feet. She looked both beautiful and terrifying. Yvonne, hiding behind one of the pillars, felt her limbs go weak.

Susan stopped immediately before the throne.

"Well, well, what have we here?" The queen spoke in dulcet tones. "Look what my rose has brought me. Where did you come from, my dear?" She addressed Susan kindly, while the flower stem that Susan still held disintegrated.

"From Lowdar," Susan said, in a dream-like voice.

"Lowdar," the witch repeated softly. "And what are you doing so far from home?"

"Taking Lucky home."

The witch looked at her with dislike. "Indeed? You must be one of the six. My immense magical powers warned me that trouble would come from six children. I heard how five children rescued that idiot prince from the trap I left him in. I dispatched some of my minions to search for you, but that dolt Cable could not even hold two when he had them. When I saw that *thing* at the conference, I should have guessed it was through your interference she made it back here. I would have enjoyed learning of the demise of that meddlesome creature, my enemy for so long. But no matter, it will make little difference now."

Susan stood immobile and silent before the throne. The witch stretched out her arm, and with one long finger tilted Susan's chin so she could better observe her face. Susan did not resist.

"Something about you," the witch mused. "Some – feature – resists my influence, yet your eyes tell me that you are wholly mine. You tried to be a nuisance to me, but you failed, as your kind will always fail against me." She laughed, a deep hollow laugh drawn up from the evil roots of her castle. Yvonne shuddered at the sound.

"You have gained nothing by freeing the prince. I only needed him in case I was refused access to his country. I had troops on standby, but the fools were happy to let me in." The witch laughed again. Susan did not react.

For a few moments, Witch Rose silently studied Susan.

"Power emanates from you..." The witch's voice grew harsh as she grasped Susan by the shoulder and pulled her forward. "You don't have that *thing* with you, do you? No, I would have felt her presence the moment she entered my domain. You have something else: what is this?" A hand slipped under Susan's collar. Yvonne heard a snap, and the witch held aloft a slim velvet pouch. From it, she pulled out Susan's flute, its sheen dulled by the red glow. The witch laughed a third time, and this time her laugh grew louder as it reverberated around the mighty hall. Louder and louder. Yvonne covered her ears and the statues trembled, some starting to crumble, little grey flakes falling softly to the floor.

"Do you have *any* idea of what this is?" The witch spoke in silken accents. "No, of course you don't, you poor fool. But you have given me a powerful gift, and my success is now assured." She clapped her hands and instantly a number of Nilken guards stepped forward. Yvonne was startled, she had not been aware of their presence. "Take this child away and imprison her somewhere. And all of you leave me."

The Nilkens led away an unresisting Susan. Yvonne, hidden behind a statue halfway across the room, was left alone with the witch. The queen remained on her throne, smiling in Yvonne's direction. At first, Yvonne thought that the witch was staring at her. Soon she realised something else was absorbing the witch's attention. A wave of the witch's hand had transformed a large section of the black wall behind Yvonne into a kind of screen. A confusion of colourful images played against it, each briefly appearing before being rapidly succeeded by another. Every picture contained scenes of agony and suffering, of death and destruction. Yvonne gasped at the horror of it. At the same moment, a hand with fingers of cold steel gripped her shoulder and a vice-like grip dragged her out from behind the statue.

"What have we here? A spy?" an angry voice demanded. Yvonne peered up, terrified, into the burning eyes of the witch.

Queen Rose dragged Yvonne behind her as she stalked back to her throne, and flung Yvonne on the floor before her.

"I shall grind you into fertiliser for my roses," the witch snarled. "Or feed you alive, limb by limb, to the nearest dragon. Or merely have you horribly tortured by my faithful Nilkens. Which is it to be?"

Yvonne couldn't answer. Terror stole her voice,

"What are you doing here?" The witch leaned over her.

"I know you: I saw you outside the council earlier. Speak before I truly lose my temper."

Yvonne opened her mouth to answer, swallowed, and tried again. "I want my sister." Her voice was a croak in her ears, and she barely managed to force the words out.

The witch laughed. "You fool. She is under an enchantment – it would take someone very powerful to make her leave here. You shall join her, and I will send you both to the Pit of Eternal Sighs."

Yvonne quaked in terror. "No, no, please don't do that."

A cruel smile played about the lips of the witch. "You are not the first to beg before me. Nor shall you be the last. Look about you – see these statues? Every enemy I ever had stands in this room. After each one's defeat, I sculpt their effigy so that I can contemplate my past victories and laugh. Perhaps you shall adorn this room one day? Look at those images yonder…" The witch nodded at the wall where all this time the pictures had continued to blink and flash. "They are my memories, which I had bottled. See." She pointed a finger at them. The light died, the images faded, and Yvonne could see a clear panel was set in the wall. In the recess behind it was a glass phial filled with a sparkling green liquid. The witch pointed her finger again, and instantly that section of the wall was covered with quickly passing pictures of battles and oceans, dragons and ogres, and creatures that Yvonne could not even guess at. But human or otherwise, they all had one thing in common: despair was etched on every face.

"I look forward to including the sorry end you and your sister shall have." A gloating smile lit up the witch's face. "As friends of my most hated enemies, it will be particularly satisfying."

Yvonne feared for herself and Susan. Her only hope lay in Vicky. She tried not to think of the long walk back to the lake or whether Vicky could get to Lucky in time.

"And now to deal with you." Queen Rose raised her finger once again, and the pictures on the wall faded to nothing. She clapped her hands, and instantly half a dozen solemn-faced Nilkens ran in.

"Take this prisoner to join the other, and guard them closely."

Yvonne was surrounded by the Nilkens and hustled away.

Chapter Twenty-Four
THE THEFT

Vicky watched Yvonne walk down the slope towards the pyramid, awed by her sister's courage. Though mostly she was overcome with shame by her own cowardice. In Lowdar. she boasted of being brave – no building too high to be climbed, no dare too wild to be taken. Now it dawned on her she only did things that frightened others but not her. Faced with *real* danger, she wanted to run like a coward back to Lucky, abandoning Susan to the witch.

"I won't let you be a snivelling scaredy-cat," she said aloud. Exerting all her willpower, she raised her right foot and placed it firmly in front of the left. "Yes, you're afraid, but so was Yvonne, and she went in. Are you going to let everyone know that Yvonne is braver than you?"

Her left foot reluctantly followed her right. Keeping her eyes on the ground and trying not to think of the witch's castle, she forced herself down the slope and into the witch's domain. She hesitated momentarily at the fiery curtain, took a deep breath, and stepped through. It didn't burn or vaporise her, as she expected. Instead it felt soft and damp. She made her way through the chambers and passageways, using the faint sheen from her telescope to help find her way.

The sight of the throne room, with its statues and pillars, terrified her, and she shrank into the shadows at the doorway. Hearing voices, she held her telescope to her eye. Now she could see the statues clearly, and Yvonne hiding behind one of the pillars. The telescope moved to Queen Rose. The close up of the witch's face was too much for Vicky. She dropped the telescope, fortunately managing to catch it before it clattered to the floor.

It took her a moment to gain the courage to look again. She was in time to see Yvonne's horrified face as the witch seized her and dragged her to the throne.

With the telescope pressed against her eyes, Vicky could hear every word of the conversation between the gloating witch and her eldest sister.

"They are my memories, which I had bottled," Queen Rose said. "See."

Vicky followed the witch's pointing finger and shook in revulsion at the images on the far wall, the telescope displaying every agonising detail. It occurred to her that if the phial contained all the witch's memories, perhaps it was also the witch's evidence, proof of her claim to Nivram.

Yvonne was taken away, and Vicky left alone with the witch. She gripped the telescope tightly, afraid to look at the witch but more afraid to look away.

Queen Rose gazed at the replay of her memories with obvious enjoyment. Eventually she snapped her fingers and the images extinguished. With a swish, she rose gracefully to her feet and departed.

Vicky slowly let out her breath. While the witch watched her memories, Vicky had been struck with a brilliant idea. If she stole the phial, the witch would not be able to prove her claim to Nivram.

Which would be a good thing. Nivram would be safe from her wickedness.

Trembling with a mixture of excitement at her daring plan, and fear of being caught, Vicky slipped quietly over to the far wall.

She couldn't open the panel. It had neither handle nor catch. Vicky kept searching, her fingers running over the cold surface.

"Aha." Her fingers discovered a tiny keyhole. If only she could find the key.

But she *had* a key. She was carrying Yvonne's gift. Fingers trembling in anticipation, she drew the delicate silver key from her pocket. She knew it would not work for her. After all, no one else could use her telescope, only Susan could play the flute, and the words on Cathy's compass were incomprehensible to the rest of them. The key would only work if Yvonne was there to turn it.

Yet she still went ahead and fitted the key into the keyhole.

She glanced nervously over her shoulder. Nothing stirred in the dim and dismal hall. Holding her breath, she twisted the key.

The key turned easily, the glass door clicked open, and her fingers wrapped around the phial. It was icy to touch, and she placed it carefully in her pocket. It would be awful to drop it.

She had to get out of the pyramid castle, quickly, before she was discovered. Vicky tried not to think of what the witch would do to her if she were caught. Retrieving Yvonne's key, she hastily retraced her steps through the pyramid.

She couldn't rescue Yvonne and Susan on her own. Their best chance lay in her getting to Lucky as quickly as possible. As she returned to the fiery entrance of the castle, she expected the thumping of her heart would bring on an army of guards.

She met no-one.

A few moments later she was through the red curtain and out of the pyramid, blinking in the sudden light of early morning. She ran through the witch's gardens and exited her realm. Nobody came after her.

Ahead was the steep climb out of the desolate valley. Her route looked more precarious by dawn than it had by moonlight. Halfway up the slope, she found she could only lift her feet with great effort. Her night time exertions and lack of sleep were taking their toll. Even the witch's memories, small though the phial was, weighed her down. By the time she reached the highest ridge and was back on Nivram soil, she was exhausted. She dropped down behind a large boulder for a breather.

"Two minutes," she murmured, closing her eyelids.

She woke to the sound of marching feet. Her sleepy eyes fell on a line of more than a hundred uniformed Nilkens tramping towards Crocodile Lake, a blue gleam visible in the distance. In their midst, a couple of inches above the ground, floated the witch.

Vicky crouched down behind the rock, terrified. Fortunately, no one glanced in her direction, for they could not have failed to see her. The cavalcade moved on tirelessly. Soon Vicky would have been unable to catch up with it, even if she wished to. It was only when they were well ahead that she risked continuing her own journey, furious with herself for having fallen asleep. Maybe the witch was looking for her, for the theft must have been discovered by now. How had Witch Rose reacted when she realised her evidence was stolen? What would she say to the Diamonds? Maybe the king would hand the thief over to the witch for punishment? Or perhaps the witch had already inflicted retribution, but on Susan and Yvonne instead of the real culprit?

Driven by these thoughts, Vicky rushed down the hillside. She wasn't sorry she had taken the phial, but the dread of repercussions dominated her thoughts. Recalling Yvonne and Susan's plight after a little while, she forgot her other fears.

Vicky hurried as fast as she could, but it still took her the best part of two hours to scramble down the slope. By the time she arrived, the conference had already begun.

She hesitated before running to the lakeside. To her relief, Charlie was there, paddling aimlessly.

"Charlie! Charlie!" she called.

Charlie swam over. "Hello. There you are. We thought you and your sisters had done a bunk with the valuables:

where have you been? I was almost worried."

"Susan and Yvonne are prisoners of Witch Rose."

Charlie gaped at her. "What?"

"Susan had a spell cast on her and went to the witch's realm last night. Yvonne and I followed, but Yvonne was captured as well. So I stole Witch Rose's memories and ran back here for help." She didn't mean to mention the phial but couldn't help blurting it out.

"You stole her memories?" Charlie looked confused.

"Yes, she keeps them in a bottle. It's her evidence, proof that Prince Caralan was her father…"

"Never mind that now. Go at once to the pavilion and hand the phial over."

"But…"

"You'll be in bigger trouble if the witch catches you with it. Tell Lucky about Susan and Yvonne. I'll get the Nilkens together and we'll go immediately to rescue them. We've no time to waste."

"But she'll prove her claim to Nivram. She'll destroy it," Vicky cried.

"You don't understand, do you?" Charlie said. "If she is truly Caralan's heir, she is entitled to Nivram, half anyway, if not the whole country. But we will never allow her to destroy it; we are still guardians of Nivram."

Vicky hesitated.

"You must tell Lucky," he urged.

"All right."

"Good girl." Charlie gave her an encouraging smile. "Now hurry."

Chapter Twenty-Five
EXPOSED

Paul rose late, for the council was due only to reconvene at midday. The absence of all three sisters did not unduly concern him. He assumed they were on some business of their own, and so he told Current, who arrived with breakfast.

Afterwards, he resumed the same place at the council table and waited in trepidation for the witch to return. Reminding himself that Lucky and the king were there, and Charlie close by, he still could not banish his fear of seeing her again. What was worse, if the Diamonds allowed Witch Rose to take control of Nivram, he was sure that the kingdom of Kyle would be next on her list. After all, it was a much more beautiful country, with a vast amount of wealth, and many industrious and loyal people. Could his army defeat a witch who had been able to snatch Lucky against her will? He doubted it.

Queen Rose arrived punctually, floating into the presence

of the King of the Diamonds as she had done the previous day – proud, arrogant, and supremely confident. The darkness that surrounded her again seemed to absorb and diminish the pure light of the Diamonds.

Paul shifted in his seat, and didn't look at her face.

An air of tense expectancy rippled among the Diamonds.

The witch was accompanied by two Nilkens bearing a large oaken chest, which they placed carefully on the ground. During the exchange of formal greetings, Paul could not keep his eyes from the chest.

Queen Rose remained standing, towering over all the occupants of the room, and spoke sweetly. "I have brought my proof – where is yours? I'd like to meet your heir."

"Let us hear your case first," Lucky said.

The witch waved a languid hand. Two Nilkens sprang for the heavy casket. Both strained to throw open the lid, releasing a cloud of fine dust. Paul coughed. It was probably a magical or poisonous powder, specially prepared by the witch. He looked at Lucky but she hadn't reacted. Maybe he was wrong about the dust.

A huge leather-bound volume was removed from the chest and tenderly handed to Queen Rose. She placed it gently on the table. It looked ancient, with frayed covers and disintegrating yellowed paper that crackled as she turned the pages.

"My father's diaries," the witch announced.

Paul craned his neck forward. He could see, though not decipher, a tiny spidery hand that closely covered page after page. The King of the Diamonds rose from his throne.

Together with Lucky and a Diamond who was bent and elderly, they made their way down the table for a closer look.

"I can't read this." The old Diamond's voice was weak and faded. "It's in code, a code resembling that used by Prince Caralan, but I cannot be sure without a closer examination. May I spend some time with this volume?"

"I cannot allow that," the witch said. "My father bequeathed little to me and I shall not allow anything but a cursory inspection."

"It looks genuine," the ancient Diamond said after a few minutes. "It is old enough to be so."

"You should know, Dulstar," the King said. "You taught Prince Caralan how to write."

"I believe it to be the prince's handwriting," Dulstar finally pronounced. "As far as I can tell without further study."

Triumph radiated from the witch. She seemed to fill the lopsey with her gloating presence. Paul dreaded the moment when the king would recognise her parentage.

"But surely that is not proof?" A young Diamond said nervously. "I mean, the fact that Prince Caralan's belongings are in her possession is not conclusive proof of paternity."

"True, true," the king said.

"How else would I have them? Who else would know where my father kept them hidden? I have more evidence to follow. But first I would like to know whether I am proving my claim to all Nivram or not."

"You are establishing your relationship to Caralan," the king corrected her severely. For a moment, he shone with such intensity that Paul had to shield his eyes. "As for my daughter, she believes that she has found the Lost Flute of Thule."

"The Lost Flute of Thule," the witch repeated softly. The smile lingering on her lips frightened Paul. "The Flute, the gift of the Goldener People, handed down for generations through Scatherina, until it was eventually lost along with her descendants. The legends say that it will always remain with the lawful owner – you think that possession of the flute is evidence enough of someone's ancestry?"

The king nodded.

"Deny my claim no longer," the witch thundered. From the recesses of her gown, and with a scattering of more of that golden dust, a flash of silver gleamed as she cast something onto the table. It was a flute, wrought from the purest silver, and etched with intricate designs. Paul had never seen such a beautiful instrument. Except for Susan's flute.

A startled tinkling ran among the Diamonds.

Orange, red, and blue light flashed through the lopsey as the king shot off a kaleidoscope of colourful sparks before speaking.

"That is indeed the Flute of Thule. Without any doubt."

"No doubt," Lucky repeated in a dazed tone. "Where did you get it?"

Queen Rose inhaled sharply, and the lopsey once more darkened. "You, of all things, should know that the Lost Flute of Thule will inevitably make its way to its rightful owner."

Dulstar walked the length of the flute as it lay shimmering on the table.

"Hmm. It is damaged, I believe. Some of the ancient symbols are missing. It is as if the lower section was removed, or a small part of it, leaving it somewhat shorter than the original…"

"You fool." The witch spoke contemptuously. "Can you not see the power emanating from it?"

The flute shone with a pure silver light that equalled the white light of the Diamonds, and the symbols etched upon its length blazed with fire.

"Indubitably," Dulstar said, "it is very powerful. And certainly of Thule workmanship."

"It is clearly the flute in question," the king said. "You concur, Dulstar?"

"It is ancient enough. The symbols look authentic, I believe…" As if he felt that the king was anxious to hurry him along, Dulstar quickly added, "It is slightly damaged, but undoubtedly it is the legendary Flute of Thule, as claimed."

The king cleared his throat. "In that case –"

He was interrupted. Vicky burst into the council.

"I'm sorry, Lucky, but Charlie said I should…" She spoke breathlessly, as if she had been running. "The witch has Susan and Yvonne."

Paul gasped.

"And she's bottled her memories, and I took them so she couldn't prove that she's heir to Prince Caralan, but Charlie told me to take this directly to you." She held up a cut-glass

253

phial filled with a shimmering green liquid.

Witch Rose gave a shriek that shook the slanted lopsey and must have ruffled the waters of Crocodile Lake. Her arm shot out to grasp the phial. Vicky dodged the witch's hand, but stumbled as she did so. As she tried to regain her balance, the phial flew from her fingers and across the table where it shattered into a thousand fragments.

A cry of alarm rose from the Diamonds as hundreds of flickering shadows instantly leaped up and towered over them. Some were of strange inhuman shapes, others of deformed animals, and still more grotesque creatures. They filled the tent, their shadowy heads brushing against the ceiling as they gyrated around the table in a macabre dance.

The silver flute rolled off the table, and Vicky dived to retrieve it.

"Thieves! Scoundrels! Traitors of a sacred trust!" the witch shrieked. "You will regret this!" She moved away hastily, thrusting aside everything in her way, and stormed out, forgetting her casket, Caralan's diaries, and the Lost Flute of Thule.

Paul ducked for safety beneath the table. The shadows emitted terrible groans of despair as they circled the table at an ever-increasing speed. Vicky and the Nilkens guards shivered beside him, and the quaking of the Diamonds vibrated the table.

"Somebody get a bottle to contain these horrible things. Hurry!" The king shouted.

Everybody was too terrified to move. Paul covered his ears in a vain attempt to block out the fearful noise of Queen Rose's memories.

Then the shadows were gone.

Paul breathed a sigh of relief and crawled out from under the table.

"Such miserable unhappiness I have never seen before," the king said, much moved. Paul had only seen shadows, but it was obvious that the Diamonds had been able to perceive more substance to them. "What have they been captured in? I must dispose of them… He broke off.

Paul stared in astonishment.

Lucky had turned bright green.

"No container to hand," she gasped.

"Quickly," the king said. Without the shadowy forms to terrify him, one of the Nilkens scampered off, returning almost immediately. A moment later, a small glass bottle was filled with the memories of Witch Rose, and tightly corked. Lucky still retained a faint greenish tinge.

Paul found his voice. "How did you get such a thing?"

"Yvonne and Susan," Vicky said frantically, not answering his question. "The witch has captured them. They're in her castle, over the hills –"

"Why didn't you say so earlier?" the king grumbled. "She has a good head start on us now."

"Is Charlie outside?" Lucky said.

Vicky nodded.

Lucky addressed her father. "Lift your ban on Charlie, allow him to take passengers. He can fly us all to the witch's den. We'll get there before her."

The king hesitated, but only for a moment, before consenting.

Charlie was waiting outside, standing awkwardly on his paddle-like feet.

"I've sent a contingent of Nilkens to the witch's castle," he said.

"Please fly us there too," Lucky said.

"Certainly," Charlie said, as if he normally flew with passengers. "Hop aboard."

Paul clambered into the canoe, and held on tightly to the sides. His stomach gave a lurch as Charlie rose into the air.

Chapter Twenty-Six
THE REALM OF QUEEN ROSE

Vicky's hair was blown back from her face, and the air pumped from her lungs as Charlie flew over the Little Hills towards the border with Paul's country. Fear that they would be too late for Yvonne and Susan fought with terror of the dreadful reprisals the witch would carry out for Vicky's theft. She couldn't speak, even if she wanted to. Grasping Charlie's side, she peered at the hills thirty feet below.

It didn't take long to fly over the Nilkens Charlie had despatched to Kyle. They marched purposefully up the lower slopes, but it would take them several hours to reach the black pyramid.

Where was the witch?

In the distance, a streak of black appeared. Charlie increased his speed. Vicky could see the witch's guard scattered on the hills, unable to keep up with her.

The thought of Susan and Yvonne held captive by the

witch tied Vicky in a knot of anxiety which tightened every moment, until she convinced herself the witch had already done her worst to them.

If only she hadn't fallen asleep...

She felt for her telescope for comfort. Somehow its warmth through the velvet pouch gave her hope that Charlie would beat the witch to the pyramid and rescue the others before Witch Rose could make her whole realm vanish elsewhere.

Charlie gained on the witch, and soon Witch Rose was only several canoe lengths away. She sped effortlessly a foot above the stony earth as she approached the border. The canoe drew level, and although Charlie was twenty foot above her head, Vicky could feel the menace emanating from Queen Rose, and the power of her dark gaze. Charlie drew ahead, and passed into the kingdom of Kyle.

The black pyramid was in sight, and despite Lucky's presence, Vicky felt all the horror of the place once more.

As Charlie began the descent into the valley, a flock of birds rose from the pyramid and headed towards them. As they drew nearer, Vicky saw that the birds were catchills, their beaks open to attack as they dived at Charlie.

Charlie cried out but kept going. More catchills surrounded the flying canoe. Vicky screamed as razor edged feathers brushed against her cheek. A catchill grasped her shoulder, and she whacked it with her telescope. It fell back with a shriek. Another attack came. Two catchills seized her at the same time and pulled.

With both arms gripped by the creatures, Vicky couldn't

lash out with her telescope. She screamed, as she rose upwards, the catchills lifting her into the air.

A shower of light burst from Charlie's interior, hundreds of tiny sparks converged on the catchills, penetrating their feathers. Vicky was released, and she dropped onto Charlie's wooden floor, as one by one the gigantic creatures of the air wheeled away from the flying canoe and fell to the rocky valley below.

Vicky, her cheek bleeding and arms aching, scrambled back to her seat and looked for the witch. The catchills had delayed Charlie, and Witch Rose was almost at the pyramid.

Charlie strained harder as the canoe and the witch raced neck and neck. Slowly Charlie inched ahead, and all of a sudden, he had beaten the witch. He flew over the hedge and landed with a thud in front of the fiery curtain.

Vicky stared at the imposing walls and the red mouth that was the entrance. For a moment, she didn't move.

"Come on, Vicky." Paul jumped onto the black grass. "Where to?"

Vicky trembled, dreading entering the pyramid again. Where would she even look for her sisters? But then she heard voices. One of them sounded like Yvonne.

"Over there." Without waiting for the others, she leaped out of the canoe and raced around the side of the witch's castle.

Thick, healthy rose bushes, heavily laden with dark blooms, surrounded a wrought iron bench where Yvonne and Susan sat. Half a dozen Nilkens stood guard.

"Oh no!" Yvonne looked devastated. "Vicky, I was sure you had got away."

Before Vicky could reply, Paul appeared by her side, followed by Charlie who was awkward and slow on land. Lucky and the king remained out of sight.

Yvonne jumped joyfully to her feet. "Charlie! I'm so glad to see you. Though the Nilkens have been quite nice to us. Once they saw how upset we were this morning – especially Susan – they let us sit out in the sun. But they won't let us move from this garden."

"They won't be able to stop me," Charlie said. "Hop aboard and we'll be off."

Yvonne stepped forward eagerly, dragging Susan, and they both climbed into Charlie. The Nilkens watched helplessly.

Vicky had barely taken her seat when a black shadow fell across the canoe, and the day felt cold as night.

"I can stop you, you miserable canoe." Witch Rose towered above Charlie and his passengers. "None who enter my domain can leave if I withhold my permission."

Charlie made an effort to rise into the air, but could not leave the ground.

The witch laughed evilly. "See? Here shall you stay, and you shall fuel the fire that will fry your human friends." She broke off abruptly.

The Diamond king appeared. He stood on Charlie's head and gazed sternly at the witch.

"Foolish creature. Miserable wretch, to think that you can defy the guardians of these lands."

"You are on my domain now, over which you have no control. My land was never under your miserable guardianship."

She laughed, a low sinister noise that sent a chill into Vicky's heart.

As the sound persisted, the witch started to grow. Taller and taller, with fire and lightning darting from her eyes and scorching the ground around Charlie, until it seemed as if the whole sky had darkened, so great was the shadow with which she covered them. Vicky cowered in the canoe, hiding her head beneath her arms, too terrified to raise her eyes to the horrendous spectacle the witch presented.

She couldn't understand why Lucky was so silent in the face of the enemy who sent the half-grolsch to destroy her. Surely the Diamond wasn't going to allow the witch to win? Peering between her fingers, Vicky saw the others cringing on the floor of the canoe. Where was Lucky?

In the darkness which covered Queen Rose's realm, only the king stood before her, shining brightly in the gloom.

The witch's voice boomed as she said: "Why, I could pick you up and crush you between my fingers." She held up an enormous hand, her fingers gigantic cruel talons.

"Paul," Lucky's voice was weak. "Paul."

It took Vicky a moment to spot the Diamond. Lucky, a faint unhealthy tinge of green, stood close to the prince. When she called his name the second time, he raised his head slightly to look at her.

"Paul," Lucky spoke again, still with difficulty. Vicky had to concentrate to hear the words. "We are in *your* land – you can banish her by revoking her permission to be here."

Paul looked pale. He swallowed nervously and replied: "Yes. Of course I can." Raising his head above Charlie's rim, he shouted up quickly at the gargantuan figure high above him. "I am Prince Paul Alexander Rovesvitch Ivan Kylovsky. You have been resident in my country by consent of my regent, which was fraudulently obtained. By the throne of Rowena the Great, I revoke this permission. You are no longer welcome in my land."

The witch laughed in amusement. She swooped down to stare more closely at the prince, who immediately ducked low in the canoe.

"Who can make me, you miserable specimen?" As she straightened up, she grasped the King of the Diamonds and held him between two claws. "Why, this has worked out even better than I thought. I never thought I'd able to lure you into my realm where I reign supreme. I shall crush you to Diamond dust."

Vicky was sick with fear at these words. She looked to Lucky for help but the Diamond merely smiled faintly in response.

"You forget one thing," the king said. "You are no longer welcome here, your powers count as nothing."

"Really?" The witch sounded contemptuous and squeezed her talons around the king.

Vicky wanted to turn away but something compelled her to look at the king radiating brightly, and the flashing eyes of the witch. As she watched, a mysterious thing happened. At first, there seemed to be a struggle, a battle of wills between the two. The witch lost her smirk and frowned in anger, trying to crush the king. The Diamond king started to glow intensely. Brighter and brighter he shone, while the black figure of the witch began to diminish. Soon the shadow she cast above them shrank back and the sunlight shone throughout the garden once more.

"You broke the ancient ordinances of your existence." The king spoke again when the witch was once more her true size, although she was many times angrier than before.

"I *shall* have control of Nivram. My armies are already attacking and winning," Witch Rose said, her face distorted with hatred. "I shall not spare a single drop of Nivram blood." She glared defiantly at the king, but he held and returned her gaze as he became increasingly luminous. Finally Vicky could bear the blazing light no longer, covered her eyes and turned away.

"You shall not *shed* a single drop of Nivram blood," the king said irritably. "Not today."

A soft hiss faded to nothing, the light died, and when Vicky opened her eyes, she saw no witch. Only a bad-tempered mottled green lizard which scuttled away behind a rock.

"Is she gone?" Susan whispered, her arms still covering her face.

"For the moment," Lucky said faintly.

The king stood once more on Charlie's head and addressed the Nilken guard. Their blank expressions and empty eyes were replaced by dazed confusion. The witch's enchantment must have been broken with her defeat by the king.

"Now, you silly straying Nilkens: hurry home to your families, while you can. For I hereby banish Witch Rose and her flying floating prison. I banish her from entering any realm under our care, for a thousand years. May she enjoy her sentence of exile in the form that she has just chosen. Now, let us hasten back. I intend not to leave my home again for at least that length of time."

Charlie ran a few steps and gently rose upwards. Half afraid to believe that the witch was truly vanquished, Vicky looked back. She was in time to glimpse the whole of the witch's domain rising up into the air before disappearing so rapidly that she couldn't tell which way it went. She took out her telescope, held it once more to her eye, but no matter in which direction she looked, the black pyramid was gone.

Chapter Twenty-Seven
THE END OF THE SIEGE

The Nilken army swarmed up the slope towards Alan. It wouldn't take them long to reach the pass. Twenty minutes perhaps, while it would take the best part of an hour for the scout to reach Tremere, another hour for any help to come from the Forest men.

It looked like it would be up to Cathy and him to defend the pass, but Alan wasn't sure how they could do it.

Not against so many.

"Maybe the scout will meet Tremere on his way here?" Cathy said, as if reading his thoughts. "He might get here first."

"Maybe." Alan didn't think that was likely. He fingered his arrow, and wished it was a sword.

Cathy tugged on his sleeve. "We're not going to fight them. We're *not.*"

"Only if we have to." The entrance to the pass was narrow. A large boulder would block it. He looked around.

Plenty of small rocks lay scattered along the path but nothing of the size he needed.

"Should we run back to Tremere?" Cathy said anxiously.

"Here." Alan bent down and gathered up some stones which he gave to Cathy. "Go up to the scout's post. We can hide there."

He filled his own pockets and climbed up after Cathy. The lookout was a shelf of rock, positioned in such a way that it was hidden from both above and below. The Nilkens would never see them. It would be a perfect place to defend the pass.

His hand closed around one of the rocks he had picked up. His aim was good, perhaps he could delay the first charge long enough for Tremere to arrive. He could see plenty of stones piled up close by. The scouts must have had the same thought.

"We'll be safe here," Alan said. He put as much confidence as he could into his voice.

Despite his words, Cathy looked worried. "I hope so."

The lookout post commanded a good view of the countryside. Alan could see Scatherina's castle, and in the distance Mount Slant with the blue of the lake gleaming at its base.

The Nilken soldiers continued to advance, their pace slowed by enormous screens they carried. At first Alan was puzzled by these, but then he guessed the Nilkens expected arrows to rain from the pass once they neared it, and held the screens as shields.

A small group of men were approaching the pass from

the castle. The Nilkens didn't appear to see them. Perhaps the way the land fell around the base of the mountain hid the men from the Nilkens' view.

He nudged Cathy. "Look."

Cathy turned her head. Her anxious expression didn't change as she eyed Bardey and his men.

"Oh," was all she said.

The Nilkens reached the pass. Their numbers swelled about the entrance, leaving Alan to doubt that Bardey's contingent would have a chance against them. The Forest men still had some ground to cover. The Nilkens could charge into the pass, unhampered. His fingers tightened on the rock.

A Nilken soldier peered into the pass. When no one challenged him, he stepped forward.

Alan took careful aim and flung the rock as hard as he could.

The rock bounced off the Nilken's forehead. He cried out in pain and scampered out of sight.

Cathy elbowed him. "No fighting, remember."

"That's why I did it," Alan said. "To scare them off so we don't have to fight."

For a few minutes, nothing happened. Alan waited for the Nilken response. Would they come pouring into the pass, or would they venture in one by one? Bardey's men crested the hill beyond the soldiers, but the Nilkens paid no heed.

Then a hail of arrows flew into the pass. Most hit the rocks below Alan, although one or two came close to the lookout post before falling to the ground.

At the same moment, one of the Nilken shields entered the pass. Alan couldn't see how many it took to carry it, but he guessed three or four. Another shield followed, and Alan moved back from the edge, pulling Cathy with him. His plan with the rocks wasn't going to work. All he could do was try to defend himself and Cathy if the Nilkens came after them.

The shields dropped to the ground and six Nilkens gazed at each other in bewilderment. With one accord, they turned and exited the pass.

Alan was stunned.

He scrambled back to the ledge for a better look. The men from the castle were still some distance away. The Nilken army dropped their shields and weapons and raced back to their camp. As Alan stared, they ran past their tents, unheeding.

"The spell must be broken." Alan couldn't think of any other explanation. Which meant – Alan couldn't think what that meant, except maybe Lucky had woken up and defeated Witch Rose.

Or Witch Rose had changed her plans.

Or perhaps the Nilken army realised going into the pass was a really bad idea.

"Are we safe?" Cathy said.

"From the Nilken army, yes."

He saw the Forest men split into two groups, some headed towards the Nilken camp, the rest entered the pass.

"Hello, Smolley, Banto." Bardey's voice echoed in the rocky channel. "Tremere, you up there?"

Alan peered over the ledge at Bardey. "Tremere is at the

forest end. Cathy and myself are in charge here."

Bardey looked unimpressed. "Things are worse than I thought."

"It's true," Cathy said. "Alan hit one of the Nilkens with a rock and two minutes later they all ran off."

Bardey scratched his head. He clearly didn't believe a word but didn't know how to respond. Then his face cleared. "Ah, here he is."

Tremere and the scout were hurrying towards them. Tremere carried a sword in his hand and looked grim and determined, but when Alan and Cathy scrambled down from the lookout post, his expression lightened and he put away his weapon.

"Smolley said the Nilkens were attacking. I take it you defeated them, Bardey?"

Bardey grunted. "Ran away."

"I know you can be a fearsome sight, Bardey," Tremere said with a smile. "But I didn't expect a whole troop of soldiers to run from you."

"*They* must have done it, for the Nilkens never even saw me," Bardey said, pointing to Alan and Cathy. "What is going on with this Serand?"

"Did the rest of Serand's men attack?" Alan said. He didn't like the Forest men, other than Tremere and Tom, but he hoped Serand's men didn't kill them.

Tremere looked grim. "It seems Serand had a hundred more soldiers secreted in the forest. It is only a guess but I believe some beast devoured them while they waited for Serand to call on their services."

Alan was glad he and Cathy hadn't met the monster capable of killing a hundred soldiers, but he felt sorry for the soldiers. It wasn't their fault they were in the forest.

"Bardey, we have dozens of soldiers captive. I would release them to return the way they came but they have begged for mercy. What would you do with them?" Tremere said.

Bardey gaped at him. "Me?"

"It is time you resumed your old position as leader. I must take Alan and Cathy to meet some friends of theirs. I do not feel like returning to the forest afterwards. This business with Jensen and Serand has sickened me of it. Although it is not up to me, I can think of no one more worthy to lead these people."

"Discuss it when you return," Bardey said. "I'll take charge while you're gone. Bring an armed escort with you, there may be dozens of those Nilkens out to ambush you."

Tremere turned down the offer of an escort. Alan was glad. He didn't know how Lucky would react to Tremere, let alone a band of Forest men.

"We'll go to the castle first and get Firefly," Tremere said, as they left Bardey and the pass behind.

In the castle, Tom was delighted to welcome them and pressed some refreshment upon them. He seemed disappointed to have missed the siege.

"You were lucky to be in the middle of it," he said. To Alan's surprise he begged them to come back to the palace for a visit. "It's nice having other young people around."

"We'd love to," Cathy said.

It didn't take long for Firefly to reach the Great Road. As they rode, Tremere asked for more details about the Nilken attack.

"You did well," he said after Alan told him. "You must have good aim."

"Stones wouldn't have been any good against anything bigger," Alan said. "I need to be able to shoot."

"An archer requires a steady arm and good eye. You seem to have both. I'd like to see you with a bow."

Alan looked up excitedly. "Would you show me how?"

Tremere smiled. "If you'd like. I'm self-taught so I lack technique, but I can vouch that it works."

Alan smiled too, picturing himself as an armed adventurer travelling the world.

"I've never come this far from the castle," Tremere said. "The open countryside looks strange to me, but it is a pleasant experience."

The journey along the Great Road as far as the monument did not take long on horseback. When Alan saw how substantial the monument was, he was amazed that they had passed it without noticing.

"The debris lying about the road makes me think the marvinlings may have been here," Tremere said. "Perhaps they recently destroyed much of the monument?"

"If we'd noticed it before, we'd never have met you," Cathy said.

"It was fate that led you to me. Which way now?"

Cathy produced her compass. "It always shows me the true path. I never get lost."

"Indeed?" Tremere said. "Though after hearing of your adventures, nothing should surprise me."

As Cathy promised, the dial led them unerringly to the shores of Crocodile Lake. Alan was pleased to see Tremere's amazed look as the horse mounted the last ridge and the blue waters of the lake spread before them.

"Your compass is truly amazing," Tremere said, as Firefly broke into a trot for the shore.

Cathy gave a squeal of delight and pointed excitedly. A canoe rapidly skimmed across the water towards them. He carried four passengers and a bright light blazed at his prow.

Chapter Twenty-Eight
REUNITED

After the defeat of Witch Rose, Charlie flew back to the lake. Lucky, the king, and Charlie returned to the Rock, leaving the rest to their own devices. It seemed a terrible anti-climax after the battle with the witch. The Nilkens were already dismantling the lopseys. Everyone else seemed to have something to do or some place to go, and paid little attention to any of them.

They sat by the lake, and Vicky gazed into its unfathomable depths.

"Cathy and Alan missed out all the fun," she said. "They won't be happy."

"Fun?" Yvonne shuddered. "Captured by the witch and held in her dreadful prisons? I really believed she would crush the king. I thought she had won."

"She would have, but for me," Paul said. "If I had not revoked her permission to be in my land, her powers would have stayed strong."

Vicky wanted to dispute this but remembered how Lucky had urged Paul to speak to the witch. And it was only after the prince had said she was unwelcome, that the king overcame Witch Rose.

Susan sighed. "I wish I had my flute. Now the witch and her realm are gone, and my flute with her."

"Oh, I forgot." Vicky fumbled among her clothes. "Here." She tossed a shimmering silver object to her sister.

"My flute!" Susan exclaimed. "How did you get it?"

"I had to fight Witch Rose for it," Vicky said immediately. "It wasn't easy – her talons are so sharp. So I challenged the witch to a deed of daring – the first to reach her highest turret could keep the flute."

"And naturally Vicky won," Yvonne said with a smile.

"Don't listen to them. They're lying." Paul sounded disgusted. "It rolled off the table when we were in the lopsey. Vicky must have grabbed it when we were hiding beneath the table."

"I forgot, you don't know what happened at the conference," Vicky said, noticing how confused Susan and Yvonne looked.

"I was there for it all, I'll tell the story," Paul said and proceeded to relate how Witch Rose had produced the evidence for her claim. Vicky saw Susan blush when Paul related how the witch tried to use her flute.

"It wasn't your fault," Vicky said. "You were under a spell."

"Do you think she could have persuaded the Diamonds she was who she pretended to be?" Susan said.

Paul shook his head. "Not Lucky. I could tell that she didn't believe a word of it."

Susan fingered her flute. "Is this really some ancient treasure?"

"I don't think it's the same one," Paul said. "Dulstar said it was too short, or missing important symbols."

Silence fell, but Vicky couldn't stay quiet for long.

"What do you think our reward shall be?" Vicky said, lying on her back and gazing up at the cloudless blue sky.

"What is your dearest wish?" Paul asked her. "Lucky is sure to grant it – if it's possible."

"I'd like to see a Demera," Vicky said instantly. The glimpses she had crossing the plains were not enough.

"I bet Cathy would love to find that puppy from the Wood of Witches," Yvonne said. "I'd like a home, a proper home."

Vicky squinted at her in the sunlight. "What, stuck in a town again? Things like cleaning and housework and stuff?"

"No, and not in Lowdar. I meant soft beds, hot water, and a cosy hearth. Somewhere clean and comfortable, where we wouldn't have to hide." She smiled as she said this, and Vicky knew that Yvonne pictured herself keeping house and looking after her family, no longer living in fear. It didn't sound too bad. As long as Yvonne didn't try to boss her around, of course.

"I wish our parents were alive," Susan said wistfully. "And Uncle Matt."

"I'm afraid that wish is classified as impossible," Vicky said. She mused on the promised reward some more. "I'd

275

like to enter the Rock of Diamonds."

"Where will you live?" Paul said. "If you don't return to your home town?"

Vicky was determined not to return to Lowdar, but where else could they go?

"You could stay with me if you wish," Paul added in an offhand manner. "My place has plenty of room."

Vicky glanced at him in shock. The prince was looking at the water, and his cheeks flushed with embarrassment. It was the first time he hadn't said the word *palace* when mentioning his home.

"I wouldn't mind a visit," she said.

Paul looked relieved. Vicky forgot all about his invitation as she spotted Charlie paddling towards them. Lucky glittered on his prow.

"Hop on!" Charlie called. "We thought you might like a chance to talk to us."

"Are you better, Lucky?" Vicky said anxiously as she scrambled aboard. "I'm so sorry about stealing the witch's memories and breaking the phial and all that." Although Lucky had lost the green tinge, Vicky still felt bad about it.

"Breaking the phial turned out for the best," Lucky said. "By containing the witch's memories, terrible though they were, I learned finally what had happened to Princess Varya."

She said nothing more for a few minutes while Charlie swam out to the middle of the lake. Vicky dared not break the silence.

The canoe was far from shore and surrounded by miles

of blue water before Lucky spoke again.

"I have always wanted to know the truth about her demise, for better or worse. And I believe you should know it too."

Vicky waited to hear the story, hardly daring to breathe.

"Long ago and far away, beyond these realms that we consider ourselves guardians of, lived a race of people. We know little about them except that they were tall and arrogant, proud, and with a deep thirst for knowledge. But they drank too deep and beyond their powers and so destroyed themselves. Cast from their homeland, they were condemned to wander eternally in their floating castles. Such was their punishment. One day, one of these people reached, not Paul's land, but the country beyond it. There, she settled for a while, and walking about one evening met Hestrane, the son of a local chieftain. She thought him young, handsome, and brave, so she decided that he would make her a suitable husband. Unfortunately, he did not feel the same.

"You find me repulsive,' she cried, for she had the long curved nose and chin of her race, and a scaly skin. Although he denied that this was the reason, she was convinced it was so. She spent the next three years searching the world for means of beautifying herself. She paid a terrible price for she bartered her mortality, but returned truly beautiful.

"She was too late. By the time she came back, Hestrane had met and married Princess Varya, and the twins had been born. In her rage, she murdered first Hestrane, then Varya, and was about to finish off the twins when she was disturbed by the arrival of Varya's younger sister. So, she hastily removed and buried Hestrane's body, ensuring that everyone believed that it was he who had committed this dreadful deed.

"Some years later, she visited Nivram once more. Prince Caralan had already planted the Great Forest; at that time, he loved trees and animals. She claimed to be a distant relative and assumed the guise of an older woman, and he trusted her blindly. Under her influence, he quarrelled with Scatherina until the Blackhand Mountains were raised, dividing the country in two. She encouraged him to experiment deeply with magic, sharing some of her own dark arts. Many twisted and evil creatures now dwell within the Great Forest as a result. Hidden in west Nivram, her presence and influence went unnoticed by the Diamonds, still grieving for the loss of Varya. When Caralan died, she was satisfied that at least one half of Nivram was destroyed, and she wandered off to other lands, there to cause trouble and mayhem for her own enjoyment.

"Occasionally she re-entered Nivram, always with evil intentions to ruin what she could. It was she who inspired the mirehogs to destroy all Scatherina's descendants. But when she learned that one might have survived, she came again with this false claim. It is out of hatred for the Diamonds and Varya's line that she wishes to destroy this country. She will not rest until every last descendant is dead.

"All this I learned from the phial you stole, Vicky. It *disproved* her story, not proved it."

"So that's why she tried to snatch it back from me." Vicky shivered. "She must be so old."

"I'm glad she's gone," Susan said. "She stole my flute. Luckily, Vicky got it back."

Charlie abruptly stopped paddling. Lucky threw a triumphant glance at him and said: "I knew that *had* to be your flute, even before we heard that you were captured by Witch Rose. But, for *one* moment, we thought that the flute the witch showed us was really hers. We nearly believed she was who she claimed to be when she threw it on the table."

"We've been searching for it high and low since we came back," Charlie said. "If the witch had taken it with her when she left the conference, she would have tried using it on the king, so we reckoned it must have been left in the lopsey. But the Nilkens said they didn't see it."

"I knew it was magical," Susan said. "But why is it so important?"

Lucky sparkled so much in the warm sunshine that Vicky had to look away.

"The Flute of Thule was given to Scatherina. It was a great honour, and was one of the treasures of the castle by the pass. It was passed from generation to generation until the castle was raided by the mirehogs, and all those living there killed. The flute was lost on that occasion but it was always believed that one daughter escaped with it and lived among the Nilkens. Legend has it that the flute must be passed from parent to child and will always remain in the possession of a true heir. It was given to you by your mother, Susan."

Vicky gasped.

Susan looked dazed. "But…but…"

"Lucky believes your mother was a direct descendant of Princess Scatherina," Charlie said. "It's merely a theory…"

"Based upon the Lost Flute of Thule," Lucky said.

Susan shook her head. "My mother made it. She told me herself when she gave it to me, that she had designed it."

Vicky found her voice. "Paul said that it wasn't the same, that some symbols were missing?"

"My theory is that your mother removed a small section of the flute to make something else," Lucky said.

"It's speculation," Charlie said. "Even if it is the lost flute, it does not necessarily prove anything."

"What of Cathy's compass?" Lucky said. "It has the ancient symbols of Thule. And Yvonne's magical key. It, too, must be made from the flute."

"It's a nice theory," Charlie said. "I hope it's true, but you'll never be able to prove it."

"You mean, we've Diamond blood in us?" Yvonne stammered.

Vicky couldn't believe it. Descended from Princess Varya? "Brilliant. Can we…?"

"It's very thin at this stage," Lucky said severely. "If, as Charlie says, it's there at all."

Lucky hadn't mentioned her telescope. Vicky knew it was special, and she held it up for the Diamond to see. "What about this? Is it made from Susan's flute as well?"

"I don't think so," Lucky said. "I would like Dulstar to examine it. It seems to me that it is the same workmanship, possibly another treasure of the Thule people, one that the records say nothing about."

"It's very potent," Charlie said. "All your gifts are

powerful, much more so than you know."

Vicky was delighted to hear this. "What else do you think it can do?" Her words were lost in the burst of the chatter from the others, as everyone talked at once.

Lucky laughed. "One at a time please."

"I wonder what Alan had?" Susan said. "Such a pity he lost it."

"Our mother told us to keep the gifts secret. We were almost afraid to tell each other what we got," Yvonne said. "Our father was dead, and after our mother died, Uncle Matt was arrested and executed. We had to go into hiding..." She sighed. "I guess we never asked and then it was all too late."

"I don't think Alan *can* remember," Vicky said. "He was only five."

"Maybe we can help him find it again?" Lucky said.

Alan's gift was lost somewhere in Lowdar. Vicky doubted if even Lucky could find it.

The further shore was rapidly approaching. Charlie was taking them away from Mount Slant.

"Are you getting rid of us?" Vicky said, in alarm.

Charlie chuckled. "No, no. I was informed that two young friends of yours were heading for Crocodile Lake."

Charlie, as usual, was reliably informed. As his passengers disembarked, a horse trotted into view. Vicky didn't know the man who rode the horse but she recognised the twins. She stared suspiciously at the stranger.

"Who is that man?"

Yvonne stood beside her. "He looks familiar – oh!"

Vicky felt Yvonne's fingers dig into her arm. "Ouch."

"Don't you know him?" Yvonne didn't loosen her hold. "Isn't that…? Could it be? It looks so like him."

"I don't know who you're talking about." Vicky shook her arm to free it from Yvonne, and shot an indignant glance at her.

The riders had seen the canoe, ridden over, and dismounted.

"It is!" Yvonne exclaimed, and finally released Vicky's arm. "I'm sure of it."

The twins ran over to their sisters while the stranger followed at a little distance. Alan was the first to greet Vicky.

"We were kidnapped by mirehogs, taken to the Great Forest, and survived a siege," he said. "What have you been doing?"

"And we made friends with a baby mirehog!" Cathy added.

Vicky looked at the twins' companion. "He doesn't look like a mirehog to me."

Cathy laughed. "This is our friend Tremere."

"Good afternoon," Tremere said, stepping forward.

"Uncle Matt," Yvonne said. "It *is* you."

Vicky gasped. Had Yvonne lost her mind? Why was she calling the stranger Uncle Matt? Uncle Matt was dead.

Tremere looked blankly at Yvonne.

"Don't you remember me? Yvonne?"

Tremere slowly shook his head. Susan stepped beside Yvonne and his expression changed. He looked confused and unsure.

"Remira?" he said doubtfully.

Susan smiled. "I'm Susan. But I'm meant to resemble my mother closely."

Vicky gazed at Tremere in stunned amazement as he said hesitantly: "Victoria?"

She nodded, not sure that she wasn't dreaming. She couldn't remember him at all. "We thought you were dead."

"And… Caralan and Scatherina…" Tremere turned to the twins.

"I can't believe it." Cathy was ecstatic. "You're our uncle. You're alive."

Alan looked disgusted. "Don't tell me Alan is short for that sissy name?"

"We've Diamond blood in us," Vicky said. "That's why you're called after Princess Varya's twins. She's our great – great – great – hundreds-of-great grandmother."

"It's a theory," Lucky said, in her severest tone. "Though it's interesting to learn of your full names, Caralan and Scatherina."

"We'll have to call you Scatty Cathy," Alan said.

Tremere still looked bemused.

"I've long wished for this moment," he said, "but I cannot quite believe it."

"Me neither," Vicky said. Banished from Lowdar, left outside the town gates for the monsters from the Forest to devour, how had her uncle ended up beside Crocodile Lake with Cathy and Alan? "Where have you been?"

"Why don't you hop aboard and we can catchup?" Charlie said.

Tremere seemed to notice the canoe for the first time. His dazed expression did not change. He merely said: "What about my horse?"

"Leave him to me," Lucky said with a smile. "Susan?" Susan approached the horse, and the Diamond whispered a few words. Firefly tossed his head and snorted, and, a moment later, galloped gracefully away. "He'll meet us at the other side of the lake."

Vicky was dying to hear all about Tremere but Lucky insisted the twins tell the tale of their adventures first. After that, she requested Vicky and Paul pour out the story of Queen Rose's claim and subsequent defeat.

"She was terrifying," Vicky said, when it came to her turn, recalling the witch towering over Charlie. "She picked up the king and was about to crush him…"

"Only for my intervention," Paul said.

"What could you do against her, Paul?" Cathy looked astonished.

It was Lucky who answered. "Paul revoked her permission to be in his land. She could no longer wield such terrific power."

"I am amazed by how much magic she had," Charlie said sombrely. "I did not realise she was that strong."

"She has been banished from our realms so she will trouble us no more," Lucky said. "I pity the people she has cause to bother in future."

Finally, it was time for Tremere to talk.

"You heard how I met Cathy and Alan," he said. "Before that, the Forest men found me wandering in the Great Forest. Yvonne tells me it's five years since I left Lowdar. Why, I don't recall, nor can I explain how I survived on my own in the forest for over two years. I would have thought two weeks were beyond the ability of most ordinary men."

"Maybe you have Diamond blood too?" Vicky said.

"If your valuable inheritance has come through your mother, no. Ramira was my brother's wife."

Yvonne asked Tremere more about the past. "I'm the only one of us who remembers you. Yet I remember you so well."

"That's because you went to the trial," Susan said. "You wouldn't let any of the rest of us go."

"Trial?" Tremere looked disappointed. "I had hoped for a noble past." He smiled almost immediately. "I jest. I only hope I wasn't a murderer or violent brute."

Yvonne looked at her feet. *Don't say it,* Vicky pleaded silently.

"Treason," Yvonne said. "You were a convicted rebel."

In Lowdar, traitors were considered the lowest of the criminal classes. To Vicky's surprise, Tremere laughed.

"In that case, I was a fitting companion for my forest friends. I'm sure I had good reason, though I don't recall it."

"Don't you remember *anything* about Lowdar?" Vicky said.

Yvonne tried to jog his memory. "We lived in a little cottage near the harbour, didn't we?"

"I remember nothing," Tremere confessed. "Other than an image I have of your parents and the five of you."

"Not even the trial?" Yvonne said.

"No."

"The forest? How you survived? Lowdar? Our parents? How they met? The house? What happened?"

In answer to each of this barrage of questions, Tremere shook his head.

"It will take time," Lucky said. "But I'm sure your memory will come back."

"This is like a dream come true," Susan whispered to Vicky. "Meeting Uncle Matt – Tremere – again."

Vicky smiled. The defeat of Witch Rose, the discovery of their Diamond kinship, and the reunion with her uncle filled her with happiness. Was it really less than two weeks since they had been scavenging to survive in Lowdar? Now the future looked wonderfully bright, like the Diamond glittering in the sun, as Charlie carried them across the sunlit waters of Crocodile Lake.

Epilogue
THE LUCKY DIAMONDS

I t was three days since the defeat of Witch Rose. On a grey overcast morning, Cathy joined the others to climb the steep path to the entrance to the Rock of Diamonds. She was more excited than nervous to get so close to Lucky's home. Current told her that they were first humans allowed on Mount Slant since the original Scatherina and Caralan. Not that they were actually going to enter the Rock, the king had balked at that, but the ceremony would take place on the plateau half way up the mountain.

"You'll be fine, Cathy," Yvonne said, as the mountain path twisted around a corner and opened on to a broad ledge.

"I know," Cathy said. She only had three lines to say after all.

A large crowd of Nilkens were gathered at the lower entrance to the Rock of Diamonds. A huge arch was cut in the rock, normally guarded by the Nilkens. Beyond this yawned darkness with numerous pinpoints of light, moving, shimmering, and speaking in tiny silvery voices. Immediately outside the arch, the king, Lucky, and a host of Diamonds were there to conduct the ceremony.

When her name was called, Cathy stepped forward eagerly, Alan beside her.

The king started the proceedings speaking of Prince Caralan and Princess Scatherina, of how noble and fair they were, and how, tragically, a rift took place and drove them apart. They would not have long been estranged but for the evil influence of another.

"For hundreds of years, Nivram has been unnaturally divided," the king proclaimed. "But a united Nivram has been ordained since the beginning of time. The era of Nivram in division is about to be ended."

Alan stepped forward and addressed Cathy. "Er, Scatherina, my sister," he began, stumbling slightly over his lines. "We are tied by blood, both to each other and to the most gracious and royal Diamonds. Let us put aside our differences and fulfil our destiny." He extended his hand.

"Brother Caralan," Cathy responded excitedly. "Long have I waited for this moment. Together we shall live out our fate. Let all Nivram rejoice, for once more is Nivram united." She clasped her brother's hand and shook it warmly.

A gleam of sunlight from behind a cloud fell on them. The Nilkens cheered. The king resumed his speech, and prophesied a glorious future for the country.

Afterwards, Cathy, her siblings, and Paul returned to sit by the shores of the lake, Lucky and a strange Diamond accompanying them.

"Thank goodness that's over," Alan said. "I was afraid the Blackhand Mountains would be swallowed up into the ground."

"It is far too late for that," Lucky said. "The ceremony was merely symbolic. West Nivram still remains outside the Diamond control. Much work remains to be done to clear the evil from the Great Forest."

Tremere approached, leading his horse. "I must leave now," he said.

Cathy was disappointed to learn that her new-found uncle was leaving them already. In all the fuss in preparing for the ceremony, she hadn't seen much of Tremere.

"But only for a few days. I wish to confer with Bardey about Serand and his men. I have received confirmation that the troops Serand confidently expected never arrived. Bardey believes that they must have met with some marvinlings, or perhaps something worse."

"I think marvinlings should be left in peace," Cathy said instantly. "They have a right to their own section of the forest too."

"They'll have to behave themselves a little better in that case," Tremere said. "I'll be back in time for the wedding." He mounted his horse and rode away.

"What wedding?" Vicky asked.

"Ours," Lucky said, indicating the strange Diamond, who bowed graciously in acknowledgement.

Cathy stared in dismay. It seemed wrong, considering how close Lucky and Charlie were.

Nobody said anything, and the atmosphere grew uncomfortable. Finally Susan spoke.

"Where's Charlie?" she said. "I haven't seen him for ages. He wasn't at the ceremony."

Lucky looked astounded.

The strange Diamond chuckled. "I've forgiven the king," he said in a familiar voice. "After all, I suppose he was only being over protective."

"And he's forgiven you," Lucky said. "And finally consented to our marriage."

"Charlie!" Cathy had forgotten the canoe was really a Diamond. Now that she knew who the stranger was, she was delighted to hear about the wedding.

When the congratulations had finished, Cathy sighed and murmured: "I miss the old Charlie. And I never had a flight in you either."

"Well, I'm not really supposed to, but I'm sure something could be arranged." Charlie winked.

Some time later, Charlie resumed his old form and Cathy, accompanied by her family, Paul, and Lucky the Diamond, climbed in for one last sail and a final flight. Charlie flew the way he swam – his feet pulling through the air with strong even strokes, and Cathy couldn't imagine anything more exhilarating.

Charlie flew over much of the ground that they had journeyed by foot. Cathy gazed, fascinated, at the Great Road stretching into the distance, the fields and homes of the Nilkens, now once more fully exposed to view. It was amazing, sitting in that open canoe, enjoying the sweep of landscape that passed thirty feet below. She even spotted the castle by Peacemaker's Pass, a tiny jewel on the Blackhand

Mountains. Charlie swooped and turned and they were soaring once more over the rivers and the plain. The sun was sinking low in the sky before Charlie returned to Crocodile Lake and the imposing Mount Slant.

"Our adventures are over," Yvonne said. "And now we can go home."

Yvonne meant the little cottage the Nilkens had offered them. Cathy didn't think it would be their home for very long. She had overheard the king tell Lucky that Cathy and Alan should live in Scatherina's palace. It was wonderful to be reunited with their lost uncle, and she hadn't forgotten that Lucky had promised a reward for returning her to Mount Slant. Perhaps best of all was that they would never return to their old miserable life in Lowdar, all thanks to the Lucky Diamond.

Author's Note

Thank you so much for reading *The Lucky Diamond*. I hope you enjoyed my story. I would be really grateful if you would leave a review on Amazon or GoodReads, even if only a few words. Reviews are so important to authors, especially those independently published. It helps readers find our books.

I owe immense thanks and gratitude to so many people for their help and support in bringing *The Lucky Diamond* to publication. First and foremost are my family and friends, in particular Iseult, Madeline, Marvin, and the Disreponsible Nodpot society. I would like to mention also my niece Lily for all her encouragement in bringing this book to publication.

I am so grateful to Livi Michael and Lindsay J Sedgwick, two writers I hugely admire, for their kindness in reading my book and providing blurbs. Special thanks to Elizabeth Eckstein for her fabulous cover, Dewi Hargreaves for his amazing map, and Joseph Sale for editing this book. To all my writing friends, those I only know virtually, and those I know in person, thank you for all your support, advice and encouragement.

Finally, thanks for to my parents, and especially to my mother for immersing me in books and writing from my earliest childhood.

SIGN UP TO MY READERS NEWSLETTER!

Sign up to my readers club occasional newsletter and get news of upcoming releases, updates on my writing, and learn more about Nivram and other fun stuff. Simply scan on the QR mark below for the sign up page. *If you are under 13, please ask a grown-up to sign up for you.*

As a welcome, I'll send you a FREE eBook of my short story collection *Once Upon A Time.*

This free collection features a mythical water dragon, an overworked dragon put up for sale, a boy who make a bad deal with a puppet master, and a girl who needs the help of a dog and a bird to find her father in a retelling of *Beauty & the Beast.*

ABOUT THE AUTHOR

Valinora Troy has been writing since she was a child. Her first story popped into her head when she was 5 or 6, about a little girl who found a magic diamond.

Recently she completed a M.A. in Creative Writing, specialising in Children & Young Adult fiction. Her short stories for adults have appeared in numerous venues. She hails from Blackrock, Co Louth, Ireland, and after living in Dublin for a number of years, recently returned to Louth to live in a magical writing cottage.

The Great Forest is her third published novel, and completes *The Lucky Diamond* trilogy.

The thrilling sequel to *The Lucky Diamond*

*Book 2 in The Lucky
Diamond trilogy*

The Rock of Diamonds has been attacked, the Diamonds sealed inside, and Susan and Vicky have disappeared. Everything points to Queen Rose instigating the attack but how can this be the case when she has been banished from Nivram for a thousand years?

Twins Cathy and Alan must travel to the distant land of Thule in search of answers in this action-packed exciting sequel to *The Lucky Diamond*.

"A fast-paced sequel packed full of magic, adventure – and monsters!" The Wishing Shelf

"Another action-packed fantasy adventure to add to the series" LoveReading4Kids UK premier book recommendation site.

The exciting conclusion to *The Lucky Diamond* trilogy

*Book 3 in The Lucky
Diamond trilogy*

T wins Cathy and Alan are thrilled to be asked by the
king of the Diamonds to enter the Great Forest on their
eleventh birthday to complete the cleansing of the land. After
all, Queen Rose is dead and all darkness gone from the trees.
But when their home is attacked by a horde of vicious boars,
and Alan and Cathy unwillingly taken to the Great Forest, the
twins realise that evil remains there. Now they are faced with a
terrible choice: escape from their captors and take their chances
at survival, or find out who is waiting for them in the centre of
the forest, and why?

Cathy and Alan are about to face the deadliest battle of their
lives, against the forest, the monsters, ... and each other.

Made in the USA
Middletown, DE
06 December 2023

43688585R00176